LOVE MATCH

Acclaim for the Cain Casey Saga

The Devil Inside

"Vali's fluid writing style quickly puts the reader at ease, which makes the story and its characters equally easy to get to know and care about. When you find yourself talking out loud to the characters in a book, you know the work is polished and professional, as well as entertaining."—*Family and Friends*

"Not only is *The Devil Inside* a ripping mystery, it's also an intimate character study."—*L-Word Literature*

"*The Devil Inside* is the first of what promises to be a very exciting series…While telling an exciting story that grips the reader, Vali has also fully fleshed out her heroes and villains. *The Devil Inside* is that rarity: a fascinating crime novel which includes a tender love story and leaves the reader with a cliffhanger ending."—*MegaScene*

The Devil Unleashed

"Fast-paced action scenes, intriguing character revelations, and a refreshing approach to the romance thriller genre all make for an enjoyable reading experience in the Big Easy…*The Devil Unleashed* is an engrossing reading experience."—*Midwest Book Review*

Deal With the Devil

"Ali Vali has given her fans another thick, rich thriller…*Deal With the Devil* has wonderful love stories, great sex, and an ample supply of humor. It is an exciting, page turning read that leaves her readers eagerly awaiting the next book in the series."—*Just About Write*

The Devil Be Damned

"Ali Vali excels at creating strong, romantic characters along with her fast paced, sophisticated plots. Her setting, New Orleans, provides just the right blend of immigrants from Mexico, South America and Cuba, along with a city steeped in traditions."—*Just About Write*

Praise for Ali Vali

Carly's Sound

"Vali paints vivid pictures with her words…*Carly's Sound* is a great romance, with some wonderfully hot sex."—*Midwest Book Review*

"It's no surprise that passion is indeed possible a second time around"—*Q Syndicate*

Calling the Dead

"So many writers set stories in New Orleans, but Ali Vali's mystery novels have the authenticity that only a real Big Easy resident could bring…makes for a classic lesbian murder yarn."—*Curve*

Blue Skies

"Vali is skilled at building sexual tension and the sex in this novel flies as high as Berkley's jets. Look for this fast-paced read."—*Just About Write*

Balance of Forces: Toujours Ici

"A stunning addition to the vampire legend, *Balance of Forces: Toujour Ici,* is one that stands apart from the rest."—*Bibliophilic Book Blog*

By the Author

Carly's Sound

Second Season

Calling the Dead

Blue Skies

Balance of Forces: Toujours Ici

Love Match

The Cain Casey Saga

The Devil Inside

The Devil Unleashed

Deal with the Devil

The Devil Be Damned

Visit us at www.boldstrokesbooks.com

LOVE MATCH

by

Ali Vali

2012

Credits
Editors: Shelley Thrasher and Stacia Seaman
Production Design: Stacia Seaman
Cover Design by Sheri (graphicartist2020@hotmail.com)

Acknowledgments

Every project starts small, an idea that takes root during the strangest moments sometimes, like when you're walking behind a lawnmower. Once I start writing, the characters take shape, the story is always a surprise to me, and where I'll end up I really don't know until the final chapter is done. Through the process, Radclyffe is always there offering support, advice, and the wealth of her knowledge and experience. Thank you for giving me a home with BSB and for your friendship, I am grateful for both.

Once the writing is done, the next part of the process is turning it over to an editor. Shelley Thrasher has been there from the beginning of my career guiding, teaching, and editing with her usual soft Southern grace. This book was no different. Thank you, Shelley. It's an honor to work with you.

One of the best parts of finishing a book is seeing the cover for the first time. Sheri, you're a mind reader when it comes to what I want, even when I have no idea what that might be. Thank you for sharing your wonderful talent. I love it.

Thank you to my good friends and beta readers Kathi Isserman and Connie Ward. Your comments, suggestions, demands for more keep me motivated, and your encouragement keeps me going whenever I'm stuck. Thank you for never saying no whenever there's a new book on the horizon.

Thank you to every reader who has picked up the book and taken one more adventure with me. Every e-mail I receive is a treasure I appreciate tremendously, and I enjoy meeting each of you at the events I attend. Each story is written with you in mind, and I promise it will always be so. Thank you all for your support.

Each story is different, the characters have their own distinctive voice and journey, but I'm grateful for the one thing in my life that is constant. Thank you, C, for teaching me so much, for bringing so much fun into my life, and for loving me without reservation. You are my safe harbor, my best friend, and my love. *Verdad.*

For C
My partner, my life, my love

CHAPTER ONE

Whack. The sound the ball made when it connected with Parker "Kong" King's racquet echoed all the way to the upper levels of the center court at the All England Club. Her forward stroke after a long volley sent the ball over the net at 115 miles an hour, where it landed right inside the line before flying off in a wicked slice. The velocity and angle made it impossible to reach in time, and even the ball boy had a hard time chasing it down.

Parker waited—for the kid to get back to his post; for her opponent, Jill Seabrook, to get into position; and for the tingling in her finger from the power of the last shot to subside—before she served again. Some of the commentators and sports writers said she made playing tennis look easy, especially since she'd won the Australian and French titles, but that pissed her off. Maybe tennis wasn't rocket science or curing cancer, but it was her passion, and she paid for every minute of a match like this with hours of practice and work.

She'd watched similar games when she was a kid in Atlanta and thought she'd have a better chance of getting to the moon riding a cow than actually playing in one. Here she was for a return visit to the Wimbledon finals, though, and she planned to obliterate Jill's game by shoving the ball down her throat every chance she got. She served again and the same resounding whack reverberated throughout the stadium. It didn't matter to her how many royals sat in the stands; this wasn't the time for finesse or mercy. Cute, feminine Jill would pay for all her trash talk in her last interview.

"Kong is an appropriate nickname for Parker," Jill had said when the network covering the championship asked about her opponent in the final. "She's all muscle, but plays like a gorilla. All the comparisons of her to Martina Navratilova are overrated. Martina had power but could place the ball anywhere on the court with marksman-like precision."

The crowd got to their feet and chanted "Kong" when the official said "forty-love" in a clipped English accent. If Parker couldn't beat Jill to death with her racquet for calling her an unskilled ape, she'd humiliate her by trying to win every point and break every serve.

"Quiet, please," the official said right before Parker served again.

She bounced the ball her customary four times before throwing it into the air and going through the motions of the stroke. Her involuntary grunt came right after she connected with it, and the result sent the crowd to their feet again when the ace won her the third game of the first set. At least gorillas moved around. Standing there as three serves whizzed past would justify her comparing Jill to a cow chewing her cud when the match was over.

Parker was the current darling of the tennis world. She wasn't exactly polished, but the crowds that filled the venues loved her, and companies lined up wanting her to wear their logos and sell their products. At a little over six-one, with sun-streaked, light brown shoulder-length hair, skin tanned by her daily hours on the court, and eyes the color of blue ice, she made her manager's job easy.

Only the voluntarily blind or cynically thinking who'd seen her on a court could dispute her number one ranking. Her style of play had earned her the nickname Kong from the fans, and Parker hadn't disappointed them during the tournament by reaching the final with a blistering pace, not dropping a set and losing only eight games total.

Jill rolled her shoulders as if trying to relax, and Parker could see her lips moving as she bounced the ball before she served. If Parker had to guess, poor little Jill was giving herself a pep talk to will herself back into the game.

That's right, serve and move to the net, she thought as Jill rolled her shoulders again. It was the only thing Jill hadn't tried yet and where she'd shown the most moxie in all her matches so far. Jill's first serve hit the net so she had to reset and try again, sending the next one to Parker's backhand. Parker hit it to the baseline, and the only save Jill could manage was a lob. One single word popped into her head before she returned it—"gorilla."

The crowd shouted "Kong" as the ball bounced so hard it landed in the stands after hitting just inside the line. "That's me, baby," she said softly as she smiled at Jill.

"Love-forty," the judge said a few shots later, pointing to her side of the net, followed momentarily by "Game, Miss King."

"I don't care if you don't feel like running." The Tennessee twang of Parker's coach, Beau Bertrand, pinged around her head as Jill crouched into her return stance, appearing wiped. "You're going to love me when it's hotter than shit and there's a hell of a lot of tennis left to play." Beau said the same damn thing every day, and she almost laughed as she caught the balls the ball girl threw to her. It was hotter than shit, all right, but she planned to chip away the rest of Jill's game a ball at a time, her legs as fresh as when she started.

She glanced up at Beau in the stands before she served and smiled. He was wearing the same Longhorns ball cap he wore when they worked out and chewing on his thumbnail like she was losing badly. Some things never changed, and Beau's sense of paranoia until she hoisted the trophy was one constant that she counted on.

She also glimpsed her other guest sitting next to him. Alicia, the pop-star sensation who topped the charts with her latest album, stood waving, and Parker lost concentration for a split second. The cute redhead was another mistake who'd climb to the top of her disaster list when it came to women after this was over.

Divas in the making were as welcome in her life as tobacco, drugs, and joining a cult that worshipped flamingo droppings. If the landscape of the dating world was peppered with land mines, she'd blown herself to shit and back more than once. After her time with Alicia, "land mine" was being kind. The singer was more like a bunker-buster bomb that went off in stages.

It hadn't taken long to figure that out and she was ready to go home. She missed her stretch of beach, her dog, and the quiet. After three months on the road that's what she wanted, but hell if she was going back empty-handed.

Her next serve sent the ball a few millimeters over the net, landing just inside the line. She pumped her arm, sending the crowd to their feet after Jill got back on hers. The grass on center court, she was sure, was the only reason Jill didn't pop back up with skinned knees.

"Quiet, please," the umpire said as the crowd chanted "Kong" so loud she came close to beating her chest.

The second set went faster than the first, and Parker curtseyed and held the women's singles trophy over her head as the crowd still shouted. The match had probably gone faster than they liked, so she took her time walking the circuit of the court to give everyone a chance to share this moment with her. In her every interview she said the victories belonged equally to the people who supported her and came to see her play.

She saved the last stop for Beau, who smiled like a proud father when she blew him a kiss. Beau had been a rising star until the day he collapsed on center court at the US Open with a blown knee. No amount of rehab would strengthen his leg enough for him to play professionally again, so he turned to coaching.

His favorite story was about finding a tall, gangly kid as his first student. She'd been his reward for the tennis gods screwing him over, but it became so much more than that to both of them. Finding each other had saved both their lives, or at least kept him from drowning in a bottle, which is what he'd wanted to do when he first looked at his leg after the initial surgery. He'd saved her from simply giving up on more than tennis.

❖

"Come on, Alicia, let's go congratulate the new champion down in the locker room," Beau said as Parker waved to the crowd one last time before heading in for her interview.

Alicia had been able to attend the prestigious tournament because her band's tour schedule put them in the area during the finals. It had been complete pandemonium a couple of nights before when the three of them went out to dinner and people recognized Parker and Alicia. In a country that thrived on sensational tabloid stories they had been like a gift from the heavens, or hell, as Beau thought every time a flash went off in his face and left red dots in his line of sight for hours.

"Excuse me, Mr. Bertrand. I have a message for you." The young man wearing traditional Wimbledon colors handed him a note.

He came close to sneezing from the sensation of relief and frustration as he read the two words followed by an exclamation point. It sucked when Parker used him to blow off a date, but it was time to stick a fork in Alicia and scream, "You're done." Not that *Come alone!* was really a note, but Parker wrote like she played tennis. Nothing fancy and to the point.

"Alicia, honey, you're going to have to head on back without us. Something must have happened on one of those last serves and Parker's in with a trainer." Alicia's expression of concern made him feel like an ass, but he wasn't falling for that face again. This girl was a horror movie in the making, and he was ready to return his small part.

"Will she be okay? I don't mind waiting to help her through the paparazzi."

"I'm sure they're more interested in pictures of you, so go ahead and take off. An hour or so with the trainer and Parker will be fine. Believe me, this happens sometimes when the tournament's over," he said, trying not to smile at the last thing he'd said. If Alicia only knew what came next he'd fear for his safety, but he figured the publicity-hungry, narcissistic singer would be fine.

If Parker was true to form it'd be the last time he'd see Alicia, except by chance. Like in a restaurant, where the typical scenario ended with Parker wearing a drink before the dessert cart came out. It still amazed him that women would chance going out with her, considering her track record, but they were all convinced they were the one who'd tame the badass Kong. After a few weeks of fun it was clear Alicia wasn't in the running, and he hadn't even had to resort to saying novenas.

He entered the green room softly singing a line about a notch in a lipstick case as Parker finished her post-game interviews. He shook his head, making her laugh. The note might've been short, but translated it meant they were going home and she didn't want the complications the increasingly demanding party girl Alicia would pose.

Beau congratulated her with a scowl for using him as the heavy before he cuffed her on the back of the head and sent her into the locker room to change. He'd cut her some slack, like he always did, considering they didn't have any time to just kick back and not worry about the next tournament.

The US Open was not only where he'd gone down, but it was the only title that continued to elude Parker, the American champion who had more trophies than women she'd slept with. It wouldn't take much prodding on his part to get Parker to work hard for the title that'd make her mark on the game. The Australian, French, and now the Wimbledon trophies were going home with them, and he could almost taste the Grand Slam.

❖

"Would you care for anything, ma'am?" the waiter asked as he balanced his order pad on his tray. "Our special today is kidney pie."

Captain Sydney Parish slid her hands from her thighs to her knees, the fabric of her uniform pants scratching her palms. She did her best to not show a reaction to the dish, which wasn't her favorite. "Just a large tea with milk, please."

The employee lounge at Heathrow was fuller than usual, with

most of the waiting flight crews watching the large television screens throughout the space. She'd picked a comfortable chair next to the wall of glass overlooking the tarmac, wanting privacy and peace before her flight to Miami.

The recap of the upcoming women's final at Wimbledon didn't bother her as she took out her organizer and reviewed the list she'd made in her three days off in London. She'd found a Realtor for her condo in Atlanta and a mover—both important, but not her top priority of things to settle before she was free to take her new promotion. After a few years of these overseas routes, she was excited about doing day runs strictly in the States. Flying out of JFK in the morning and returning the same afternoon would make her job like a cool desk position.

"Here you are." The man put down her tea with a small plate of cookies. "The sweets are on me." He winked and she wasn't so wrapped up to not notice that he was flirting, but he was harmless. Sometimes on flights all men saw were a cute ass, pretty face, and blond hair and figured it for some kind of invitation to become obnoxious. Sydney wasn't egotistical in thinking herself beautiful, but come-ons weren't foreign to her. Not as foreign as some of the ideas of men she'd come across throughout her career when they found out she was their pilot.

If she had a dollar for every time a dimwit told her, "A pretty little thing like you in command of this big ole machine could probably handle me in a bedroom," she'd be rich. She figured those guys didn't have any professional relationships with any woman.

"Thank you," she said as she took a small bite of a cookie.

"Are you a tennis fan?"

"Every match I've watched has been in an airport waiting for my flight." She took her cup and stood before he got too revved up. The guy seemed harmless, but he also struck her as earnest, so it was best to stop him before she had to out herself to get rid of him. That line, while truthful, never worked either because men always took it as a more creative way to say "get lost."

She moved to one of the phone booths and dialed the number of her partner, Gene Hines, on her cell. It was three in the morning and she thought it rude to wake Gene, but she hadn't been able to reach her since her arrival in London and refused to call midair, so Gene would have to get over it.

Gene didn't answer at the condo, and her cell went to voice mail after ten rings. Sydney checked her watch again and recalculated. She couldn't imagine why Gene wouldn't be available or would sleep through both calls unless she was in a coma.

Sydney didn't leave a message and placed a check mark next to Gene's name. She wasn't trying again.

❖

"Over here, sweetheart." Gene Hines waved to the bartender before pointing to her empty glass. She'd even consumed the ice trying to get the last bit of scotch. That was the drawback of a crowded bar with a younger clientele. The only problem with the quiet places where they fell over themselves to pour was the type of woman who went there. Every single one of them you picked up in the low lighting was ready to sign a lease once you fucked her, and Gene had her fill of the questions and accusations that came with committed relationships.

"Are you trying to avoid me?" she asked when the cute college-age girl made it back.

"Did you have a really bad day or are you trying to work up the courage to head home?"

"Which answer will get you to pour me another drink quicker?"

"If you're driving it'll get you cut off, so think that over while I take care of the bill at the end of the bar."

She was holding up her empty glass when the bartender returned. "I already have a girlfriend, thanks, and I have a cab service on speed dial, so save the concern for someone who needs it. Maybe if I'm nice enough you might take me home when you get off. I could show you a great time."

"The music's not loud enough for me to miss the word 'girlfriend.' If you actually have one, it's not a smart move to pick up other women in bars." She poured another two fingers and plopped another two ice cubes, obviously remembering Gene's previous requests.

"She's a real understanding woman." She sipped this drink slower, with a hundred-dollar bill folded in her fingers. Big tips were the best bait for getting laid and making a clean getaway.

"That's great for you, but I'm not that understanding, so we'll stick to me pouring and you drinking. How about it?" Her ice was still fresh so the bartender poured another before she could ask.

"Are you married?" she asked, and the woman shook her head. "Let me give you some relationship advice, then." She glanced at her watch and pointed to the empty glass again. "Before you take that plunge off the cliff of no return, make sure you take inventory of the person you're about to chain yourself to."

"What do you mean?"

"Frigid women do not thaw, whether you're faithful or not. I got sidetracked by the cute ass and blond hair, and now that's all I got. It's kind of like having the most beautiful sports car in the world sitting in your garage." The bartender laughed and put her elbows on the wood separating them. A little more small talk and Gene would get a ride home. "You can sit in the damn thing, but it doesn't have an engine and the only channel on the radio is Bitch 101.2. It's about as much fun as the plague."

"Maybe you should try flowers and a ring instead of spending the afternoon with me."

"Or maybe I should shop the car lot again," she said, laughing at what she considered a hilarious joke.

"Let me know if you need anything else aside from kicking my tires. That's not on the menu tonight."

"We'll see," Gene said, taking her phone out and noticing she'd missed a call. It was time to deliver the bad news, and she was lubricated enough to take the bitching Sydney would unleash. The sooner she got this behind her, the sooner she'd be peeling off the thong she was sure the bartender was wearing.

"You want one more?" the bartender asked, "or do you want to settle your bill and call that cab?" She tugged on the hundred as she asked.

"When do you get off?"

"I got another twenty minutes."

"One more, then. I can wait." The young woman smiled and turned for the bottle. Gene had a short window to deal with Sydney before the real fun began.

❖

"I can't make it this week," Gene said. "If I put in some extra hours I might be able to salvage the weekend."

Sydney gripped the telephone, and the pain behind her left eye caused by talking to Gene flared to the point that her breath hitched. Some poetry and songs said love hurt, but this was ridiculous. "Where are you?"

"Working."

The late hour, the sound of music and people in the background ordering drinks amplified the lie. "Did the judges get together and have a bar put in with late-night specials?"

"Sydney...baby, you know most deals happen outside the office. Do you think I want to be here instead of on a private beach with you?"

"What I think is I was stupid enough to give you another chance after your last batch of relationship amnesia, which makes me a total idiot."

"Come on." Gene suddenly sounded as if she was in a tunnel, and Sydney guessed she'd cupped her hand around the phone. "You took that completely wrong."

"I'm sorry, but no one on my crew has ever stripped down to their bra and panties to show me how well they fit, in case I had an urge to buy some."

"She was only showing me how much she liked the gift I'd given her. It was totally harmless."

If Gene had been standing before her, she would've strangled her. "Is this the kind of defense you put on in court? Or do you believe I'm brain-dead?"

"Syd, calm down." Gene laughed, and Sydney could imagine the perfect dimples in her cheeks. "Let me figure out something, and we'll see each other this weekend. Believe me, we'll be laughing about this ten minutes after I get there."

Gene had been hard to miss when Sydney and her friends ventured down to Buckhead her first weekend in Atlanta after her move. The attorney had bought her a drink and completely charmed her before she'd finished it. The warnings her friends had given her about the beautiful, tall, sexy-as-hell Gene didn't make a dent in how she felt after months of dating.

In all that time Gene had pitched her like a carny tent vendor about how perfect they were as a couple, how she'd changed her, and how they were destined to be together. But Gene neglected to share how she planned to keep sleeping with anyone willing and breathing in her vicinity and not help with anything having to do with the condo they shared but Sydney paid for.

Ignorance was bliss since she was away so much, taking as much airtime with the airline as she could. Her absence was perfect for Gene and her addiction to women and a good time. That happy fantasy blew up when she surprised Gene at her office a day ahead of schedule to find her giving her secretary a special kind of dictation. She'd fallen for the sincere apology Gene had sobbed out, and now she realized that lying was simply part of Gene's makeup, like the gorgeous face and the perfect tall body. The piece of shit was incapable of fidelity or telling the truth.

"Don't worry about it, and take your time with your case. After this week it won't matter anyway."

The background suddenly quieted, only to be replaced by traffic noise. "What are you talking about?" Gene asked.

"Obviously you weren't paying attention when I explained why we were going away this weekend, so let me recap. The airline is transferring me, so we were supposed to plan how to proceed with our relationship. It's hard enough having one, given the little time we spend together, so being so far apart will make it impossible." She'd always wondered what it'd be like to simply let Gene go after so long, but emotionally nothing was holding her back. She wasn't hysterical, numb, or hurt. This actually had been easier than changing her address.

"You don't have to deny yourself anything because of me, especially Bimbo in your office or whoever else you're talking up." The women's match had started and she watched Parker King win the first set. "The movers will be there for my stuff at the end of the week, so please don't lock the dead bolt. Let me know when you find a new apartment so the Realtor can have the place cleaned once you're out."

"You're seriously breaking up with me over the phone? I won't give you another chance, Syd."

"I would've made an appointment, but I'm in London, so yeah. No hard feelings, and take care of yourself."

"Wait a minute."

She hung up and moved to one of the leather chairs to finish watching the match. Football she knew, but watching Parker work the ball around the court made her envy the fluidity of her movements. It was a good way to kill time before her flight. Her vacation was waiting, and the planning session for the future would require a different mind-set. The first thing on her list was not repeating her mistakes.

One good-looking womanizer was enough in this lifetime.

CHAPTER TWO

The women's doubles final was still going on when Parker and Beau arrived at the airport. Parker was anxious to get home after being out of the country for over three months. The two police officers assigned to them kept the crowds back as they sat waiting for their flight. The bobbies stood far enough away to give them some privacy, but close enough to send a message to any overzealous fans. They'd let a few autograph seekers in at a time, most of them young girls thrilled to sit this close to their idol, before putting their arms out and closing ranks. These security measures were courtesy of the airline after they'd become one of her sponsors. Every deal had its perks.

Parker asked the hopefuls about their own tennis game and gave pointers to those who seemed serious about the sport. She'd replaced her tennis whites with a lightweight linen suit over a tight, white T-shirt. After they called for boarding she walked through the crowd autographing everything from tennis balls to tournament programs.

The crew of flight 756 waited at the door to greet passengers, as was their norm, and Sydney would've recognized their famous passenger even if she hadn't been carrying a large bag full of racquets. She'd spent the morning trying not to dwell on the death of her personal life and watching Parker King completely obliterate her opponent. Seeing her now, she had to agree with the whispers of her crew—Parker was better-looking in person.

"Welcome aboard, Ms. King. I hope you enjoy your flight, and congratulations on your win," Sydney said. She'd stepped out of the cockpit, as was her habit before every flight, leaving the coat with her rank draped over her seat.

"Thanks," Parker said, and shook her hand as she smiled. "It's good to be going home, and I won't even mind being trapped in here for hours with such a good-looking flight attendant."

Sydney felt her crew freeze after taking deep breaths. Granted, her pants did resemble those of her fellow crewwomen, but the comment had jangled her last un-tense nerve. "I'm not your flight attendant." She managed not to completely clench her jaw as she spoke, not wanting to be rude.

"Don't tell me your company still calls the position 'stewardess'?" Parker's smile widened. Dimples, she had goddamn dimples. Sydney had the urge to slap the wide smile off her face. "I'll be happy to e-mail your CEO and let him know that's really archaic." Parker placed her bag in the overhead compartment so she took the opportunity to clench her hands into fists. "I realize you're still preboarding, but could I bother you for a sandwich or something? If you can deliver that with the biggest mug of hot chocolate you can find, that'd be great. I'm starved after running around that court for hours."

Her crew lifting their hands to their mouths in an almost practiced synchronized motion ratcheted Sydney's anger. They were hiding their smiles and the tennis imbecile was still talking, obviously not hearing the ice breaking under her feet. She'd earned her reputation as a great pilot and as a perfectionist by a perfect record at the yoke. The latter made her hard to work for, and those who did knew better than to laugh out loud. She wouldn't hesitate to reassign them. Her crew might not have been laughing, but she was sure they were enjoying this.

"I'll see about that right after I finish my preflight checklist so *I* can fly you home safely." Her smile was so tight her face hurt, and it took control not to add, "You egotistical asshole." Before she turned around she did notice Parker at least had the decency to appear apologetic, since she'd blushed.

"I'm sorry, Captain," Parker said to the back of her head, but she didn't turn around. "It was an honest mistake, really, but I didn't mean to insult you." When Sydney turned around again, Parker was already seated with her eyes closed.

You're sorry all right, she thought with one last glance at Parker, *and you're a complete asshole.*

❖

"Way to go, champ," Beau said, and laughed. "Your way with women is legendary. I'm sure there's a warning article about you in every issue of the good-girl newsletter, so have fun back there in the tiny seat if the captain sends you to coach just to prove a point." He stowed his bag and took the window seat. "Not that Alicia is getting that particular issue, but now that we're alone, you want to tell me what happened?"

They both smiled as the other passengers started streaming in, offering congratulations like they were old friends as they passed. Parker nodded at each well-wisher, ignoring Beau for the moment.

When there was a break in the traffic, he leaned closer and whispered, "Come on, Parker. Sitting next to me at a tournament is the kiss of death for any of your relationships. I want you to have a life outside of tennis and be happy, kid. Believe me, it'll instill the desire to win in you more than this bullshit you've been doing."

"I have the desire to win, so give it a rest. You aren't my mother, and you don't have to worry that I'm trying to win the prize for the most *Enquirer* front pages. I want to go home and take it easy for a while without the whining about how boring and old I am because I want to go to bed before five in the morning. Alicia's got her own gig to worry about, and the last few weeks had more to do with the publicity than me. I get enough press without fanning the flames. I'm not stupid or naïve enough to think she gives a good goddamn about me. Trust me, when I meet the one all the fairy tales talk about, you'll be the proverbial first to know."

"Great to hear," he said, and smiled.

"Besides, are you seriously sitting here giving me shit for dropping Alicia? If you are, then look deep into my eyes and come back from the dark side. She was hot, but certifiable."

"I'm not vouching for her, but I do want you to keep your eyes open for someone who'll make you happy."

"Sure thing. I'll start working on that right away."

When the first-edition copy of *To Kill a Mockingbird* came out of her carry-on, Beau knew the conversation was over. Parker tuned him out as she got lost in another classic story. *This is the Kong no one writes about*, Beau thought. Parker was so much more than just the game, but she kept those other parts hidden except from the people she loved and let in, and he could count those on one hand.

The bad girl of tennis was in reality a very private, intelligent person who loved to read as many books as her schedule allowed for. But that didn't make as interesting a headline as Alicia would the minute she figured out she'd been dumped. Beau's anger over the unfairness of the press vanished when he saw the captain walk down the aisle with a tray in her hand. Maybe she did have a sense of humor.

"Sorry it took so long, but we had to send out for marshmallows. We go the extra mile to make our passengers happy." Sydney's sarcasm stopped when Parker snapped her book closed and looked at her.

"I hope Godiva is good enough?" She didn't straighten up and moved her face closer to Parker's, prompting Parker to close her eyes and take a deep breath. The brief break in eye contact gave her the opportunity to glance down Parker's body. The move wasn't blatant, but it reminded Sydney so much of Gene, she was disgusted with herself.

"Actually, I'm more of a Hershey girl, Captain." Parker opened her eyes as she spoke and drew out her title. "I really am sorry. It never occurred to me that you're the captain, which probably makes you think I'm an asshole."

"I'd never think that," she said, and smiled to cover up any insincerity in her tone.

"Sure you didn't," Parker smiled and shook her head, "but even if you don't believe me, I'm not so much of an asshole that I go out of my way to make people feel bad. Thanks for the hot chocolate and the sandwich. I promise I won't bother you again."

"It's not a bother."

"I'm willing to bet you have other things to do than to make me a snack, so I'm sorry for putting you out. If nothing else I'm glad I picked the book I did. It's a good story about people making wrong assumptions with a bit nastier consequences."

When Parker finished, Sydney looked at the book on her lap. The title wiped away any assumption that Parker was simply a dumb jock, and it wasn't fair to take her bad mood out on her. Any other passenger would've been demanding her name and employee number for trying to embarrass them like this, so she relaxed her shoulders a little but stayed leaning across Parker's tray.

This kinder side of Parker made her more attractive, and Sydney really looked at her. Standing in line at the supermarket she'd read enough about Parker's love life to think she knew more about her than Gene, who'd been in her life two years. Being this close to her made her wonder what kind of date Parker would be, but thoughts like that were extremely premature.

"It's all right, Miss King. You aren't the first person and you won't be the last to think that. I apologize for taking all my frustrations out on you. I hope you enjoy your flight." She placed her hand on Parker's shoulder as she straightened up and smiled before she returned to work.

It was a good thing she was taking a vacation after this. She seldom blew up at anyone, much less a paid spokesperson for the airline, and seldom let her imagination skitter off to think about someone on her flight as anything but a passenger. Parker's beautiful face, though, didn't give her a choice. She wondered now if she'd chosen Gene because deep down she knew she wouldn't be able to commit, no matter how hard she worked at the relationship. And because Gene hadn't, Sydney had dedicated herself to getting her career on track. Settling for someone like Gene had helped her avoid the arguments that inevitably crept up about her unpredictable schedule.

Fortunately, this would be her last transatlantic flight for a while, and she'd be back to a more normal workday that'd allow her to be home more. That change, coupled with letting Gene go, would hopefully spark a social life to balance out the long hours. If not, then what the hell was this all for? One of the greatest gifts you could give yourself, her mother always told her, was to find someone to share your success with and, more importantly, your sorrow, since it was better to weather the ups and downs that marked anyone's life in the arms of the one you loved.

It's too early and you have too much to do for such deep observations, she thought as she walked slowly up the aisle to her to-do list. *Especially since you thought Ms. King was an asshole six minutes ago.* She shook her head and kept going, putting Parker out of her head the farther she got away from her.

Sydney walked back to the cockpit without another word, leaving Parker leaning into the aisle watching the sway of her hips. The way the pants fit was a sure sign she did more than just sit and fly the plane. She was beauty in motion.

"Forget it, tennis pro," one of the male attendants said. "She's dating someone."

"I've already had my ass handed to me on a nice tray today, so I was just looking. Hopefully she's easier to work for."

"Some of the crew call her the Ice Queen, but she's okay. Believe it or not, I still get the shakes when one of these bad boys takes off, but Sydney makes me feel safe."

"And you think I'm playing her?"

"I just saw you staring and thought I'd warn you."

Glancing at his name tag, Parker smiled before answering. "No worries, Willy. If you believe everything in the *Enquirer*, you know I've got them lined up. I don't have any reason to go chasing after lost causes."

"You aren't going to disillusion me and tell me it's not true. Some of those pictures I see standing in line at the grocery store have to be real."

"If the woman next to me is beautiful and looks like she wants nothing more than to rip my clothes off with her teeth—then yes, it's all real."

Willy laughed, then moved on when she lowered her gaze to her book. She dropped a handful of marshmallows into the cup Sydney had delivered before taking a sip.

Ten hours later Sydney's voice came over the speakers, informing everyone of their impending arrival at the Miami airport. The navigator followed, providing last-minute instructions for the customs forms, as well as a list of connections and gate numbers. "So, ladies and gentlemen, if you would, please bring your seats to their full upright position and we should have you on the ground in about ten minutes. Again, thank you for choosing us for your flying needs and we hope to see you on board in the future," Sydney said.

"The Nike shoot is scheduled right when we get back, so you're going to have to hit the gym starting today. If your naked ass is going up in Times Square, we want it to look pumped," Beau said. The schedule book had come out of his bag twenty minutes before so they could review upcoming events. Being trapped in a plane gave Parker no choice but to listen to him run through the month.

"Whose idea was this again?" The sponsor had approached her before Wimbledon with the idea to add her to the list of athletes that had appeared in the ads clad only in their shoes, illustrating that just the footwear and the body were necessary to succeed in sports. She could've sworn she'd turned them down.

"It was Nick's idea, and I forbid you to give him a hard time about it. You know how sensitive he is, and I'm the one who has to live with him. All the shots will be from the back, and he got Annie and her all-girl crew to do it, so quit your griping." Beau pointed his finger at her as he spoke. "The last thing I need is for you both to give me a hard time about this for weeks to come."

"I just asked a question, Beau. I hardly see how that could be construed as griping. Are they coming to the house or will it be done in a studio?" She put away her book and stood to pull her jacket back on.

"Do you need anything, Ms. King?" Willy asked when she stood up. She smiled and shook her head as she sat and refastened her seat belt.

The crew had seemed surprised that, besides her initial hot chocolate and sandwich request, she'd stuck to bottled water. The fourteen she'd consumed kept her hydrated and active with constant trips to the bathroom. No amount of free alcohol was worth jet lag, so while most of the other passengers fought fatigue, she'd be lifting weights for the rest of the afternoon.

"You get to stay home, kid. Annie thought the court there would make for good shots. Let's hope we didn't miss our connection. You know how Nick hates to wait around in airports."

"Now who's griping?" Parker asked, trying her best to get his accent right. She was pulling her hair into a ponytail when the wheels of the plane hit the tarmac once, followed by three hard bumps before the engines were thrust into reverse to kill their speed.

Not expecting the jolts, she came close to smashing her head into the seat in front of them despite having her seat belt on, the jolt of the landing was so rough. Aside from the earlier announcement, this was the first time Sydney had crossed her mind.

The sound of everyone unfastening their seat belts and jumping into the aisle filled the plane as soon as they reached their gate, but she and Beau waited, knowing from experience their patience was usually rewarded by an empty waiting area as passengers headed toward baggage claim or connecting flights. They had a few hours for their connection, so she wasn't in a hurry.

Parker finally opened her eyes to an empty plane and Willy waiting at the door with her large bag of racquets and a pen. "Alicia and your coach weren't the only avid fans who got to watch you win," he said as he handed her bag over. "Would you mind?" He held out his program.

"I didn't know you were interested in tennis." She accepted his pen and sat down in the first set of first-class seats, waiting to hear his answer before writing something in the glossy book.

"I had to trade some really bum flights to be able to go watch you play. The final match was awesome, though I wish it had lasted longer. If that first ace you rocketed over the net hit Jill, I think the match would've been over because of a chipped bone. Having you on our flight home was an added bonus." He stopped talking when she started writing. She handed his program back with a thank-you note for his hospitality, then took the time to sign the various other souvenirs some of the crew produced.

"It would've served her right for the name-calling," Beau said.

She laughed at Beau's pout and spotted Sydney at the door of the cockpit, but didn't acknowledge her when she didn't come closer. The last thing she autographed was one of the racquets she'd removed from her bag. She wrote *Parker "Kong" King* and the date along the grip.

"Sorry you didn't get to see more play, Willy, but I was anxious to catch my flight. You might get your wish at the Open since it seems to be my Achilles' heel." On the other side of her name, Parker wrote "first-ace racquet Wimbledon." "I hope this makes up for your shitty schedule. It means a lot to me when people go so out of the way to come see me hit some balls." The racquets were custom-made for her and were a valuable collector's item for the few fans who'd gotten one as a gift.

The one she had used for the majority of the match would rest alongside the trophy at home. Both she and Beau laughed at the squeal Willy let out.

"Oh, my God, thank you. This is the best gift I've ever gotten, Parker. Thank you." Willy hugged her as she stood up and laughed again when Parker hugged him back. "I knew all those tabloids were full of shit."

"Thanks for thinking so." She squeezed him one more time before releasing him and shaking hands with the rest of the crew who still stood around. "Don't play with that one. Save it for your next vacation. If you list it on eBay it should get you to Hawaii."

"No way, this one's a keeper." The crew bade them safe travels as Parker shouldered her bags and stepped off the plane, noticing that the cockpit door was now closed. The impromptu autograph session meant she wouldn't get to apologize again, which left her with a sense of something undone.

❖

"Is Nick going to pick us up?" Parker asked. The next leg of their trip to Mobile, Alabama, appeared less crowded, judging by the people sitting outside the gate, so they finished their calendar review without interruption.

"Yep, he is. Some of your contracts were coming up, so hopefully he's re-signed all of them and is over having to miss this trip."

Beau sighed, and she didn't have to ask for an explanation. Nick Spoli was a sweet man but could whine for days, given a reason to. He and Beau lived as well as worked together at keeping her both happy and ranked. It was amazing they got along so well, considering Nick came from a wealthy family in Greece and Beau was a country boy from the mountains of Tennessee. She loved to remind him that it'd been Nick who'd finally gotten him out of jeans and combed the pine needles out of his hair. As much as they fussed at each other, they were still madly in love.

"Like you said, you're the one who has to live with him, buddy, but remind him of his commission if he gets out of hand. The smallest one alone should get him that new sports car he wanted, along with a new wardrobe to go with it." She wiggled her eyebrows and laughed when he frowned. Nick and the flight attendant they had just met, Willy, could compete on the flamboyancy scale.

"If he buys me one more doggone pink shirt, I might strangle him with it."

"No, you won't, and I can't wait to see if he spotted that picture of you in France when we left that bistro he recommended."

"You cut it out, didn't you?" Beau covered his face with his hands. "Lord, my daddy would croak all over again if he saw me wearing pink pants."

That Beau would do something like that even when Nick was nowhere in sight was the reason they were her role models for a loving relationship. They'd been together fifteen years and had built their home close to her on Press Cove. The small island near Orange Beach, Alabama, was a gated community with only a handful of buildings.

"You'll survive." She laughed as she patted him on the back. "This has been a hell of a run so far, huh?"

"One more and we can relax." He faced her and smiled. "I hope to hell you know how proud I am of you. You make my life fun, Kong, and I'm as happy as a pig in slop that you've stuck with me this long. After your first year you could've asked anyone in the business to coach you, and I wouldn't have blamed you for picking somebody else."

"Anyone wouldn't go through the trouble you guys do for me, and they aren't my family. If you couldn't bring the Slam home when you were playing, I'm going to try my best to give it to you now. It's the only way to thank you for keeping me in line and showing me that building a home was better than blowing my money into the wind."

Her house had everything she needed to train for upcoming tournaments while giving her the solitude she needed to prepare for the weeks on the road. She knew Beau looked forward to these trips home as much as she did, since it gave him and Nick time together and her the opportunity to strengthen her mental state as well as her body. Having every vice imaginable at her fingertips would've ruined her career early on if it hadn't been for their influence, along with that of her two sisters.

She seldom complained about the hours of practice and the grueling schedule, knowing her career wouldn't last forever. She had a small window of opportunity to accomplish all her goals before she retired either to her house or to the commentator's chair. At twenty-four she had plenty of time to contemplate her future, barring any injury, but what happened to Beau was always in her thoughts. Knowing it could be over in a spilt second drove her to train harder in case her time on center court was fleeting.

"You could coast from here on out and not win another tournament, and I'd still put you in the top ten of all-time best players," Beau said.

"You're a generous grader, Coach."

"I'm tough as shit, so don't argue with me." He laughed.

Beau and Parker stood and handed over their boarding passes when the announcement for first-class passengers was made. When Sydney saw the two go on ahead of her, she couldn't believe her luck. *Don't tennis superstars live in New York or something*, she asked herself as she slowed her pace, not wanting to be noticed.

After flying around the storm from hell only to have to land in the middle of it, she'd been looking forward to her own first-class leather seat for a nap before arriving at her final destination. The thought of having to share the space with Parker King made her veer into the cockpit in search of an empty seat. She'd settle for some mindless conversation with the crew rather than having to make small talk after her spectacular day so far.

Granted, Parker had apologized, and their brief encounter had ended amicably, but any other contact would be a huge waste of time. There was no chance, even if Parker was remotely attainable, that she'd put herself out there again so soon. Especially after that initial meeting.

People often assumed she was anything but the actual pilot, usually men who came close to patting her butt and asking for a beer, but this was different. Having a successful woman do the same thing made it seem worse.

It was hard enough to compete in a male-dominated field without someone like Parker piling on. No, Parker King could keep her wisecracks, good looks, and slew of women. Sydney wasn't interested. What she needed now was some time alone in the sun, but without permission, her brain drifted back to seat 4A and the tall Wimbledon champion occupying it.

CHAPTER THREE

O ver here, guys," Nick said. He stood at the Mobile Regional Airport gate with two dozen roses in his arms. After kissing them both hello and alerting everyone within a ten-mile radius of their arrival with his loud yell, he took their carry-ons and handed them each a bouquet. "Come on, I have the car parked outside and the Terminator's down waiting for your bags."

"Kimmie's here?" Parker asked.

It had been six months since the King sisters had seen each other, due to conflicting schedules, but Nick had worked for hours to get them this window of time. While Parker dominated women's tennis, her sisters Kimmie and Gray did the same in the sand, playing volleyball, and all of them were his clients.

"Yeah, she and Gray are here for twenty-four hours. They're heading out in the morning for a tournament in Palm Beach, so they're cooking you dinner and crashing in your guest rooms tonight." He pointed them toward the exit since he, Kimmie, and Gray had more than exceeded their welcome outside. Then again, they didn't call Gray the Viper for nothing. One look had sent the young security guard back to his booth for the hour they'd been waiting.

"Remember, workout first, then family reunion," Beau said.

"Yes, master, I remember."

"A night of fun won't hurt anyone, so cool it," Nick said, pinching Beau's earlobe.

The two women who stood next to the Land Cruiser outside looked almost exactly like Parker, except for the hair. Kimmie and Gray both kept theirs cut short for easier maintenance when they played, but all of them had the same powerful build. They weren't that far apart in age, with Parker the baby of the family and Gray the oldest, but all of them were stunning.

Only Nick and Beau knew the complete backstory, but for each sister, sports had been an escape from overly conservative parents who wanted prim ladies and lots of grandchildren to show off and dote on after their careers were over. Their father, Francis, had been a super sports dad when they'd started, especially with Parker, but soon lost interest not only in their time on the court, but in his daughters as well, as soon as the truth of who his daughters were came to light. Instead of the three darlings Francis had fantasized about, he'd ended up with three of the most famous lesbians in sports, which had been more than enough reason for him to disown them.

Their mother, Susan, still kept in touch, not wanting to alienate the three golden geese she'd given birth to. Short conversations at least once a month before her allowance check arrived kept Susan King's country-club membership up to date, her Mercedes running beautifully, and the young tennis pro of the month interested in spending as much time with her as she could get away with on and off the court. Susan wasn't known for either her discretion or her motherly instincts.

It gave him a sour stomach when he made the bank transactions, since neither Francis nor Susan deserved the children they were blessed with. They sure as hell didn't give a damn about how much their rejection had affected them. For Susan, at least, it seemed to be all about the money.

With Nick's careful management, all three of the King sisters had no financial concerns and more than enough to share. In their conversations with Susan, though, the subject of their father's hurtful eviction from his house never came up. Susan acted as if he didn't exist because of his small-minded opinions about his children and life in general. When she did talk about it that was how she often explained it, but Nick knew her well enough to know Susan's view of the world never went much past her own concerns and comfort.

"Is that the Wimbledon champion we see?" Gray asked as she hopped out of the driver's seat.

"I had to win something big so I could keep up with you two." Parker started laughing as first Gray, then Kimmie picked her up and spun her around.

"Any more big wins, kid, and you'll be way out of our league," Kimmie said, opening the back door for her.

"I thought you two had a tournament coming up?"

"It's worth cutting a couple days of training to come see our baby sister," Gray said as she started the car. "We're so proud of you, babe, and it killed us not to be there to see at least a few matches."

"We didn't make England, but we cleared our schedule for the entire Open. No way we're missing that," Kimmie said.

"Don't skip anything important to be there." Parker squeezed Gray's shoulder from the backseat.

"Nick's already taken care of it, so don't worry about it," Kimmie said. "We haven't been together for more than a few days in years, so we're due. What better time than when we get to see you bring home the Slam."

"Or watch me get slammed. You never know which might come first."

❖

From the door of the baggage claim, Sydney stepped out in time to see Parker get into the Toyota. The heat prompted her to remove her jacket and smile at the guy who took her bag and placed it in the bin of the rental-car van. She closed her eyes and pictured how much she wasn't going to do during the next week.

She hadn't thought about vacations since her promotion three years ago, not anything over three days, anyway. With the change in her schedule coming up, flying only domestic runs, she would relax and plan her newly single status.

Her sister always made fun of her planning, saying ninety-nine percent of life happened no matter what you did, but she felt comfortable doing it. She set goals and did what she had to do to achieve them, then when she hit those milestones she sat and made more goals and a plan to achieve them. So far that approach had been successful only at work.

Her career was where it needed to be, so for the next week she'd think along a different line. She doubted she'd take a chance like she had with Gene, but she didn't want to abandon the idea of a committed partnership. She was tired of being treated as if her feelings didn't matter. No, it was time to be swept off her feet, as it were, and she wouldn't settle until she found the woman who would do just that.

"Are you in a bikini with a drink and your woman yet?" said her sister, Margo, in lieu of a greeting when she answered her phone.

"And you call *her* barbaric," she said, and laughed. "*My woman* sounds so crass."

"I'm trying to be understanding when it comes to the...never mind that."

"To answer your question, I'm in the rental-car van, so sadly I'm still in my uniform." The van pulled away and passed the car Parker was riding in, and Sydney briefly wondered what she was doing here.

"Where's Gene?" Margo whispered something else, and she assumed it was "frigging idiot," since that was her sister's nickname for her ex-girlfriend. The word sounded so pathetic, considering she was over thirty. Girlfriends were something you had in high school.

"She confirmed she was coming a week ago and canceled before my flight this morning."

"What was your response to that?"

A bucket of tired fell on her as the van meandered off the airport campus. Any depression she'd ever suffered through came in the form of exhaustion, so she sat up, refusing to give Gene the satisfaction. "She called from a bar, so I told her I'm moving to New York and she's staying in Atlanta. She has a month to vacate my place, and she's free to date."

"Not to rub it in, Syd, but the truth is, she's free to fuck."

"Thanks. I feel much better after hearing that."

"Sorry, but ripping the Band-Aid off fast is less painful in the end." The van stopped at a light, and the driver tapped his fingers on the wheel to whatever was streaming through his headphones. "You don't need to hear this from me or anyone, but you made the right decision. I know you realize my total disdain for the moron, but you deserve so much better."

"I know, and I feel like I should be sad or something equally tragic, but I'm not."

"Shit on that. You did your best and Gene didn't appreciate it. Tell me you'll use your time down there trying to get laid. You're entitled, and some mindless sex is easier on your head than tequila."

"Tell me there aren't people standing around that can hear you?"

"I'm safely ensconced in my office, thank you, and you didn't answer me."

She laughed at Margo's answer to everything. No matter if you felt sad or had something to celebrate, a rousing orgasm could make it all better. "I'll be on a private island, so if someone swims up and doesn't have homicidal tendencies I'll consider it." She kept her voice low since the driver now seemed more interested in her conversation than the road.

"You sure you'll be okay by yourself?"

"I've been dreaming about this vacation for months." She rested her head against the window and wished the nosy guy driving would take her all the way to the beach house she'd arranged. Her job had always been fun and fascinating enough to make her ignore a lot of things, but she was tired of forgetting what it was like to be truly happy. "I'll be fine, and after I recharge I'm looking forward to being closer to you and Mom. What happened today was for the best."

"Well, we can't wait either, but do me a favor. If someone does swim toward you and they're hot, jump them." She laughed along with Margo. "If you need me to, though, I'll take some time off and come down there with you so you won't have to be alone. Even forgetting Gene, this is the first time you've been there since Dad died, and you might like the company."

"I sure miss him." Their dad had needed open-heart surgery eighteen months before, and both she and Margo had taken six weeks off to stay with their parents to help their mother take care of him. The staff had rolled him into surgery with him still cracking jokes about the kind of pie he wanted as soon as he woke up, then that night, before he ever woke up, he died.

He was gone just like that, and the pain of losing him had faded the world around her so much she missed not only him, but finding beauty in the simplest things, like she had all her life.

"Why there, Syd? You work for a damn airline and could get free tickets to the moon, if it was a route. Why go to the one place that'll remind you?"

"I need to go to the place we had some of our best times, to get moving again. I want to visit some of the shops we went to and drive by the old place we always rented. I'm going a little more upscale this time since Shelley and Connie built on Press Cove. We would've never made it past the guard onto the bridge out there, no matter how charming you were." When they slowed, she opened her eyes and fought the craving to tell Margo to come down, but she wanted the solitude more.

"I worry about you, you know that, right?" Margo had lost her teasing tone, which only added to the heaviness in Sydney's chest. "I miss him too, but right now I miss you more. Have fun, but it's good to know you'll be here soon. You've been away from us too long."

"Don't let my morose mood ruin your day. A lot of it has nothing to do with Daddy or Gene."

"What's wrong?"

"I had an interesting preflight, but I'll tell you about it later. I have to run in and get my car, so call Mom and tell her I got here and I'll call her tomorrow once I'm settled." She dug in her purse for a tip, since the driver had been kind enough to put her luggage in the trunk of her rental. "I love you."

"I love you too, don't forget to call me, and try to have fun. And if you're interested, I just read that sex is good for your skin and boosts your metabolism."

❖

"So, are you going to give us an exclusive on Alicia?" Gray asked as she spotted Parker while she did some chest presses. "I'm beginning to think you're trying to set the record for the most time between the sheets." Kimmie laughed so hard she had to slow down on the stationary bike she was pedaling.

"If you're planning on a career in comedy after volleyball, you might want to rethink that." Parker was starting to feel the burn from so many reps, but she wasn't about to stop. She'd learned her work ethic from her sisters and they didn't often get to spend time like this, so she didn't intend to waste it. "Your act needs work."

"At least tell us you showed her a good time," Kimmie said.

"You taught me that, didn't you? I may date a lot of them, but I'm not making any promises I'm not planning to keep. Alicia and I went out a few times and had a good time. What's the harm?"

Gray took the bar from her, placed it in the rack, then leaned over Parker. "We just worry about you, kid. Our schedules have been crazy, and phone calls aren't the same, so we want to make sure you're okay."

"I'm fine, and I promise no more psychotic singers if I can help it. Workouts and practice are the only things on my schedule until we board the plane for New York and the Open." She toweled her face off and sighed. "I'm not getting any younger. I feel like I'm chasing this title, and it's going to outrun me." It was a relief to be able to let all her façades go and be totally honest without thinking her words would come back to bite her in the ass in four-inch letters with pictures to make a better story.

"This is your year," Kimmie said. They all stood close enough to put their hands on each other's shoulders. "And it's time to start running *toward* that title." She held up Parker's jogging shoes and smiled.

"Get going and we'll have dinner waiting for you. Kimmie's making spaghetti and we're serving it on that fancy plate they gave you in England. She's not making her famous chicken soup until you give her more kitchenware from New York," Gray said, which made them all laugh.

❖

Parker stretched on the deck at the back of her house and enjoyed listening to her sisters in the kitchen. Having two older siblings had left her on the receiving end of all their protective instincts, especially after being on their own since their teens. But at moments like this when she was on the outside listening in, the loneliness pressed in. Gray and Kimmie were her family, but they had a bond that came from being born so close together. Being only ten months apart in age made them as close as twins, and their choice of career had made that connection even stronger.

Parker wasn't bitter or envious as she listened to them kid around in her kitchen. She simply enjoyed their joking, feeling connected to her family after standing on a court alone for so many months. Even after the long flight and workout, she anticipated finishing her run so she could get back and share a meal with her sisters.

She walked down to the beach, taking deep breaths to reacquaint herself with all the aspects of this place. This stretch of paradise was one of the things she missed most when grueling tournament play kept her away for weeks. The pristine white sand and blue-green waters were like a blanket of calm in an otherwise busy life. She loved it so much she was sure she could one day walk away from tennis and not miss the crowds or the action.

Her house was built at the end of a large island close to the Florida border that rarely showed up on any map. Beau and Nick lived on the other end, with only a couple of houses between them. Only one bridge connected them to the mainland, and at night if she walked to the westernmost tip she could see the lights of the more populated Gulf Shores. This was her haven and she didn't mind sharing it with her neighbors, since they were mostly weekenders who came in the fall to enjoy the still-warm but cooler temperatures and kept mostly to themselves. Thankfully the houses weren't rented out, like most of the ones on the mainland, and the manned security gate kept away any curiosity seekers.

She stood on the shoreline and took another deep breath, enjoying the scent of salt water before she bent to go through her final set of stretches. Her usual route took her five miles down the beach before she turned around and headed back. No matter the weather, she ran it almost every day, thinking of lines of poetry along the way. Gorilla, indeed.

Since it was a gated community her companions were mostly the gulls flying past and the sandpipers fleeing the oncoming water. She ran without the headphones popular with others, content to enjoy the sound of the Gulf and her feet hitting the sand. Those were the best forms of meditation she'd found to clear her head. She was enjoying her surroundings and the joy of being home so much she almost tripped over the woman lying on her stomach on a red blanket close to the water.

Parker admired the way the blonde's backside looked in the suit but didn't stop to chat. The way her forehead was resting on her folded hands made her think she was asleep, so she returned her gaze to the water and ran past her. It was unusual for her neighbors to rent out the house or to lend it to someone, but the woman appeared harmless, so Parker cleared her presence from her mind as well.

She had two months to enjoy these snippets of calm before she immersed herself in the madness of big-tournament play, and she didn't plan to waste a second of it.

❖

Sydney lay on the blanket with her eyes closed for over an hour before getting up and going for a swim. After her cool-off she'd moved her blanket closer to the dunes, not wanting to soak it with the incoming tide. She'd heard the runner earlier, before she'd drifted off to sleep, glad that they'd respected her privacy.

Well into chapter two of her book, Sydney peered up to see who the footsteps belonged to. She was sure the runner was the same person who'd passed earlier, since this place was about as isolated as she'd ever been on a beach. This time, though, she passed oblivious to her presence, and Sydney held her breath at her luck. She held her book high enough to hide her face and prayed those memorable eyes stayed focused on anything but her, because there in all her sweaty glory was Parker King, wearing only running shorts and a sports bra.

The distance between them gave Sydney the opportunity to just stare without guilt or fear of being caught as she peeked over the top of her book. Parker resembled a fine work of art found in museums. She had visible muscles on every uncovered part of her body, and the expression on her face made Sydney think she was happy. *And she should be. I thought a six-pack like that was only possible with a great air-brush artist.*

This version of Parker who'd slowed to a walk held no trace of the passenger she'd met. Parker had been nice enough, but she'd seemed guarded on the plane. The thought that perhaps she'd misjudged Parker had occurred to her after she finished the first two chapters of *To Kill a Mockingbird*. She'd stopped to buy it before heading out of Mobile, falling instantly in love again with the characters she'd read about years earlier. That Parker could get so engrossed in one of her mother's favorites had to mean she had some redeeming qualities. Right? There was only one way to answer that.

She had put the book down and opened her mouth to call out, when Parker stripped naked and jumped into the surf in front of the house next to the one her friends had lent her for the week. She really hadn't noticed the beach house a ways down when she'd arrived, she was so anxious to start her holiday, but the tennis court built on pilings over the water would've given her a good clue.

"So this is where the Romeo of the circuit lives," she said softly to herself, shaking her head when two other naked women ran out of the house and joined Parker in the water.

"Yep, she's a pig with a soft spot for classical books."

After another hour Sydney walked back to the house, carrying only her book and bag. Staying for a week would certainly magnify the difference between her life and Parker King's, so she decided to not let it bother her. She probably wouldn't have anything to distract her from Parker's antics. So far Parker had a lot in common with Gene, which wasn't winning her any points.

They both cruised through life without worry or guilt about anything or anyone. What made a person like that? She pondered the question as she took one last look at the three women having fun in the surf. They certainly looked like they had the answer, and unlike her, they appeared thrilled to revel in the moment.

Chapter Four

Sydney woke the next morning to a carbon copy of the day before, with plenty of sun and high temperatures, so she decided to head in to Gulf Shores and save herself from the sunburn that'd keep her from enjoying the rest of her week. She'd visited the area with her parents and sister every summer until she'd started college, and she thought of all the shopping excursions with her mom and Margo.

Almost as if her dad had a premonition of his future, he'd invited Sydney and Margo here for a long weekend a few months before he died. She hadn't laughed that much in a long time, since her parents seemed to have perfect recall when it came to every second of their childhood. The stories had filled their time, and she'd left with a certainty about her life because no matter what, she belonged somewhere. Even if she wasn't thrilled with Gene at the time, and much less now, she had a family that loved her, and they represented the place in her heart where she'd always be safe. Their last family photo had been taken on the beach in front of the house they'd rented, and her mom had placed a copy of it in her dad's pocket before they'd closed his casket.

Losing him had been hard, but her mom had been the rock who'd reminded them to dwell on the happy memories, like the ones they'd made here, instead of dwelling on the grief. Sydney found the coffee shop in Daphne they'd frequented years before and stopped for breakfast before trying to find birthday presents for Margo and her mom. The place had been remodeled and had a different name, but it still had the row of tables with a great view of the street and its quaint shops.

She relaxed as she waited for her order and tried to forget the list of shitty things that had happened, trying instead to put herself in a mind-set to have fun. Her mother was always preaching about that in every phone call they'd had recently. She sat with her eyes closed, running through a litany of questions in her mind, when a familiar voice interrupted her thought process and she frowned.

"Sorry it took so long, ma'am, but I'm still recovering from a bumpy landing in Miami yesterday." She opened her eyes to Parker holding a tray with her cappuccino. The heat in her ears, she knew, was a combination of a blush and anger over Parker's flip comment. Bad weather and wind shears had made for a less-than-perfect landing, and she didn't want to take anyone's shit about it.

"I'm sorry, Captain, I was only kidding. You seemed so lost I thought I'd cheer you up by bringing over your order. It looks like you could use a shot of caffeine."

"Why are you harassing me on my vacation, Miss King?" Sydney asked. *Oh no, I will not fall for a cute smile and a cute butt. She sleeps with two women at a time.* She repeated that mantra three times in her head to remind herself of who she was dealing with as Parker's smile showed off her dimples. *Today her eyes are sky blue*, her internal lecture continued as a way of chipping bricks off her defenses. She'd gotten a good look at Parker's eyes when she'd leaned over and set her coffee down.

"I was on my way home from the airport, Captain, and I love the hot chocolate here. I'm sorry for bothering you, it won't happen again. Enjoy your day and the rest of your stay." Parker's smile disappeared and she stepped back, turning around and heading to the counter again without another word.

"Do you like hanging out in airports? Or is it where you perfect your sarcastic comments for airline employees?" She spoke loud enough for Parker to hear her, and the question was her effort, against her better judgment, to get Parker to stay after she'd snapped at her.

"No, it's your job to love airports, I'd guess, and I'm not stalking or harassing you. I was just dropping my sisters off for their flight this morning. They surprised me with a visit yesterday before their next tournament. One night wasn't enough, but they had to fly out this morning." A teenager with acne walked up and handed Parker a tray with large steaming cup and a gigantic cinnamon roll. "That's more information than I'm sure you needed, but I don't want you calling the cops."

"There's more than one of you?" She was disgusted when she thought Parker could eat something like that and still look fantastic. She looked up at Parker with her hands full and realized she was waiting for an invitation to join her. "I'm sorry, would you like to sit?" She waved to the empty chair at the table, suddenly wanting Parker's company even though a loud alarm was flashing in her brain.

"Thanks, and yes, there are three of us, but Gray and Kimmie are a lot different. First, they're both taller, and they're into sand." Parker took a big bite of the gooey roll, then held it close to Sydney's mouth as an offer to take a bite. With a sigh she shook her head, knowing she had the metabolism of a lazy slug. The alarm was replaced by Margo's damned comment about sex and metabolism. She was sure Margo would've had Parker naked in the parking lot by now, despite the fact she wasn't gay.

"Sand?" She regretted not taking a bite when Parker rolled her eyes back with a blissful expression.

"They play sand volleyball and can make you eat the ball if you're not paying attention."

She watched Parker continue to eat the roll and stop every so often to lick icing off her fingers. *God, that looks good*, she thought, and had a hard time deciding whether she was commenting on the roll or the long fingers holding it. She was clearly either losing her mind or had a natural talent for finding hot, philandering women.

"Sort of like their sister serving the ball at over a hundred miles an hour." Her mouth engaged without permission, and the second the words came out she could have kicked herself. All Parker needed was encouragement, and her smile with a slight chocolate mustache was a clear sign of her screw-up.

"Why, Captain, I didn't know you cared," Parker said in a teasing way, and Sydney's face got hot again.

"I watched a little of your match at the airport lounge because nothing else was on. Your talent on the tennis court impressed me, Ms. Parker. Then I met you and you called me sweetheart and essentially asked me to make you coffee and a sandwich." She felt like she'd served an ace when Parker lost her smile and squirmed a bit.

"It was hot chocolate. I don't drink coffee."

"A splitting of semantic hairs, Ms. King. I don't serve either."

"Ah, I beg to differ. Yes, you do, and so you did," Parker said, and stopped talking when Sydney narrowed her eyes in warning. She changed the subject. "I never did ask where you're staying?"

"The Pelican Villa house." The question had been the bell that'd ended the round, and they retreated to their respective corners. *Yes, the house right next to yours, oh naked swimmer, though now I know who the two other women were. I was wrong about you yet again*, Sydney thought, berating herself for being so judgmental, but it was hard to overcome a learned response.

"Hey, we're neighbors," Parker said, sitting up and smiling. "How about I take you out to dinner to make it up to you? Better yet, I could cook for you."

Okay, off beverages and onto flirting. Did she just ask me out? Jesus, she moves so fast it's hard to know. Gene would be taking notes by now. "Is there a catch to your dinner invitations?" The coffee encounter, if she was honest with herself, had slid into flirtation the minute Parker had sat down, and it was time to pull back some. This vacation was supposed to be a planning session as well as a break, not a chance to play footsie with Parker King.

Parker's photogenic smile faltered a bit but didn't completely fade. "Sure, I have a pole in my living room you'll be expected to dance on before the appetizers," she said without sarcasm. "I'm sure that's what you're thinking anyway, but there's no catch. It's only dinner. If you're interested I have practice and workouts until around five thirty every day, so just let me know. I hope you have fun in town." Parker got up and left without waiting for an answer, and this time she made it out the door.

"Well, this ought to be a lesson for any future encounters I have as I start dating again," Sydney muttered softly. "So far I'm batting a thousand with this one," she added before grabbing the last bit of cinnamon roll Parker had slid across the table to her before she left. Now she had two things to feel guilty about, though a high-calorie treat was safer than giving any thought whatsoever to Parker King. She was the kind of woman her mother was forever going on about and the reason the next person she allowed into her life would have to pass a long and grueling psychological test.

"I thought you were going home?" Sydney entered the small gallery next door after spotting Parker through the glass door staring at a canvas. At the angle she was standing she couldn't see what it was, but judging by the reflection in the store window it was infused with color.

"Captain, I'm beginning to think you're following me." That easy smile Sydney was starting to expect reappeared, a testament that Parker was joking. It was a wonder, after how rude she'd been.

"Do you often have these delusional fantasies?"

"My fantasies revolve more around the…well, never mind about that." Sydney enjoyed the blush that suddenly appeared on Parker's face. She didn't know why, but she figured Parker wasn't one to be flustered easily.

"Had a sudden urge to buy a piece of art before you headed home?"

"It's a gift, actually, but I feel kind of egotistical hanging it up. And I have a feeling you already believe my head is swelled up enough."

Sydney walked around the easel slowly, trying to stall so she could think of a good comeback. The piece knocked any thought of sarcasm from her mind. She took a step back as if afraid she'd get hit by the ball frozen in time at the top of the canvas. Below it, with her racquet at the ready, Parker stood in the middle of her serving stance.

LeRoy Neiman had in his unique way captured the essence of Parker's power and style of play. Even though Sydney had only seen Parker play on television, standing this close to her she could almost feel the energy she seemed to exude, even while standing still. Neiman had captured the energy in a riot of red, yellow, and blue thick paint.

"I'll let you in on a long-time belief of mine, Ms. King," she said, speaking softly and not taking her eyes off the painting. "When you're this good at something, you have a right to be a little swell-headed."

"Then I'll have to see if he'll consider doing one of you at the controls of a plane."

"After that landing yesterday I'm sure you have a definite opinion of how good a pilot I am." She took a quick peek at Parker's profile. "Perhaps you think I'm more suited to serve the coffee and sandwich you asked for."

"Headwinds of close to thirty miles an hour are just a small summer storm around here, but when you're trying to put down a large airborne object it can't be too easy. You did a good job and I was only kidding in the coffee shop. I may not know anything about piloting a plane, but I travel enough to know the experienced pilots from the beginners."

"You checked the weather?" The painting had lost all of its allure as she concentrated on the live subject. "Why?"

Parker nodded when the gallery owner pointed to the painting. It was a gift from Kimmie and Gray, so no matter how conceited she thought owning it was, it was going home with her.

"I'm the Curious George of my time. When things happen, it's usually for good reasons. Yesterday it was bad weather up against a good pilot. The fact we're both standing here talking about it means the good pilot won, so sorry for teasing you about it."

"Are you busy for the rest of the day?" Sydney asked.

"I'm playing tennis later, why?"

"I thought you might like to have lunch."

Parker laughed as she glanced at her watch. It was a few minutes past ten. "Did the coffee not fill you up or did you have something else in mind?"

"Just forget it."

"It's only a question, calm down." She took a chance and put her hand on Sydney's shoulder to halt her retreat. With Sydney's vacillating moods she half expected to be slapped. "Let's start over, okay?"

"Start over how?"

"First, I'd love to have lunch with you, but nothing's open this early so we'll have to kill some time. What would you like to do?"

Sydney's shoulder under her hand relaxed. "I came into town to get some gifts for my mom and sister."

"What are their names?"

"I think they're past the name on a license for their bikes." Sydney's smile helped cut the sharpness of the comment.

"I was just—"

"Curious? My mom's name is Lucia and I have one sister, Margo."

"Do Lucia and Margo like pottery?"

"They love it, actually. My mom loves to garden, but with only a small space behind her place in the city, she keeps everything in containers." Sydney hesitated, as if having an internal argument, but she slipped her hand into the bend of the arm Parker had offered and started walking.

Parker told the gallery owner she'd be back later for the painting, then ushered Sydney out the door. They walked two blocks in a comfortable silence, enjoying the day since the dark cloud cover from late the day before had cleared. The building Parker was headed to was one of her favorites to visit when she was in town. It housed a huge collection of some of the most unusual and eclectic things the owners of the place could find in their frequent travels.

Sydney pulled them to a stop when they arrived and just stared at the side of the old brick façade. The entire thing was covered by a large mural of whales and other sea life, so well done everything on it seemed to have paused momentarily before swimming off. In addition to the artwork, the huge collection of wind chimes on the large front porch lined with rockers sounded to Parker like they were harmonizing.

"Is this place new?"

"It looks like it's been here for years, doesn't it?"

Sydney nodded. "I don't remember it from my family vacations."

"The owners are transplants from New Orleans and it took them about eight months to get it together, but from the day they opened, it had a comfortable feel about it. I think it's because they go about life the same way they go about putting their inventory together. It's a little jumbled, but in the end it all fits."

"Sounds interesting," Sydney said as she squeezed her arm.

"Let's go take a look, then. I'm sure you'll find something unique for your family. If not, there's a surf shop closer to the water where we can find some of those license plates with their names."

They separated at the door, strolling through the large place admiring the variation of furniture, pottery, and odds and ends scattered throughout. When they met at the back of the store Sydney ran her fingers along the design of one plant container Parker found and pointed it out. It was too big to carry home, but the girl behind the counter said it could be shipped with no problem.

In the back Parker found a wind chime made of salvaged driftwood from the Amazon and made another mailing arrangement for Margo's gift. Parker spotted another smaller chime close to it, crafted from the same wood. The birds in flight carved into the wood reminded her of Sydney.

They headed back to the counter and Parker pointed it out to the one of the clerks and asked her to wrap it. Altogether they had shared maybe an hour in each other's company, but she liked Sydney. Customarily guarded with who she let around her, Parker found that a welcome surprise.

"What else does your family enjoy?" Parker asked as she accepted the bag with her purchase.

"My mom's a retired kindergarten teacher who likes to garden and read, and my sister likes to read too and enjoy a good glass of wine. She says it's a good way to unwind every so often."

Parker led her farther down the block away from the coffee shop where they'd started. "What's she getting wound up about?"

"She's a VP in lending for the Chase Group." Sydney followed

Parker into a small wine shop a few doors away, attached to a small café with a large chalkboard touting the day's specials.

"Maybe after lunch we can add a good bottle of wine to her bounty of gifts," Parker said. Only two tables were left, and one of the servers waved them to the one closest to the windows. "You are still interested in lunch, right?"

"Since you've obviously been here before, what do you recommend?"

"The crispy duck in raspberry sauce, and a crab cake to start."

Sydney took her advice and shot her a teasing glare when she ordered a salad and a glass of water. "I'm practicing this afternoon and it's a pain when we have to stop to clean off the court when I start spitting up duck," she said, and shrugged.

"Do you ever get tired of it? The playing, I mean."

"In the beginning, tennis was fun." Parker laid her napkin in her lap and leaned back so the waiter could put down their drinks. "When I was about to turn pro, it got to be more of a chore, but with a few changes in my life, I've gotten to a place where I've found the joy in it again."

"You certainly looked like you were having fun a couple of days ago on center court."

She laughed and shrugged again. "My coach might disagree with you. He believes in the money shots, as it were—don't prolong the game too much and go with what works to win. When I start pushing those baseline shots, he gets nervous, but that's what all the practice is for, I figure." She stopped talking when Sydney's crab cake arrived. "You know enough about me. Tell me more about yourself, Captain."

They had a pleasant lunch, and Sydney shared her appetizer and some stories about her family. If the mundane lives of a retired teacher, banking executive, and pilot were boring, she couldn't tell from Parker's face. She asked engaging questions every so often, sending her off on another tangent and making it clear she was not only interested but paying attention. Sydney avoided anything that had to do with Gene, since that part of her life was over and not worth rehashing.

For dessert Parker insisted they share a piece of key lime pie, then asked for the bill. "To make up for the order of a sandwich and hot chocolate yesterday," she said, referring to the tab. "And this," she picked up the bag at her feet and set it on the table, "is just because I thought you'd like it."

The chime had been laid in the tissue with care, so Sydney left it and only lifted one section to admire the carving. "I should say you shouldn't have, but I'm just going to say thank you. It's beautiful."

"Every vacation should be marked by something special, don't you think?" Parker put her credit card back into her wallet and stood to pull Sydney's chair for her. "Want to get your sister something or would you like me to walk you to your car?" Parker put her hands up as if to stop her from correcting her assumptions. "Of course, if you have more shopping to do, feel free, but I have to get to my afternoon practice session. Thanks for having lunch with me, and let me know about dinner. All my days are pretty much the same, so whenever you'd like to come over just let me know. I'm looking forward to it."

She shook the hand Parker offered, wishing the day could have gone on a little longer, but she understood. "Thanks for the tour and for lunch. I'm going to look around a little more. Talk to you soon."

"Have fun, then."

After she waved good-bye, Sydney stood in the wine shop until Parker disappeared into the gallery, obviously to pick up her painting. This had been a fun way to spend time, but she had no illusions once she lost sight of Parker. From what she'd read about her, she had a better shot of piloting the space shuttle than of taming Kong.

❖

Sydney decided to skip the wine for Margo and go back to the beach house. Shopping had lost its allure after Parker left. She strolled and window-shopped to kill some more time since no one was waiting for her. For the first time in hours she thought of Gene and their breakup. If Gene really wanted her back, she had a lousy way of showing it. No one had called since her arrival.

"That should tell you something, Syd," she said to herself. "Margo's right, I need to get out and find a little fun." The morning and lunch had been more enjoyable because of Parker's company. "What the hell, let me go work on my sunburn."

The chilly interior of the house was devoid of sound, so she figured the sound of the surf would make a good white noise while she read her book. Outside the back windows, the sun sparkled off the soft waves and the tops of the sea oats bobbed gently with the slight breeze. She stripped as she walked through the house to the bedroom to put on her bathing suit, relieved not to have a schedule to worry about.

Half the contents of her beach bag slipped onto her beach blanket, which was still in place, but she didn't care as she ran into the surf. The water was shockingly cold at first so she dove in head-first to acclimate. When she came up she heard a popping noise.

Next door, on the court that seemed to float above the water, Parker and another woman seemed to be trying to kill each other with a tennis ball. Parker had changed into a T-shirt and baggy shorts, but even that couldn't hide the raw power she used to wield the tennis racquet like a sword. It brought to mind the painting she'd seen earlier.

Whoever Parker's opponent was, she was holding her own in a volley as blistering as the sun. Sydney, who could hear a man barking out corrections, was happy Parker still looked like she had fun playing what was essentially just a game.

"Natasha, hit them more toward the forehand, please. Boris needs more work on that right now since the ball will bounce differently at the Open. Park, pay attention and lengthen the shots. We already know you're a big girl who can hit it hard. Let's try finesse now, sweetheart." Sydney recognized the man from the flight. Parker's service stance swiveled a bit and the man dodged the bullet she'd shot his way. "Not funny, Parker, not funny. Okay, one more round, you two, and then we'll call it a day."

Sydney laughed at Parker's playful, free-spirited side. Sydney was only thirty-five but had lost that part of her inner child when her dad passed. It was refreshing to see someone exhibit such gusto even when no one was watching. One of Parker's lobs went over the fence and into the water, making Sydney think that was the downside of the court's location, and also that Parker was tired to make such a mistake. Parker's order of "Abby, go," told her differently.

The ball of fur that dove into the water was the biggest conglomeration of dog she'd ever seen. A big black blur swam for the yellow floating ball, then met Parker on the beach, dropping the ball at her feet and shaking the water from his body.

"You big goober." Parker's fussing at the surprise shower sent Abby running down the beach.

He stopped when he spotted Sydney in the water. Dripping, he danced from paw to paw, the equally wet ball sitting in front of him. She laughed. If Parker had been a dog, this would be it. He was wooing her in a way that made it sound like he just wanted to play and his master had headed for the house.

"Come on, Abby, time to go, boy." Parker's voice came from

behind the dunes, but the dog sat and waved his paw in Sydney's direction, then nosed the ball into the water as a gift, like he wanted her to get out. "Abby?" Parker sounded closer now.

"He won't eat me, will he, if I come out?" Sydney yelled from her spot when she noticed Parker.

"I just fed him, so you're safe." Parker picked up the ball and tossed it down the beach.

Sydney started out of the water and had the sudden urge for a robe. She didn't normally wear this bathing suit in public, but her friends who'd lent her the house had kept talking about how secluded it was. "Finished for the day?"

"If you're talking about tennis, then yes, I am. But if you're talking about dinner, I'm still in limbo."

Abby came back and gave Parker the ball, then turned to see where on the beach it would land. He was off again as soon as Parker put her shoulder into it and sent him running toward the water.

"Can I do anything about that limbo?" Sydney started toward her blanket, smiling when Parker let her go ahead. When she turned around quickly, Parker's eyes were definitely not on where the dog was running to next.

"I was thinking about this nice seafood place on the bay." Parker put her hand out for the ball when Abby made it back. "And this is just like our lunch date."

"We had a date at lunch?" Sydney picked up her towel, but instead of wrapping it around her hips as she started to, she just held it behind her back.

"Not like a date date." Parker sounded flustered.

"What, I'm not your type?" Margo seemed to have possessed her momentarily.

The question made Parker laugh. "You don't date much, do you?"

If Parker's return question was a joke, she didn't get it. "What?"

"Pummeling the asker right out of the gate might not get you many second dates."

Sydney wrapped her towel around her hips and folded her arms against her chest. "Is this your idea of charm?"

"Have dinner with me and you'll find out. Is seven okay?" The dog made it back again and dropped the ball at Parker's feet, then turned his head from one to the other, trying to get someone's attention.

Without taking her eyes off Sydney, Parker held her hand out and Abby delivered the slobber-covered ball, which she threw toward her house this time.

"Since you've made *me* curious now, I'll be ready," Sydney said, and smiled when Parker picked up her bag. This time Parker walked next to her and dropped her off at the back door.

Chapter Five

They sat across from each other in the restaurant, and Sydney perused the menu while Parker relaxed and enjoyed the piano player. Parker had arrived early and had tried to be the perfect date so far, opening doors and staying on her best behavior. She caught Parker staring and dropped her eyes back to her menu to escape the intensity, brushing a strand of her hair behind her ear as if she could cover up her embarrassment. Their time together so far reminded her of her first date with Gene. It seemed ages ago, and she could barely remember how wonderful she'd once felt to be with her since their relationship contained too many betrayals for her to forgive.

"Any more recommendations?" she asked after the heat in her ears had faded a bit.

"The filet."

"You brought me to a seafood restaurant and you're recommending a steak?"

"Did I steer you wrong at lunch?" Parker pushed her menu to the side and rested her elbows on the table. "If you're feeling really adventurous, you'd let me order for you."

"Why do I feel like I'm being challenged?"

"Oh, you are," Parker said with a big smile.

The waiter took their order from Parker as Sydney just relaxed and enjoyed the atmosphere. Parker, for someone so much younger than her, certainly knew how to set a mood. She accepted the glass of wine Parker poured after she sent the server back to the bar and clinked her glass against Parker's when she held it out.

"To a successful vacation," Parker said.

The pinot Parker chose was delicious, and for the first time in months Sydney enjoyed being pampered and feeling like the center of someone's attention. That's what her heart was telling her, but her head was having a harder time following suit since she also knew Parker's reputation. It was hard to miss it every time she stopped at the airport newsstand to pick up a magazine before her flight. One of the rags featured a picture of Parker with some beauty on her arm at least once a month, as did the more traditional newspapers.

"Are you happy?" she asked Parker.

The wineglass came down and Parker twirled the stem, making the rich liquid cling to the side of the crystal. "In what context?"

"It's not a hard question, Parker. Are you happy with your life in general?"

"Are you, in your life in general?" Parker asked in return before taking another sip of her wine.

"I'm happy with my job, but when the workday's over, it's a little different," she answered simply.

"What's different?"

She tapped the top of Parker's hand, which lay flat on the table. "I asked you a question first."

"I'm happy with my life on the court, but off it, it's a little different." She smiled.

"It can't be because you're lonely."

"I didn't take you for a tabloid reader." Parker laughed, but it didn't sound like it was because she was having a wonderful time.

"I'm not…but you have to admit that you make life look like a romance novel. And from what I recall, the characters filling their pages have sex every sixty pages or so. You definitely would make the cut."

Parker put her hand up to her chest and grimaced. "Ouch, Captain."

"I didn't mean that as an insult."

"Of course you didn't." Parker had interrupted her before she could go on, then the waiter came and put their entrées down.

"You were right about the steak," Sydney said as she looked at her filet covered in lump crab meat and sautéed shrimp.

"Thanks." Parker only nodded, the playfulness seemingly knocked out of her.

For the rest of the night they stuck to safer topics, since no matter how hard Sydney tried to get them back on track, Parker was annoyingly polite but didn't return the banter. At the end of their meal, Parker walked her to the door and thanked her for joining her. After that she turned around and never looked back.

Once Sydney was alone, she mentally kicked herself for what had happened. Her dad was famous for stating that a person's actions, not what other people say about them, should matter. So far the Parker she'd spent time with was vastly different than the one people talked about. Her fear of her growing attraction for Parker had caused the stupidity that had come out of her mouth at dinner. Her heart and her head were warring over the enigma of Parker, and whichever one won, it would involve heartache. Besides, it was too soon to even fantasize about something that wouldn't happen even if she were open to it.

The full moon and clear night made her decide to go outside. The night was warm but the water was cool as she started her walk down the shoreline. Outside, with the waves coming ashore burying her feet in the sand, she indulged in a game of "what if."

The annoying buzz of her phone cut her smile, especially when she saw Gene's name on the readout. "Hello." With one word the wonderful time she'd shared with Parker washed away like her footprints in the sand.

❖

The sound of the doorbell took Parker by surprise as she sat down to read with Abby at her feet for company. With the twenty-four-hour gate and guard, people rarely came to the house, and even less often actually pressed the button.

"Can I help you?" she asked through the crack the security chain made in the door.

"P. King?" the FedEx guy asked. The large truck in her driveway bolstered his identity as a legitimate driver.

"Like I said, can I help you?"

"Sorry to call so late, but I had trouble finding the place. Will you sign for a package for P. King?" He slipped the clipboard through the opening in the door when it became apparent she wouldn't open it completely. That task completed, he handed over the envelope.

The label was typed just like the other thirty-seven she'd received, and like those others this one probably didn't have fingerprints, DNA, or any other clue to who the writer was. Still, she picked up the phone and called Beau before she notified the police assigned to the case. She was getting tired of having them do nothing but show up and fill out a report. An hour later that was exactly what'd happened as the detective walked out with the original letter.

"Go home, both of you." She folded the copy of what had been sent as she spoke to Beau and Nick. The original was headed to the file to join the others. "Tomorrow's soon enough for you to harass me about this, so go home."

"At least let us read it," Beau said.

"Tomorrow, I promise." She put the folded paper in her back pocket.

"Denial won't make this go away." Beau obviously ignored Nick's fingers on his bicep as he tried to pull him to the door.

"And me moving in with you won't make it go away either." She threw her hands up in frustration and dropped them just as quickly when Abby barked. "I'm not giving in to what's easy, Beau. If I do, then what? I live with you and Nick until this nut case finds a new hobby?"

"What's wrong with that?"

"Aside from the obvious reasons, you mean?" Before she said anything else she hugged him. "Go home. I'll be fine until we talk about it tomorrow. If the only way to change this sicko's mind is to change myself into someone I'm not, it isn't an option. You know that, but I love you for caring."

"How can you say that? You don't know what this inbred's capable of."

"I have Abby, and the police and I are on a first-name basis. They got here in less than ten minutes tonight. That's their personal best."

Beau laughed even though he was obviously still upset. "It's not funny, and I'm calling the FBI in the morning."

"We did that already. They told us to let the locals handle it, and that's what we're going to do." She let him go but kept her arm around his shoulder as she walked him to the door. "Get some sleep and I'll see you in the morning."

When the house was quiet again she sat in the library with Abby's head in her lap. Surrounded by such comfort, she unfolded the innocuous white sheet and read what someone else considered it their duty to write. The beautiful individual letters in the scrolling calligraphy didn't mask the violence of the words they formed, but the writer must have found it normal to live with such hatred since he, or she, had written her so many letters.

The ink, the linen paper, the calligraphy, and her sins were the same in every one, but the way she would die was always different. She stared at the copy until the words became jumbled, then forced herself to read.

P. King,

Your life is an affront to God. The Savior who gave you life, talent, and privilege is ashamed of you for defiling His holy name. At the end of your life, you will have something in common with our Lord. To purify your blood you will shed it on the cross like He did. I'll save your soul by driving the nails myself. First your hands, then your feet, so that through pain, you'll repent of your sins of lying with women in the vilest of ways. Finally your spirit will be lifted to heaven when I plunge my blade into your heart over and over again until the beast that lives within is dead.

This is my vow as a soldier of God.

After the fifth note arrived by the same method, she'd stopped asking why this person had picked her. For whatever reason, he'd proved persistent. "Everyone needs goals, I guess," she told Abby. "I just wish this jerk had picked trying to swim through the Everglades in alligator-mating season instead of becoming my pen pal."

With a pat on Abby's side, she got up and headed to the back door. Sleep wouldn't come now, so she decided to go for a walk. Abby followed with his tail wagging until they reached the water, then he ran ahead only to double back, as if to check on her.

After about two hundred yards she saw she wasn't alone: A lone figure stood in ankle-deep water just staring off into the horizon. The letter slipped easily from her thoughts when she saw how beautiful Sydney's hair looked in the sparse moonlight. A couple of poems came to mind that spoke of spun gold, and now she knew what they meant.

She gave a short whistle and Abby headed to the dunes, since she didn't want him to startle Sydney. It also made Sydney aware that she wasn't alone.

"Couldn't sleep, Captain? I hope you aren't lamenting what a horrible dinner companion you had tonight."

Sydney wrapped her arms around herself despite the warm temperatures and appeared to not want company, but she did smile when Parker stopped next to her. "My dinner date was wonderful, even though I acted like a complete idiot. I'm sorry for insulting you."

"It's okay. I'm used to being pigeonholed. No harm done."

"Don't let me off the hook so easily." Sydney sighed and dropped her arms. "To answer your question, I was out here enjoying the solitude."

"Should I keep walking?"

"Solitude isn't all it's cracked up to be. Please stay."

"Let's walk," she said, and pointed away from the houses.

"What brings you out tonight? Tell me it's not so you could think of ways to avoid your annoying neighbor?"

"As if. It's more like I have divine questions and thought the water might hold some answers."

Sydney laughed and looked up at her. "Aren't you a little young to have such deep questions?"

"Wickedness doesn't care about age," she said, and laughed too, "or so I've read recently. Sorry. I'm in a morose mood tonight, so I wouldn't blame you for thinking I was horrible company."

"Should *I* keep walking?"

"If you have to get back to your vacation then don't let me hold you up, but I'd really enjoy spending time with you."

"What do you mean?" Sydney appeared confused.

"That even though you keep me on my toes, I'm sure you didn't plan to spend your time off trying to make me feel better."

"The last couple of days have taught me that alone time isn't all it's cracked up to be either." The waves seemed to catch Sydney's attention after she fell silent.

"That sounds like the true definition of a dilemma. You don't want to be alone, but someone you think is in it only for the sex isn't a good choice either." She sighed loudly for effect. "There's only one middle ground."

"A rubber room and lots of pills to make me forget my problems?"

"I see morose is catching," she said, and whistled. With the abandon of a heart that carried no burdens, Abby ran out of the dunes with a stick in his mouth. "I had Abby in mind, and he's really not into rubber or pills."

"We haven't officially met." Sydney held her hand out for inspection and smiled when Abby readily licked it from her hand to her elbow. Sydney looked at Parker again and wiped her arm off on her shirt. "So you were really just walking your dog and not asking divine questions."

"Of course I was. But Abby doesn't have an answer for me, so maybe you do, because I do have just one question."

Sydney started down the beach. "Ask away."

"If there are two roads along everyone's path, why do so many people choose the wrong one?"

"What do you mean by wrong?"

"You know, good and bad. I realize we can't all be good all the time, but why do some of us choose bad so many times it becomes a way of life?"

Abby picked up his stick and dropped it in Sydney's path, so she threw it down the beach for him. "Some people can bend the meaning of bad to justify what they want to do. If you see something and know it'd be wrong to take it, I guess you could convince yourself you deserve it, so it isn't bad to take it. When you do it over and over, it simply becomes a habit, though it hurts those who care about you. Does that help?"

Parker took a turn with Abby's stick and laughed when he chose to go through the water, even though she'd thrown it well onto the sand. "It does, thanks. Can I answer any questions for you?"

"Actually, you could." While Sydney was successful at her job, standing next to her was someone who was the absolute best at what she did. According to the tabloids, Parker had enjoyed the fruits of what her labors had borne, but she and Sydney had chosen such different ways to act out their success.

Their earlier conversation had sent up a red flag about coming up with her own answers, so she'd waited for Parker's response, not wanting to have any more problems. If she drew conclusions constantly she'd never get to know Parker better, and if she constantly compared her to Gene she'd drive her away. "Don't answer if you don't want to, but it might help me understand something better."

"Shoot."

"What do you get out of the conquest of so many women?"

"Conquest? You make me sound like a caveman." Parker had to laugh but stopped just as quickly when she seemed to realize it was a serious question. "Do you think that's what this is? Me trying to get you into bed to add a notch to my bedpost? After all, it's the only reason I spend time with women, right?"

"No, I'm not that easy. I just want to know. Like I said, you don't have to answer if you don't want to, and you probably think I'm the rudest person alive, but the answer's important to me." Abby had given up on his stick and was now content to walk between them, splashing water on their legs as he went.

"I can't answer for other people, only for myself, so don't use my answer to try to figure out the dogs of this world, okay? Especially the dog you're asking about."

"How do you know that?"

"It's a guess, so remember what I said. My answer's mine. If you need more info, then you need to widen the parameters of your study." Parker smiled.

"Fair enough."

"No woman I've ever been linked to has ever been a conquest, as you put it." Parker ran her hand through her hair to comb it behind her ears, but with the breeze it wasn't cooperating. "They've all had something to teach me." She shook her head when Sydney snorted.

"Sorry. Go on."

"Is your mind out of the gutter? Since I'm guessing you're thinking sexual positions." She nodded. "They taught me something about life. Some wanted something from me. Not commitment, but the trappings of what I've achieved. Others just wanted company. Then there were the crazies who didn't come across that way until I got them alone." Parker shivered and Sydney came close to laughing. "I try never to judge anyone for their reasons, and I hope for the same in return."

"And if you ever make a promise of commitment?"

"Then it means I've met the person I'll be more than willing to give my heart to until it's either returned or has ceased to pump."

Sydney stopped walking and Parker stopped a few feet in front of her. Parker had sounded sincere, but Sydney took the answer with a grain of disbelief. "It's that simple for you?" Her thoughts were jumbled and she stared intently at Parker, trying to find any hint she was only giving the answers she wanted to hear. How ironic that she wanted to know Parker's take on this, but never Gene's. Getting the truth from Gene meant she also had to face how stupid she'd been to trust her with her heart.

"Obviously not, since I'm still in the learning process and haven't come close to meeting someone I can picture myself with sixty days from now, much less sixty years. I'm young, Captain, not stupid. Life's incredibly hard to make it through when you're alone, and I imagine it's only more so when you decide to share it with someone else." Parker turned around since they'd walked almost to the end.

A small fish jumped close to the shore and Abby took off after it. Without the barrier between them Sydney moved closer and wrapped her hand around Parker's elbow, like she had earlier in the day. "You're right, you're young but rather insightful." Her face relaxed when Parker didn't push her away.

"It comes from all the time in the sun. After a while you become delirious, so you have to think about something else to take your mind off the heat."

They walked back in silence, taking the cut that would lead up to Sydney's place. Parker walked her to the door again and kissed her forehead when they arrived. "Good luck, Captain."

"Thanks, but good luck on what?"

"Getting the answers to all your questions. You deserve the truth no matter what."

The next morning Sydney made herself breakfast and went for another walk. She was thrilled to bump into Parker as she neared the end of her run and accepted her invitation to dinner that night. This time Parker offered to cook so she'd feel free to ask as many insulting questions as she wanted without anyone interrupting her, she'd joked.

At six she walked along the shoreline to Parker's house in the same silence she'd enjoyed most of the day, either reading or watching Parker's workout. In her left hand she carried the tennis ball Abby had left.

She watched the undulations, which really couldn't be called waves, in the water as if they held the answers to what she wanted from life. Gene had called again but she'd let it go to voice mail. She might've been unsure of a lot in her life right now, but the finality of their relationship wasn't on the list. She didn't want to dwell on explaining to Gene the concept of either having cake or eating it. Doing both things was impossible.

"You go out into that sand or anywhere near the water, and I'm throwing you on the grill." Parker's voice held no hint of teasing and Sydney stopped in her tracks. "I mean it, Abby, it takes an hour to blow you dry." Sydney could see him standing on the edge of the deck looking at her hand and quickened her steps so he wouldn't get in trouble.

"Hey," Sydney called up. Abby's loud barking alerted a ten-mile radius of her arrival.

"Hey, come on up. As you know, Abby's h-a-r-m-l-e-s-s," Parker said.

She quirked an eyebrow at the spelling. Parker was right about spending too much time in the sun. "Okay then, since he's obviously harmless." As soon as the word left her mouth Abby underwent a transformation. Like a cat, his back arched and his teeth were bared in a snarl.

"Abercrombie Princeton King, down," Parker shouted. The yell made him whip his head around and instantly sit. He looked up at Parker and seemed to wait to see how much trouble he was in. "She didn't mean it, boy. Everybody knows you're the real King Kong around here," Parker cooed to him. His tail started wagging again and he started coaxing Sydney to join them again.

"Good thing he hasn't learned how to spell," she joked.

"Sorry. Abby takes exception when people call him what you just did. Makes him feel like a weenie, I guess, since he's so big. Say you're sorry, boy," Parker ordered him. Abby walked to her and offered a paw with his head bowed, which she accepted, giving him his ball back.

"Hey, I'm glad you came and I hope you're hungry." Behind Parker a huge grill was burning logs of hickory down to coal, and next to it sat large steaks of salmon. To an experienced cook like Sydney, everything looked organized and within easy reach. Cooking was one of her hobbies that she didn't get to practice very often.

"You cook, Miss King?" Did Parker know her name? They'd never used their first name in all their previous meetings.

"Please, Captain, call me Parker, and I love to cook when I'm home and have the opportunity. All those upscale hotels I have to stay in get pissed if I start an open flame in the bathroom. Can I get you something to drink?"

"I'll have hot chocolate." She noticed the thermos sitting on the table.

"With or without marshmallows?" Parker asked.

"What the hell? I'm on vacation, so make it with marshmallows."

"Why don't you entertain yourself for a minute while I get everything ready for the grill. We're having fish, so I hope that's all right and you don't have an allergy or aversion to salmon. If you ask nicely enough, Abby will be happy to run the gamut of tricks he knows. Start with 'play dead' and work your way down."

It had occurred to Parker to stop next door during her run and cancel, since Beau had moved their photo shoot up a day and she needed to look her best, even though her face wasn't the subject of the pictures. Besides, Sydney was starting to get under her skin, and as much as she wanted Sydney around, it was starting to scare her. She could've canceled for a whole lot of reasons, but she'd really wanted to see her and spend time with her, so the thought of blowing her off died before it had time to take root.

"Abby, play dead," Parker said, to start them off. She pulled an imaginary gun from her hip and shot him.

The ham put a little more into it than the usual just falling and not moving like most dogs. With a paw on his head he howled like she'd actually pulled the trigger, then staggered a bit before crumbling at Sydney's feet and moaning a few more times before he died.

While Sydney laughed at the big dog's antics, Parker went inside to get everything she needed. "Abby, dance," she prompted him again.

She kept her eyes on Sydney, who had her eyes on Abby, and left the dog to do a jig on his hind legs as she ran back inside for the last thing she had to cook. Sydney praised Abby's efforts as she prepared the rest of dinner.

It'd be fun to have someone to cook with, she thought as she watched Sydney enjoy Abby's show. When Abby finished, Sydney joined her and seemed content to lean against her as she finished cooking. Parker put her arm around Sydney's shoulders right after she placed everything on the grill, and it felt heavenly that Sydney didn't immediately tense.

"This looks wonderful," Sydney said as soon as Parker pulled out her chair for her and placed a plate of food in front of her.

"Every so often I get inspired by the company I keep. Thanks for coming over."

This time their conversation was comfortable and they posed their questions to learn more about each other instead of delving into awkward subjects. After a dessert of raspberries in Chantilly cream, Parker held out her hand to walk Sydney home.

When they reached the door, she took a chance and kissed Sydney good night in a way that opened the door to the attraction they both seemed to feel. She made it quick, not wanting to scare Sydney off, but she did intend to make her interest plain.

"Good night, Captain, and thanks again for joining me."

"Thanks for going to the trouble. You have a way of making a girl feel special."

"It depends on the girl, trust me." Parker kissed her again and made sure the door was locked before she headed home through the dunes.

CHAPTER SIX

What in the hell?" Sydney said as soon as she swung her legs out of bed and put her feet in a puddle. In fact, when she looked down she saw at least an inch of water swamping the oak floor in the bedroom. "Please, God, don't let this be something I did."

She started in the bathroom before going from room to room, trying to figure out where the deluge was coming from since the sun was shining and the stone patio outside the back door didn't appear wet from a recent shower. When she reached the kitchen she heard the source of the problem. The water heater had sprung a major leak and water was pouring out of the top at an alarming rate. The fact that it was now cold water meant it had been running for a while.

The shut-off valve at the top was stuck and no matter how hard she tried to twist, the damn thing wouldn't budge. "Great, I decide to go on vacation and end up flooding the house."

She got her robe on and hurried over the dunes to Parker's. Despite the early hour a work crew was out on the tennis court doing something, so she didn't feel guilty knocking on the door.

"Need to borrow some sugar?" Parker asked, wearing a T-shirt and a pair of boxers covered with hula girls.

"Actually I need to borrow some brawn." She held out her hand, hoping Parker came along willingly.

"Oh, wow," Parker said when they reached the house and water was now steadily pouring out the open back door. Parker put a dish towel over the valve for a better grip and was able to stop the flow of water, but the damage was done. "Nick, I need you to call that plumber you sent to the house last year and have him come by the Rider place to change out the hot-water heater. Then see if you can get in touch with the Riders and get their insurance information. With the amount of water on their floors, I'm thinking they'll have to make a claim. Then could you call the cleaning service you used after that storm a couple of years ago? Thanks."

"I can do all that, Parker," Sydney said when Parker hung up.

"Nick's got the contacts to put this back together before they see the extent of the damage, so don't worry about it. You're supposed to be on vacation, not doing home repair." Parker put her hand behind Sydney's neck and squeezed gently. "Just wait for the plumber to get here, then go out and enjoy the day."

Sydney stepped closer to Parker, liking the contact. "Interested in doing something with me?"

"Give me a few hours, then I'm all yours, but I have a little something going on today that Nick will kill me if I back out of."

"I'll hold you to that." She smiled as Parker pulled her closer and kissed her forehead. The horrible morning didn't seem as bleak now.

❖

"All right, people, let's get this stuff set up before we get one of those summer showers this place is famous for. I did the *Sports Illustrated* cover here before Wimbledon last year and ruined my favorite Nikon lens. If that happens today, heads will roll," someone shouted. "Joe, go get Nick and tell him we're ready for his final approval."

The shouting and running and music from next door grabbed Sydney's attention as she made her way to her blanket outside, wanting to get out of the way of everyone who'd arrived after Nick's flurry of calls. When Parker said she'd be tied up she figured she had practice, but this didn't look like the makings of a workout.

The music pumping through the outdoor system made her put her book down and concentrate on what was happening. Besides a whole lot of people with camera equipment, she spotted a huge selection of tennis shoes around the outside of the court. Then someone yelled to Nick and told him to get Parker. The shower the woman had been complaining about was just offshore and looked like it was bringing a dazzling lightning display with it.

Sydney watched Parker walk out of the house onto a now-clean court wearing only a robe. The fencing from around the court had been taken down and she figured they were going to photograph Parker's play. Strangely, Parker grabbed a racquet and hit a few practice rounds with the robe on. Out of sight of the camera in a small boat in the water, a man fed her some lobs over the net.

"That's great, Beau. A few more and we should have all our shots set up."

Once Parker had broken a good sweat, the photographer announced they were ready to begin and Parker dropped the robe. Thank God Sydney was sitting on the beach and not out in the water. The sight before her would've made her drown.

Parker continued to hit balls with her hair loose, wearing only a pair of tennis shoes. A superb makeup job made it appear as if she didn't have any tan lines on the most perfect body Sydney had ever seen. "Holy shit" was all she could think to say as she stared at Parker moving around the court.

Parker hit ball after ball as the photographer changed cameras numerous times. The backdrop of the incoming storm only accentuated Parker's form as Sydney noticed how her muscles bulged when she hit the ball. Without her permission, Sydney's feet moved her closer to Parker's place as the commercial shoot ended.

By the time she stood next to the deck, Parker was sitting at the table they'd had dinner on the night before with two empty water bottles in front of her. She wore the robe she'd come out in, and Beau sat with her as the crew packed up their gear.

"How's it going next door?" Parker asked. Abby's whining had alerted her to Sydney's presence before she actually saw her.

"Thanks for having Nick come to my rescue. The cleaning crew arrived and the plumber's almost finished, but they said the house will be unlivable for the next month, so I'm thinking of heading back today. I wanted to say good-bye before I go. It sucks that I'll have to cut my time short, but if you're ever in New York, please give me a call so I can return the dinner favor." Sydney crossed her arms over her chest after glancing at Beau, and Parker wondered why she was so shy about what she thought to be a gorgeous body.

"Why don't you come up for some juice or something," she said, not ready for her to go just yet. Sydney looked depressed, and the thought of not seeing her again was suddenly unacceptable.

"Parker, we need to finish this," Beau insisted. She glared at him to shut him up and he ignored her. "There's plenty of sand out there for you to stick your head in, but that ain't gonna help nothing."

The last letter she'd received from her number one fan was under his hand on the table, and he'd been pushing her to run for cover since he'd read it. That morning the detective who'd collected the letter had reported this one was clean too, which gave them no place to start searching for whoever had sent it.

They all agreed that the coverage of her ditching Alicia had prompted the soldier of God to send her the only note she'd ever gotten at home. She often got hate mail, or letters of advice from well-meaning conservatives on what changes she needed to make to save her soul, but this guy was different. She wouldn't admit it, but the letters had chilled her to her soul—and she did have one, in her opinion, despite what this whack job wrote.

"I don't want to bother you," Sydney said, and kept her arms crossed. "Thanks for everything."

"Don't go yet." Parker stood and held out her hand. Next to her, Abby raised his paw in case Sydney needed more than one offer. "This is my coach, Beau Bertrand. He's also our number one worrywart."

"When someone wants to kill you, you shouldn't ignore him," Beau said.

"What are you talking about?" Sydney asked as she sat down.

"Sydney, people threaten me all the time because of who I am, for the clothes I play in, for the way I wear my hair—you name it and they find fault with it. This isn't anything new and I'm sure it won't be the last time, so forgive me for not hiding under my bed. Apple, cranberry, or orange?"

"Apple, thanks." Beau pushed the letter on the table toward her, and Sydney started to read it, so Parker stood to get Sydney's juice. "Ah, so you do know my name. I was beginning to wonder," Sydney said when she returned.

"Of course I know your name, Captain. Willy told me all about you. Your likes, dislikes, and what kind of person you are."

The chair seemed to swallow Sydney as she leaned back. "I'm afraid to ask."

"Abby, fetch blue for me, boy," Parker said, which sent him inside at a run. "Willy and the rest of that crew think you're a hard worker and a stickler for the rules, but they love you. They feel safe with you. Hell, you can fly the plane, serve hot chocolate, and put up with full-of-themselves tennis players. Good boy," she said when Abby came back out with a red shirt in his mouth. She tossed it to Sydney as she petted Abby for his good deed.

"Thanks, Parker, but this is a red shirt." Sydney held the shirt up before slipping it on.

"I know that and you know that, but he doesn't. Abby's color-blind, but he's eager to please. Aren't you, boy?" She squeezed his face between her hands and laughed when he swiped his tongue up her cheek.

"That he is. Must've learned it from you." Sydney held up the letter she'd read. "And I understand better why you had divine questions." The noise coming from the court area made her glance in that direction to see Nick supervising the crew as they put the fences back up. "No rest for the wicked, huh?"

Parker laughed again, and as mad as Beau seemed, he smiled when she did. "Playing without the fences isn't impossible, but if you chase a ball too far that last step is memorable, depending on what side of the net you're on."

"You looked pretty comfortable out there earlier."

Parker tried to open her eyes as wide as she could and put her hand to her chest. "You peeked?"

"It was more like a glance, so don't flatter yourself."

"So how about it? Does my naked ass make you want to go out and buy new tennis shoes?"

Sydney tugged the bottom of the borrowed shirt as if trying to cover more of her body. "More like I need to buy new shoes and a gym membership, if I compare my ass to yours."

"I've seen you in uniform, Captain. You have nothing to worry about."

Beau rolled his eyes at her compliment.

"Ah, there's the Parker King I know," Sydney said.

"There's more to that saying, you know."

"And give you that kind of satisfaction?" Sydney laughed when she clutched her chest, this time acting like she was covering the wound the words had caused. "I'll let you get back to work. Like I said, I'm heading to New York today if I can, so I need to make arrangements. I guess it's a good idea to get back early since I still don't have a place to live."

"What do you mean? You're homeless?"

"With my new schedule, I'll be based out of New York instead of Atlanta, where I've been for the last couple of years. I was taking a week off for vacation, then some more time to look for a place in the city."

"There's a phone inside. Feel free to use it and call whomever you like, and feel free to pick Nick's brain before he leaves. He may live up the road, but the guy has friends all over the place. He might have some good leads on real estate." She stood after draining her glass and offered her hand to Sydney. "If he finds you something nice, maybe I'll get to keep you a while longer."

❖

"Thanks, Bobbie. I got a flight out tomorrow. Mom and Margo have started the search for me, so hopefully it'll be a matter of narrowing down their list. I'll start that process as soon as I get there, so I appreciate you giving me a place to work from." After ten minutes she'd found a flight back to New York and confirmed with her old friend that it was okay to come earlier than planned.

She waved to Parker, who was headed to the back of the house. She guessed Parker was going to change, not wanting to practice in just the robe.

"I'll see you tomorrow afternoon. My flight should be there by two, and I'll take a cab into the city."

Abby watched her finish her first call and then just stare at the phone. She absently petted her new companion as she picked up the receiver again. It was Saturday morning, which meant her mother was either tending plants or at the farmer's market trying to find new ones to fill her multitude of planters. The last time they'd talked was before her flight to London, and her mother wasn't expecting her to call yet.

It rang three times, and Sydney pictured her pulling off gardening gloves before she answered. "Mom?"

"Sydney, it's great to hear from you, but it's too early, isn't it? I thought you had another week of forced rest and relaxation." Lucia let out a long breath and Sydney guessed she'd sat in the Adirondack chair she'd given her for her birthday. "You all right?"

Her mother's insight about her made her laugh. "Define 'all right'?"

"If you aren't bleeding, sick, or in jail, then you're all right."

Sydney laughed again. "None of those, but things didn't work out for this week."

"What did Gene do now?"

"I can't believe Margo hasn't told you."

"She still has that decoder ring from first grade you gave her, so she figures she owes you the favor of keeping your secrets. If you need to talk I'm always available too, though, unlike your sister, my advice doesn't revolve so much around sex."

"Good to know, and I'll tell you the whole sad tale when I get there, but Gene isn't here." Abby put his head on her thigh and let out a long sigh, making her laugh. "It's a good thing I'm moving, and you can pat yourself and Margo on the back. You were right."

"If it's not Gene, then what? This trip is all you've been talking about."

"I'm fine, really." It wasn't until she'd heard her mom's voice that the image of her father popped into her thoughts. Not hearing him in the background was like seeing a salt shaker without the pepper. "Nothing's wrong, Mom. The vacation's over. I'm moving it to New York so I can share some time with you before I have to go back to work."

"Oh, I get it. You're obsessing about how I'm doing, aren't you?"

"I'm supposed to worry about you, so get used to it." The grief shimmered at the edges of her heart, and her mother's voice threatened to release it. "I promised him."

"You also promised him that you'd enjoy every day of your life and find something in each one to be joyful about." Lucia lowered her voice, as she usually did when she didn't want to seem to be fussing. "You're falling down on the job on that one, kiddo."

"I'm trying my best." She saw Parker heading toward her with a smile that was like a buoy in a bad storm. "I'm working hard on taking inventory and tossing out the parts that don't work. You have to give me points for Gene."

"I won't argue with that."

"Good, she's not worth the wasted breath."

"When are you coming home?"

"I couldn't get a flight out until tomorrow, so I'm going to pack up and get a room at the airport."

"Come by when you get in and I'll cook you dinner. You can eat, then tell me what happened. Where are you now?"

"At a friend's, and I'll be staying with Bobbie when I get back. I know you said I could come live with you, but I don't want to be in the way," she added before her mother could complain. After her dad had passed away her mom had downsized. She would've loved being with her, but after a few days, tripping over each other would've gotten old.

"If you're not going to let me take care of you, then tell me about your new friend. I could've sworn you said you wanted to go down there so you and Gene could work some things out without any outside distractions."

"I promise to entertain you tomorrow at dinner, but I have to run. Thanks, Mom."

"Just part of my job. I'm just glad you called."

"I love you and I'll see you soon."

Sydney stepped back outside and found Parker dressed and ready for what she assumed to be more practice. Parker was standing near the railing holding her hate mail, and from the movement of her eyes Sydney could tell she was rereading it. Beau was standing at the opposite end, staring at the water and not appearing happy.

It was weird. A lot of books and movies depicted deranged people, but most of the population wasn't the target of such twisted hate. What kind of person sat in a room and penned something that, in and of itself, brought pain to another person? Because that's what Parker and Beau appeared to be in—pain.

"All set?" Parker asked as she dropped her hand holding the note and locked eyes with her.

"Yes, thanks for letting me use your phone. I want to let you get back to work, so I'll be next door packing. After that it shouldn't be too hard to find a place near the airport until my flight late tomorrow morning." She twisted the hem of her borrowed shirt in her hands and waited for Parker to move.

"Why would you do that?" Parker asked.

"Why would I do what?"

"You're unbelievable," Beau said as he walked away headed toward the court. It was obvious to Sydney she'd interrupted another argument.

"We'll get back to our confusing conversation in a second," Sydney said, and took a step closer to Parker, "but let's talk about that letter first. Beau seems really upset about it, and after reading it, I think he has a right to be."

"I've gotten stuff like this from the time I started playing and people figured out I didn't want to date the men's champion." Parker placed the letter under the glass she'd used so it wouldn't fly away in the slight breeze. "It's never been a big deal, but Beau's upset since this sicko's a little more organized than the average critic. He sent a copy of my schedule with this love letter, which, along with having it delivered to my house, is new. Hell, I shouldn't assume this is a man. It could be a woman with a grudge, for all I know."

"You have a right to live however you want, but promise me you'll be careful."

"My admirer will lose interest soon enough, so there's no sense wasting energy worrying about it." Parker sat down and pulled a chair for her close enough that their knees would touch if she accepted the offer. "Now, why would you sit in a hotel room alone when I have three empty guest rooms inside?"

"Because you don't have to put yourself out like that, and I don't want to impose." She sat and took Parker's hand.

"Having you here would be a treat for Abby and me, not an imposition. If you accept, I promise to be on my best behavior, and I'll take you out so you don't have to suffer my cooking two nights in a row." Parker whispered in Abby's ear, prompting him to move closer. When Sydney turned her attention to him, Abby lifted his paw and placed it in her hand. "See, he's dying for you to stay. We'll even drive you to the airport when you're ready to go, and you know how much I love airports. You wouldn't deprive me of a visit to one, would you?"

"You really wouldn't mind?" She scratched Abby's head as she gazed at Parker.

"I want you to stay. How else will I get you to change your mind about me?"

"Don't waste energy worrying about that either, and I'd love to go out with you again. You're a great cook, so staying in wouldn't be a bad option either."

"Great," Parker said with a huge smile and her hand on her knee. "You need help packing?"

"You get back to work before Beau evicts me."

"The workmen should still be there, so I don't mind."

"I'll take Abby, if it'll make you feel better, then we'll meet you out on the court. I've never scored courtside tickets, so this'll be a treat. And since Abby loves to play in water, he'll be good company considering there's more than plenty of it next door."

"Just whistle if you need me to come over." Parker shouldered the bag with her racquets. "My practice partner's coming early, but I can get there quick if you need me to."

"I don't know if I can whistle that loud."

"I was talking to the dog," Parker said, and sounded serious, which made Sydney close her eyes to slits.

"No freaking way," she said over Parker's laughter and Abby's barking.

❖

It took Sydney less than an hour to gather her things and open the door of the flooded house to Nick, who carried her bags to Parker's. Abby walked with them clutching her beach bag in his mouth, which left only her purse for her to carry. She got some great tips on real estate from Nick as he settled her in the bedroom closest to Parker's.

"You need anything else before I take off?" he asked.

"Thanks for all your help and for going to all this trouble," she said as she followed him to the front of the house.

He laughed as he stopped at the door. "Beau told me what happened when they boarded your flight. It made for a great laugh, but there's something you should know about Parker."

"I'm almost afraid to hear it."

"She rarely asks for anything, even from Beau and me, and we work for her," he said, and winked. "So it wasn't any trouble, Sydney, believe me. Parker's a good kid if you're lucky enough to get to know her. She might've come off divaish, but she's nothing like that. If you give her a chance you won't find a better friend in the world."

"She's got a great fan club, that's for sure."

"Guilty as charged," he said, and laughed again.

"Do you think she'd mind if I went out and watched her for a while?" She cocked her head toward the court outside. "I don't want to be in the way."

"I'm sure Abby won't mind sharing his bench out there, so feel free." He shook her hand and pointed toward the kitchen. "She told me to make sure you knew to make yourself at home, so if you're hungry, there's stuff in the fridge."

Aside from Abby, all Sydney took with her was a bottle of water. On Parker's side of the court closest to the shore was a large double chaise lounge covered by an equally large umbrella, which Abby led her to and waited for her to sit on before he climbed up.

The tall blonde on the other side of the net and Parker were both covered in sweat but kept up the same blistering pace Sydney had seen the day before. Beau sat in a tall chair that resembled the ones she'd seen on television, but his was covered with another umbrella. The instructions he called out every so often were the only sounds except for the pop of the ball and the grunts Parker made after almost every shot.

Sydney sat and drank her water with Abby stretched out next to her, his head in her lap. He appeared relaxed but kept his eyes on the ball as if waiting for the opportunity to pounce on a missed one.

"Move the volley out more, Park, aim for the lines. If your opponent thinks the balls are going out she might not chase them all down. When that happens, you win shots and conserve energy," Beau said. Parker let the next ball the blonde hit fly past her, stopping to take a quick break.

"Why would anyone let a ball past them, Beau? I chase them all down, even the ones that look like they're out by a foot." Beau threw her a couple of balls, then pointed at her.

"Damn right you'll chase them all. You know that, but not everyone has me as their coach." Beau puffed up his chest a little. "If you want to argue with me, just think of the crappy look on Jill Seabrook's face by the third game of the first set. Now get back to work."

Parker bounced the ball four times, then went into her serving stance. To Sydney she looked like a bow drawn back and ready to fire. She watched the ball leave Parker's hand and flinched when the racquet smashed it over the net. Television didn't give that sound justice. The ball landed, in her opinion, a millimeter from the line where Parker's embarrassed practice partner took a swing at it and missed.

"Goddammit, Parker, I think the girl fancies you already. No need to show off," the woman said as she aimed her racquet at Parker and glared.

"That's Captain Sydney Parish to you, sore loser." Parker aimed her own racquet back at her and smiled.

"You know my last name too. I'm impressed, Ms. King," Sydney said when they'd stopped, which made Abby start whining. Parker turned around with her hands on her hips.

"Your name tag had S. Parish on it, so of course I know your last name. Abby, cut it out, no fly balls for you today. We have company. I don't have hours to kill grooming you, boy, so enjoy the sun." Parker turned back to her game, ready to serve again.

"And I thought you were just looking at my chest." Parker missed the ball she'd tossed up for her service, and for a second Sydney thought she'd pulled a muscle from stopping her actions so abruptly.

"Trust me, Sydney, when I start looking at you, you won't miss the meaning behind it." Parker turned toward the net and caught the balls Beau tossed to her. After they played another hour Parker called it a day. Beau didn't look happy but didn't argue when Parker started packing her gear.

"If you inspire her play this much, Captain, you should plan to attend the Open," the blonde said when she was close enough. "I'm Natasha Gering," she said with her hand out.

"You won the French Open and Wimbledon, I believe, four or five years ago, right?"

"Good memory," Natasha said. "I'm retired now, but still able to put Kong on edge every so often."

"I see that," she said, and wondered if the beautiful Swede meant only on the court.

"Have fun," Natasha said, waving over her shoulder in a way that made Sydney believe she knew exactly what came next.

CHAPTER SEVEN

A re you up for a drive or do you want to stay in?" Parker asked. Her bag of racquets was repacked and she stood before Sydney, a sweaty bundle of energy.

"Can I change first?" She plucked the T-shirt as a reminder she was still in her bathing suit.

"Why would you want to? You're dressed just right."

They walked back to the house, where Parker traded one bag for another and scooped up the keys to the old Land Cruiser parked out front. The drive took thirty minutes, and when she pulled onto a dirt road, Sydney thought something was wrong, but Parker kept driving until they could see the water's reflection up ahead through a thick line of trees.

"What is this place?" Sydney asked when they got out. Abby, who'd been sitting quietly in the back, shot off into the woods, and Parker didn't call him back.

"A long stretch of untouched and undeveloped private beach, so nothing's out here but us and the birds." There were some supplies in the back they'd stopped for, but Parker waved her off and pointed in toward the water. "You're on vacation, so go relax. I'll take care of this."

"Let me carry something," she said with her hands on her hips. "I'm not helpless."

Parker handed her a mesh bag before she hoisted the cooler onto her shoulder. "Move it, muscles, before we lose the sun."

"What's the bag for?"

"You."

She had to walk fast to keep up once Parker headed to the shoreline, only to turn around again once she caught up. They made a few more trips to the car to complete their picnic area with chairs, food, and an umbrella. Once they settled into their beach chairs, she peered down the shore in both directions and saw Parker was right. They were the only people on the beach for what seemed like miles.

"How'd you find this place?"

Parker finished reapplying sunscreen and tossed the tube to her. "I read about it, and it sounded like an urban legend, so I asked a friend who confirmed it was real. After practice one day I drove out here and fell in love with the quiet. We don't have as much coastline as Florida, so the building frenzy has been in overdrive for the last twenty years or so, which makes this stretch unusual since most developers have browbeat owners into selling off a little at a time."

"So what brought about this anomaly?"

"Old family money, and enough of it that the sole survivor doesn't need or want any more." Parker picked up the mesh bag and held her hand out to Sydney. "He keeps his sand, trees, and birds and comes out here to read to all three. I met him a few years ago and he insisted I enjoy his beach whenever I can get out here."

They were sitting too far away from the water for Sydney to figure out what the bag was for. But once she was almost ankle-deep she stared down in awe. "Look at all of them," she said of the shells littering the shore just under where the waves broke. The thousands of them were the variety usually found in gift shops.

"I thought you might want something to help decorate your mom and sister's planters." Parker handed over the bag.

It didn't take long before she sheepishly handed it back to Parker to carry back to where they'd started. She couldn't remember the last day she'd spent like this just having fun. For three hours the most serious thing they'd talked about was the best chocolate mix for milk.

Under the umbrella they shared a lunch of crab salad and crackers, until the overstuffed container Parker had bought at a local fish market was empty. When the lethargy set in, they sat beside each other in silence and watched the waves roll in. The wind had kicked up a little, creating a bit of surf.

In the distance a commercial plane flew past, too high for its noise to bother them. "What attracted you to becoming a pilot?" Parker asked.

"Probably the same thing that drove you to play tennis. It's my job, but I love it. Each flight, no matter how many times I may have flown the route, is different." She watched a small crab make its way along without displacing a grain of sand. If only it was so easy to go through life, stepping so lightly as to never cause a problem. "My airline gave me the opportunity to follow my passion for time in the air, and I've been flying the route you took home for a few years now."

"Gave you the opportunity because you're so young?"

"This from the woman who thought I was a flight attendant?" She put her hand up to her chest. "Good recovery, Kong, and yes, because I'm so young. Though I have some years on you."

"Not many, I bet."

"You know how to flatter a girl, so thank you. No, you know pretty much all there is to know about me, but I know nothing about you. Tell me something about Parker King." The chair creaked slightly when she turned to see Parker better.

"You know plenty already, at least the important stuff. I play tennis marginally well, like hot chocolate, and I have a dog."

"Come on, give up something."

Parker's laugh seemed to start in her belly at the whine, and it made her smile. "Planning to sell your story? If you are, I can tell you which rag pays the most, but you have to have pictures."

"I don't think I'll make enough for a new pair of shoes. You cook, work out, shop, and take walks on the beach. Aside from displaying all the attributes of a dream date, you're kind of boring."

"I guess that answers my question if you'll have dinner with me tonight."

"You think I'd say no after you came to my rescue?" Since it was just the two of them, she took off the shirt Parker had lent her and dropped it beside her chair. As if by magic Abby appeared, clutched it in his mouth, and took off with it. "Should I even ask?"

"Abby's got a clothes fetish."

"He's your dog. Why am I not surprised?"

"He doesn't save them for the annual pooch drag show. He just likes to bury them. It means he likes you. So if you're in love with a particular item, don't drop it anywhere near him."

Abby returned and cocked his head to the side as if waiting to see if she'd take anything else off. "Forget it. I'm keeping both pieces of the suit." Parker laughed again and this time Sydney stuck her tongue out at her. "Want to go swimming?"

"Go ahead and I'll get changed."

The memory of Parker swimming naked that first night came to mind, but she kept quiet. She'd never been skinny-dipping and wasn't about to now. She started for the shore, turning around slightly when she saw Abby take off, only this time he had Parker's shorts in his mouth.

Parker's suit was a one-piece, but it looked great when she joined her. "Thanks for today," Sydney said as they headed into the water.

"Beau always tells me a good day is a gift that makes all the bad ones tolerable, so you're welcome, though I should be thanking you. It's not often I stop playing this early. I'm glad you decided to stay."

"We have a mutual admiration thing going, since it's been forever since I've taken time off. I have a ton of stuff happening in my life, yet you've managed to salvage this vacation for me. It'll be short, but memorable."

"You want to talk about it?" Parker submerged just enough to get her hair wet. Sydney didn't say anything, and Parker seemed to understand and didn't press. "I like to take days off, but that's almost impossible when I only have a few months to prepare for a big tournament. It's good to be reminded that life isn't all about tennis."

"You don't take breaks?" Sydney swam near the shore a bit, wanting to stay where she could touch bottom.

"You have to cram a tennis career into a short period of time, so once you start it's not a good idea to stop. You do and it's a bear to get in shape again, since some kid's always gunning to sideline you permanently."

"Didn't Martina play until she was in her forties?"

"I'm not saying I plan to retire early." Parker sent a wave of water her way. "But I don't have any illusions of lasting that long. Chasing balls down and doing it well enough to play professionally takes staying in the kind of shape that's hard to maintain. Not to mention the stress to your knees, back, and your body in general."

"I have faith in you, Grandma. From what I've seen, you're in excellent shape."

"After an ego boost like that, I'm definitely buying you dinner." Parker ducked under the water just in time to avoid getting splashed with the wave Sydney had sent right back in her direction. Sydney couldn't resist moving closer and smiled when Parker put her arms around her waist and held her in deeper water.

"So after you conquer the tennis world you'll play around with Natasha for fun?" She almost cringed at how pathetic her fishing technique was.

"If you're talking about tennis, then probably yes. Natasha's not always here. She plans her stays to accommodate my schedule."

"She's beautiful," she said, looking directly at Parker.

"It's not what you think," Parker said and smiled, but she appeared almost sad.

"What am I thinking?"

"Natasha's last professional match was against me in the Australian semifinals two years ago. I beat her in straight sets, but instead of getting pissed, she asked me out for dinner. We became friends, and a year ago she bought a condo up the beach. She splits most of her time between New York and Sweden, and comes here when I'm in town preparing for whatever's next." Parker leaned back a bit but didn't let her go. "She is beautiful, and we've flirted a little, but our friendship is more important than meaningless sex. Then there's the fact that my older sister Gray and Natasha have a crush on each other, but neither of them has admitted it yet."

"You're probably counting the minutes until you get rid of me."

Parker kissed her forehead and smiled more brightly this time. "Actually, I'm scheming of ways to keep you longer."

For a long stretch after that Sydney just enjoyed Parker as she held her in the water and shielded her from the sun.

They rode back to the house in silence along a route that provided good glimpses of the water when the trees weren't too thick. Her skin had tightened from the salt water and sun, but it wasn't an unpleasant sensation.

After their rocky start she liked Parker's company and her spontaneity. For the first time she felt like she was being heard, since Parker seemed genuinely interested in what she had to say.

"Let me show you where the fresh towels are." Parker followed her into the guest room. "If you forgot anything, just look around and I'm sure you'll find it in one of the cabinets."

"I'll be fine." She undressed as soon as the door closed on Parker's relaxed smile. Even though she was a little sunburned, the hot water felt good. Not until she was drying off amid the steam she'd built up did she realize the tension that was her constant companion had bled out of her shoulders. The relief made her light-headed.

She took her time fixing her hair and putting some gloss on her lips. When she finished dressing, she walked out to a quiet house, so she did some exploring. The room at the front of the house was her first stop.

❖

"Ready?" Parker asked ten minutes later.

The room Sydney stood in was filled with trophies and pictures from Parker's career on the court. When Parker joined her, she was running her finger over the Wimbledon trophy that'd just come home with her. In a few weeks the framed photograph of her holding it up before the crowd on center court would hang alongside it, like all the other ones in the room.

Sydney moved to another picture of Parker with her sisters. Like she'd said, she was a few inches shorter, but other than that they all had brown hair, blue eyes, and the same smile. "Are these your sisters?"

Parker nodded and instantly conjured up the memory of the crowd, the win, and the joy of sharing it with her family. "That's us at the French Open last year. They had some downtime, so they came to see me play. It makes me happy to look into the stands and see them, and since they can't do it very often, it makes wins like that one special. You probably think that's incredibly immature, but they're the only family I have worth mentioning, and we really don't see each other often." She put her hands into the pockets of her linen slacks, dropped her chin toward her chest, and looked at the floor. "I miss them, and their recent visit was way too short."

Gray and Kimmie were the only two people besides Beau and Nick who didn't want anything from her. The money, fame, and the publicity weren't important to them, and that sad reality made for a lot of lonely nights with only Abby for company. Trust wasn't something she wanted to buy or barter for.

Sydney put her hand on her arm and ducked down to try to make eye contact with her. "That doesn't make you immature, Parker. It makes you incredibly sweet." She raised her head and Sydney moved her hand to her cheek. "You are so incredibly sweet. When you look at me it's easy to see why anyone would take the chance to be with you," Sydney said as she ran her thumb along her lips.

"I'm glad you think so since it's you I'm looking at right now." Parker took Sydney's hand and kissed it. Sydney's flinch was barely perceptible, but she noticed it. "You're the most beautiful sight I've laid eyes on in a very long time." Sydney didn't seem uncomfortable in her company, but she was afraid of something.

"Are your parents deceased?" Sydney asked, in what she assumed was a way of changing the subject, since she was blushing.

Parker couldn't help but tense up. "They're very much alive and living in Atlanta."

"Are they not able to travel?" Sydney scanned the room as if searching for a picture of them.

"They choose not to travel or have anything to do with me."

"I didn't mean to pry," Sydney said as she stepped even closer.

"I didn't take it that way. I never talk about my parents because our relationship is so bad it embarrasses me." She took a deep breath and tried to let out the instant anger that built at Sydney's innocent question. She always experienced pain, humiliation, and disappointment when she thought of her parents and what they'd put her through, and no amount of time away from them had changed that. She chased titles now, done trying to win the acceptance of two people who would never give a damn about her.

"Sometimes letting some of that out helps," Sydney said softly, as if not to push her.

"They have issues with my sisters and me, so we don't communicate very often. My father cut us off first, and my mother went along without question. She evidently loved her life too much to make waves. That changed when we started to win, but still she won't put herself out to have a meaningful relationship with us. Our money allows her to play tennis at the club and have lunch with her friends, so she calls me every so often. Sometimes I feel she does it so I won't cut her off. My father refuses to take a dime, but my mother couldn't care less about my lifestyle. Actually, she couldn't care less about me, or who I share my bed with."

Her parents' attitudes, combined with the letters she had been getting, were starting to dominate her thoughts. The people who were supposed to love her basically agreed with the content of the letters she'd been receiving. At least that's what her father had said in their last conversation. She'd been only sixteen, but every disgusting word was carved into her brain. He'd delivered his condemnation with such conviction it'd be impossible to forget.

"I'm sorry." Sydney wrapped her arms around Parker's waist, and she relaxed.

"Don't be. It's not your fault and it certainly isn't mine. My father had no problem tossing us out and promising us an eternity of hell for the way we live our lives. The way he sees it, one gay child would've been bad enough, but three was over the top. He'd rather we live a lie than be true to ourselves, but he's entitled to his opinion, I guess. The cherry was that one or all three of us are constantly in the sports page or on television, rubbing his nose in it, as he likes to put it." Parker made quotation marks with her fingers as she spoke. "It's like all his worst nightmares were delivered to him wrapped in pink blankets. He's religious, but if he'd gotten even a glimpse into his future I wonder if he'd have relaxed his stance on abortion. He certainly didn't want us after he saw we were damaged goods."

"You don't have any contact with him?"

"At first he was thrilled to be my coach. He pushed me harder than Beau has ever dreamed of doing, but it was his way of making sure I didn't waste my talents, he said over and over."

Sydney ran her hands up Parker's arms to the back of her neck. "The ultimate sports dad, huh?"

"That's putting it mildly. He didn't know much about tennis, but by the time I was twelve he was an expert on every aspect of the game. It was like he was pushing me hard to keep me focused so it'd validate him as a father after he'd thrown Kimmie and Gray out." She glanced over the pictures in the room, some incredibly special like her major wins at Wimbledon, and her parents had missed all of them.

"I was in a junior tournament when I was sixteen, and he caught me kissing one of my practice partners at the net after our workout. That was it. He never attended a match or spoke to me again. The gulf between us is so big now we'll never cross it, and at this point I don't think either of us wants to." She rested her cheek on Sydney's head and sighed. "I've never told anyone that story except my sisters, Beau, and Nick. You could make a mint."

"There you go again making yourself more important than you are," Sydney teased her. "Your secrets are safe with me, Parker. I promise. Thank you for trusting me. I can imagine how hard that must still be for you, but it makes me happy that your sisters are such a big part of your life." Sydney pointed to the picture she'd admired before.

"Considering he threw me out right after that, I am too. They took care of me until I turned pro a year later and Beau and Nick took me in."

Sydney's expression showed how angry she was on her behalf, which made Parker smile. "You're beautiful all the time, especially when you're mad. Don't let it ruin your night, though. I'm a stronger person because of all this."

Sydney's stomach rumbled and she flushed red, breaking the tension of the story. "You mentioned something about eating?" Sydney asked.

Parker laughed. The night before Sydney had eaten twice what she had and had eyed the piece of fish she'd left on her plate. Only after the second piece of cheesecake did she appear satisfied.

"I did indeed, but you'll have to wait until I make one stop." Sydney's pout made her laugh again. She felt so light, it was like Sydney was pumping helium into her system.

"Can't it wait?"

"Nope." She guided Sydney to the side door. "My book dealer found a first edition *Confederacy of Dunces* and I want to go pick it up. If you're patient, I promise to make it worth your while." She pouted as well, to try to make Sydney smile.

"You're an enigma, Parker King. I would've thought jocks read only sports magazines and watched ESPN." Sydney linked their hands together and moved closer.

"I only read sports magazines when I'm on the cover, and ESPN when they're showing highlights of my play," she said, as seriously as she could pull it off.

"Ah, the Parker King I know and love." From the way Sydney closed her eyes after she spoke, she obviously didn't censor the last part of her sentence.

Squeezing Sydney's hand, she let the comment slide without further embarrassing her. "I read more books than sports magazines, and I only watch television on occasion since Abby's hooked on *Animal Planet*. All the DVDs of that prairie-dog show were at the top of his Christmas list last year. That doesn't fit the tabloid image of me, but I've never conformed to how other people try to define me."

"And what about what all those tabloids stories about your nights of wine, women, and song?"

"There's no enigma there. Not so much the wine, and I suck at karaoke, but I do like women. When I get the chance I like to have a good time, but I don't apologize for that. As I said earlier, the day will soon come when people will say 'Parker King who?' when my name's mentioned, and that doesn't bother me as much as it has others who've had to retire. Some other bad boy or girl who'll make better press will replace me, and when that happens, the girls who are calling me now will move on." She grabbed her keys and opened the door to the garage for Sydney to go out first. She was taking the black Mercedes parked next to the SUV they'd driven to the beach. With her quick press of a button, the lights on the car flashed once and the doors unlocked.

"And when they do, what will you do?"

"When that day arrives, I'll live my life pretty much the way I do now. I'll play tennis, I'll read books, and I'll teach my old dog some new tricks. I haven't made the best impression on you, but I'm not all that bad. At least I don't think so. Would it surprise you that no woman you've ever read about in connection to me has ever stepped foot in my house?" She opened the car door for Sydney and helped her into her seat. Sydney smiled at her as she crossed in front of the car to the driver's side. "Hell, they don't even know what state I live in. You do realize I'm twenty-four. Hardly enough time to have earned the reputation I've been saddled with," she said when she sat down.

"Why am I here, then?" Sydney asked as she put her hand on her arm.

Parker stared at the row of gardening equipment hanging on the wall and tried to come up with the best way to answer. "The day I saw you sitting alone in the coffee shop, you looked like you were searching for or trying to run from something or someone. The best way to find or get over anything is from a safe haven, and that's what this place is to me. Granted, it's not completely secluded, but it's close enough."

"I was thinking about my dad, actually." Sydney took a deep breath and, from Sydney's pained expression, Parker knew instantly she'd hit a nerve. "He died a little over a year ago and I've been having a hard time dealing with it."

"I'm sorry for your loss, and even though I've never met him, he raised a daughter who's beautiful inside and out."

"You're making it impossible for me not to like you," Sydney whispered.

"I've got tonight to convince you to stay the week, but if you insist on leaving tomorrow I don't want you to forget your time with me." She laid her hand against Sydney's neck. "This sounds so clichéd, but something about you makes me not want to let you go. Sadly, you aren't mine to keep."

Sydney closed her eyes when she leaned across the console and kissed her, and Parker's heart rate picked up when their lips met. This woman was dangerous, she thought when she pulled back, only to have Sydney follow her in an effort to make the kiss last longer.

"So tonight I'm going to buy a book, take you to dinner, and then walk you to your room. If I make it memorable enough I might get a few days' reprieve before I have to take you to the airport." She kissed Sydney again. "If you decide you can't stay, I hope you'll want to hear from me again. I mean that, because I want it more than anything." She kissed her one more time before she pressed the garage-door opener

and started the car, stopping when they were outside to look at Sydney.
"I did forget one thing."

"What's that?"

"To tell you how beautiful you look tonight."

Sydney self-consciously smoothed down her sundress and smiled.
The bright yellow cotton garment had thin straps and looked good with
her hair and the sun she'd gotten. Sydney had mentioned a few times
how much older she was, but tonight she appeared a few years younger
than Parker.

"Thanks." Sydney initiated their next kiss before Parker put the
car in drive.

❖

"Sydney, I want you to meet Barnaby Philpot Perry." Parker stood
behind Sydney with her hand on the small of her back as she made the
introduction. She bent down a little so she could whisper in her ear.
"And yes, that's his real name."

The older gentleman with a full white beard and almost black eyes
came from behind the counter and took her hand and kissed it. "Parker,
you've been holding out on me. This creature is simply divine."

"Thank you, Barnaby, but we just met. She knows all about me
and still agreed to go out, so I don't want to keep her waiting. I just ran
by to pick up my book before taking the divine creature out to dinner."

Sydney did a slow scan of the store, admiring the stacks of well-
cared-for antique and collectible books while Parker talked to the
seemingly eccentric old guy.

"You have a lovely place here, Mr. Perry," she said in an effort to
shift the conversation from her.

"Thank you, my dear, but as lovely as you think this is, it can't
compare to the library my friend here has back home. It thrills me to
know every time she takes one of my babies away, it's going to live
in that wonderful room. I predict that in years to come, they'll talk
more of the King collection than they will of that silly game she plays."
Barnaby handed Parker her book and gave Sydney a small parcel as
well. She was about to protest when Parker shook her head from behind
Barnaby, as if warning her not to insult him by turning it down.

"Are you holding out on me, Parker? The King collection?" she
asked, which made Barnaby shoot a mocking glare at Parker.

"For shame, Parker. The best room in the house and you haven't shown it to her?" The creases around his eyes let Sydney know he was kidding.

"A mistake I'll correct when we get home, Barnaby. Now be good and call me this week for lunch. Oh, and before I forget, I brought you something." Parker stepped out to the car.

"She is a lovely girl, Parker is," Barnaby said. He directed his comment at her but watched Parker retrieve something from the backseat only to put it back when a couple approached her for what looked like an autograph. She remembered the letter Parker had let her read and tensed with irrational fear when the strangers walked toward her.

"She is. I can see there's more to her than most people would guess. She seems to be a good friend to people she cares about." She never took her eyes off Parker as she picked the bag up again and started for the storefront.

"You'd consider yourself lucky to have her call you her friend, Sydney. We met two years ago when she wandered in here and ended up staying for dinner. It amazed me that someone so young was interested in the classics."

"Parker certainly doesn't fit the image most people have of her," she said, watching Parker patiently pose for pictures when the persistent couple produced a camera.

"She goes off to play, but when she comes home, she never fails to let more than a couple of days go by before she visits me. When she bought the house she transformed one of the rooms into a library that's simply beautiful." He offered her a seat, which she accepted since it gave her a good view of the parking lot. "I've spent hours in there reading with her, or discussing a slew of things." When he spoke she could hear in his tone how much he loved Parker. "After my wife passed, spending time with Parker has been a godsend. She never makes me feel like she's humoring an old man."

The bells over the door chimed and he slapped his hands together and laughed. "What did you bring me?" he asked, suddenly transforming into a little boy on Christmas morning.

"It's not in the greatest shape, but you'll forgive that when you see the print date. Enjoy it but don't stay up all night trying to get through it." Parker handed over a leather-bound book that appeared ancient. "I went hunting for you during my off time in England and found you a first edition of Shakespeare's sonnets." Parker sat next to Sydney on the small couch and took her hand. "Shakespeare's one of Barnaby's all-time favorites, and he has one of the biggest collections of his writings I've ever seen." He looked at the book, then took Parker's free hand.

"Thank you so much for this. I'll treasure it always."

Parker helped Sydney to her feet. "You've given me more than I could ever hope for, my friend," Parker said, releasing her momentarily to hug Barnaby. "And thanks for the use of paradise again today. I took Sydney out today for some shell hunting."

"That stretch of beach belongs to you?" she asked.

"Yes, it does, and you're more than welcome to use it whenever you're in town. And before I forget…" He handed her two more wrapped packages. One had her mother's name on it and the other was for her sister. "Parker tells me your family enjoys a good book now and again."

She kissed his cheek before hugging him, charmed when he touched his fingers to his cheek when she released him. "Thank you so much. I'm sure they'll love these."

They said their good-byes, then Parker opened the car door for her and put all the books they'd left with in the backseat. They waved to Barnaby, who stood in the window with his gift under his arm.

"It was sweet of you to do that for him." She took Parker's free hand back as soon as they were on the highway again.

"I haven't gone to college yet, so I consider Barnaby my professor. He likes to find stuff for me to read and then talks to me about it. His wife died about four years ago and the big bookstores took a chunk of his business, but he perseveres through it all. The business has always been more of a passion than a moneymaker, thank God, so he's an interesting person to spend time with." Parker looked over at Sydney for a moment before turning her attention back to the road. Seeing her with her eyes closed and her head against the seat made Parker wonder what it would be like to wake up next to her.

"Will you show me Barnaby's favorite room?" Sydney asked, without letting go of her hand or opening her eyes.

"I'd love to." After that they fell into a comfortable silence until they reached the restaurant.

The place she'd picked for the night was an Italian place with romantic lighting and a great view of the water, but even better food. The young woman who showed them to their table was the daughter of the owner and had met Parker on a few occasions.

When Sydney arched her eyebrow at the friendly greeting she'd received, Parker just laughed. The setting did give the impression she had a romantic evening in mind, and from Sydney's expression that was either not on her agenda or perceived as pushing. Sydney clearly wasn't a groupie groveling at her feet to spend time with her, but the constant assumptions Sydney made about her were starting to get old.

"How are Beau and Nick?" the hostess asked.

"They're fine. I'll tell them you said hello."

"They're not joining you tonight?"

"It'll just be Ms. Parish and me this evening. How about a bottle of Chianti while we decide on what to eat?" The young woman turned and headed for the wine racks along the back wall, looking for the wine Parker had ordered.

"I thought…" Sydney acted like she didn't know how to finish.

Parker studied the dinner specials and didn't glance up to help Sydney out of her floundering. "I know what you thought, and it's kind of been a problem between us from the first moment we met. Jumping to conclusions only gets us into trouble, wouldn't you agree?"

"I just thought…"

"Like I said, I know what you thought, and while I really like spending time with you, you have a habit of giving mixed signals. All you saw when you walked in here was candles, romantic music, wine, and an ocean view, and it all added up to having to sleep with me later. If you'd given me a chance, I could've told you I come here sometimes when I'm home with Nick and Beau, and I'm sure not interested in sleeping with either of them. The guy who owns the place makes a great sauce and fabulous veal dishes I thought you might like, but if you prefer, we could go someplace better lit with a bunch of screaming kids." Before Sydney could reply, the hostess came back to the table with the wine and two glasses. She poured a little into Parker's glass, waiting for her to approve before pouring.

"I'm sorry, Parker."

"No, I'm sorry. I shouldn't have said all that. In a way you're right. I'm that fiend your mother and all your girlfriends warned you to stay away from. But I promised I'd behave, and I intend to. No matter what my reputation may be, I like you, and I'd never disrespect you. Though I have a feeling someone in your past did." She held up her glass and waited for Sydney to do the same, then tapped them together when she did. "'I shall be telling this with a sigh somewhere ages and ages hence: Two roads diverged in a wood, and I—I took the one less traveled by, and that has made all the difference.'"

"Robert Frost, 'The Road Not Taken,'" Sydney whispered before she took a sip. "Somewhere ages and ages hence there'll be a woman who'll have loved her life because she got to share it with you." She lifted her glass in salute again. "Even if you think I'm really an asshole, I swear nothing will interfere with our time together again, especially my bonehead preconceptions."

Their dinner lasted three hours by the time they'd made it through the various courses, dessert, and after-dinner drinks. They kept the conversation light, and the other patrons looked their way often as they laughed at a variety of things. Sydney made Parker feel better when she said it was the type of night she often dreamed about when she was in the middle of a boring trans-Atlantic flight. They kept talking on the way home, and even though it was late, they headed to her library.

Curling herself onto a sofa, Sydney made one request. "Read me your favorite thing in here."

Parker walked to the other side of the room, climbed the rolling ladder to the top shelf, pulled down a book, and tossed it on the coffee table. The thud made Sydney open her eyes as she looked up from taking her own shoes off. Sydney laughed when she saw the title. "*War and Peace*? You do realize I'm leaving tomorrow, don't you?"

"I wanted to see if you were still awake after those two and a half desserts you ate." She ducked the small pillow Sydney tossed at her before she stood to take another book from the oak shelves that surrounded the large room.

She read all the verses of the Robert Frost poem she'd quoted at dinner. When she finished, Sydney opened her eyes. "I wish I didn't have a job and responsibilities to get back to. Thank you for the last couple of days. It was the most fun I've had in forever, and I'm just sorry it has to end so soon." She accepted Parker's hands to help her up and her invitation to walk her to the door of the room she was staying in.

Parker handed Sydney her sandals and smiled. "Good night. I hope you have pleasant dreams." Not caring if Sydney got the wrong impression, she kissed her softly on the lips for a long, delicious moment before heading toward the master suite.

Sydney still stood at her door with her fingers on her lips and a smile when she looked back before going in. Parker was still scared of what Sydney made her feel, but she also made her lips tingle every time they kissed.

"You're beginning to sound like a romance novel, Kong," she said to herself as she untucked her shirt. "Next thing you know, you'll be renting a horse to ride through the surf followed by a full violin quartet." She laughed at the mental image, especially when she thought of someone like Alicia, who inspired no romantic notions at all in her.

The joke was, though, the minute she'd begin to have real feelings for a woman, it'd be one who was so suspicious of her motives they might not ever get past it. Also Parker had the nagging idea that Sydney was going through something she didn't want to talk about.

"If there's one thing I've learned, it's practice makes perfect." She'd keep at it until she'd blown all of Sydney's barriers to hell, and they would share each other's secrets.

CHAPTER EIGHT

Sydney wandered around the house with Abby, searching for Parker the next morning. She wasn't eager to leave, and since her flight wasn't for hours, she hoped Parker had time for breakfast and some more conversation.

She'd found Parker's bedroom empty, so she followed the music coming from somewhere beyond the kitchen. That's where Abby had run to and where he sat in the doorway waving his paw as if to get her to move faster.

Inside the large room with three walls filled with windows, through which Sydney caught glimpses of the Gulf through the dunes, Parker lay on the weight bench doing bench presses. She admired the fluidity of Parker's movements, surprised at how much commitment and effort it took to play tennis.

"Good morning." She'd waited until Parker put the weight bar back before she spoke. It wasn't even seven in the morning and Parker was already sweating.

"Hey, did you sleep well?" Parker asked before toweling off her face and neck.

"Considering how quiet it is here, I slept great." She stepped farther into the room and Abby moved with her so his head stayed strategically under her hand. "You must've started early."

"The days of practice on the court make Beau happy because it keeps my game up, but my mornings in here thrill Nick no end." Parker laughed as she reached for the juice bottle near her feet.

"Why's that?"

"I train to stay in shape, which prevents injuries, but it also keeps the sponsors lined up. Those guys really pay the bills."

Sydney moved closer and placed her hand on Parker's shoulder. "Are you almost done?"

"That's the last of my reps for today, so give me a few minutes to shower, since I sweated a gallon in here today, and I'll take you out for breakfast."

"Actually," she put her other hand on Parker's shoulder and stood between her legs, "if you don't mind, and if you'll allow me to borrow your kitchen, I'd like to cook for you." When Parker exhaled, Sydney's nipples puckered as if Parker had sucked them hard enough to make her wet. She was starting to become a little unhinged since she vacillated from anger to lust when it came to Parker. "Let me make you breakfast as a way of thanking you for going out of your way like you have."

"You sure? You don't have to." Parker's eyes drifted down as she spoke, and Sydney knew her T-shirt didn't hide much. If Parker accused her of being a tease, she'd have no defense.

"I'm positive." She gave in to the urge to hug Parker and smiled when Parker held her tight enough that her feet left the ground once Parker stood. "I don't get to indulge my passions very often, so cooking for you would be fun," she said as she ran her fingers through Parker's hair and grimaced at how wet they got.

"I told you a shower was a good idea." Parker laughed. "Sorry about that."

"Get in there, then, and meet me in the kitchen." She wiped her hand on Parker's back.

"If the doorbell rings, could you get it?" Parker said, then kissed her. "I ordered some of those cinnamon rolls you said you don't like."

"I never said I didn't like them." Parker slowly placed her on her feet. "Stuff like that doesn't fall off my hips like it does yours."

"Your hips look fantastic, and if you need some ass compliments you might miss your flight." Parker's hand headed in that direction as she spoke. "Even if you already know how spectacular I think your ass is, I still want you to miss your flight."

"Parker, you don't need me here getting in your way." The argument would've been more effective had she put more heart in it, but that was difficult with Parker's hand on her butt. If ever there was a way of getting over someone, she'd found it right here, and it was time to leave before she got any more sucked in. Parker deserved better than someone rebounding from a horrible experience.

"A few more days, then I promise I'll stop harping on it."

"That's how long it'll take for you to get tired of me?" Her promise to herself not to get mad at Parker was seriously challenged.

"The rest of the week is better than a few hours, but it still won't be enough," Parker said seriously. "Still, if those are my only choices right now," she said and kissed her, "I'll go with the longer-stay option."

"Go take a shower and I'll make some calls," she said, having decided to stay even if it meant a reprimand for changing her mind so much. Parker's face lit up with a beautiful smile. "Take your time." It was strange making someone so happy with something so trivial, but it was a new experience. Until recently, Gene had never bothered to ask her for anything except to pick up her dry cleaning. With Gene she was more motivated to try to avoid her than to spend time with her. Maybe in her next life she'd come back as an ostrich, considering how good she was at burying her head in the sand.

"You're the boss," Parker said with another kiss before releasing her. "Abby, go outside, boy." Abby shook his head and whined as he fell at Sydney's feet as if begging for a rubdown. "He'll try to cram himself into your luggage if you keep spoiling him."

"Don't think it hasn't crossed my mind to kidnap him, especially since he smells better than you do."

"You're such a good hint giver." Parker walked backward with her hands up. "Scream if you want anything."

After a call to the airline, Sydney hunted around the kitchen for all the ingredients she'd need for breakfast. She dialed her mother's number after she dumped the first of the vegetables she'd cut up into the pan. Lucia's favorite omelet was one of the first things she'd learned to make, and it was the dish her mom often woke up to whenever she visited her in Atlanta.

"Hello."

"Good morning, Mom." She turned the heat down so as not to burn anything.

"I'm glad you called, sweetheart. What time are you arriving? Your sister wanted to know so she could join us for dinner if she can leave work in time."

"Please tell me you haven't started cooking yet." She added the eggs and kept her fingers crossed that she hadn't put her mother out.

"You don't have to go to work right away, do you?"

"Actually, I thought about finishing my vacation here instead of leaving early."

"I'm dying to see you, but I'd rather you enjoy your time off and relax." Lucia paused, obviously so she could organize her thoughts to not sound nosy. "Did you find a place to stay?"

"I'm fine, Mom, and my cell is on all the time if you need to talk to me. The same friend who helped me yesterday offered to take me in."

"Anyone I know?"

She laughed. "No, but I'll tell you all about it when I see you."

"Whoever this wonderful friend is, tell her thank you from me for talking you into finishing out the week. She must be a real charmer."

"She is that." She heard Parker's voice as she and Abby got closer. "Love you, and I'll see you soon."

Parker's hair was wet and she was wearing a robe when she arrived, and Sydney stared for a moment, trying to guess what was under it. She couldn't see anything but skin down the vee of the robe on her upper chest, so she turned her attention back to the meal.

"Wow," Parker said, placing her hands on her hips when she stopped right behind her. "Hash browns, toast, and a good-looking omelet? I might keep you here permanently."

"Stop kissing up and pour the hot chocolate."

"And hot cocoa, Captain?" Parker did as she asked. "You must really like me."

"What is it about hot chocolate that you love so much?" Parker appeared to be reliving a nightmare at her question, and it made her hurt to watch.

"It's my happiest memory of my father. When I was little we'd be the first ones up and he'd stand at the stove and make some. He didn't use an instant mix either. He'd shave chocolate and stir it in slowly with sugar until it was perfect. It became our morning ritual to sit at our kitchen table and discuss all kinds of different things."

"That sounds like a wonderful memory. It's a shame to give up a relationship that obviously meant so much to both of you."

"It wasn't me who let go first. I'd wait for him before I had to leave for practice, hoping he'd change his mind, but he wouldn't come out of his bedroom. Maybe it was all for the best, since when we did talk we just screamed at each other. He could never accept us for the people we are." Sydney slid the omelet onto a plate so she could turn and hug Parker. "It was shortly after that when he said he couldn't take it anymore and threw me out."

It seemed absurd to Sydney that people who were so rigid and bigoted had children. "I'm sorry for asking."

"It's all right. All those cups I had as a kid just make me love the stuff. My parents may not accept me now, but drinking hot chocolate reminds me of a time they did."

The big smile Sydney had seen on television a million times when she watched Parker play reappeared. Her own life wasn't perfect, but she was grateful her parents had accepted her choices without censure. They'd only wanted her to be happy and find someone who'd share her life and enhance it.

"You're a wonderful person, and in time your parents will come to realize that. I've only known you a couple of days and I have at least that part figured out." Parker took her hand and kissed her palm.

"Thanks, but I've accepted how they feel and that they won't change. Upbringing is hard for some people to overcome, and my father's father was one of those old-time Bible-thumping preachers who liked to teach his kids right from wrong with a belt. At least that's what my mother told me." Parker took a deep breath and let it go before going on. "If that's true, my dad's attitude is almost understandable."

"That's kind of you to say, since I don't know if I could be so forgiving."

"All that taught me is that you can't force people to change their feelings if they're so engrained. Dwelling on it will eat you up from the inside out, and trying to change someone is a waste of your time and theirs. It shocks me that no one on the circuit has ever figured out how screwed up my family is, at least when it comes to my parents. They would've had a field day by now."

Sydney ran her hands along Parker's back and kissed her. "Don't ever change yourself," she said when their lips parted. She wanted to add the phrase "don't settle," but that would require an explanation she wasn't ready to give. Having to do so would allow the real world to sneak into their time together, and she wasn't willing to sacrifice that either. "I like the person you are."

"The only thing I want to change your mind about is staying. Have you?"

"If you promise not to try and get out of practice to spend time with me, I'm all yours when you're done."

"Remember you said that." Parker allowed herself to be led to the table. "Because when all this is over, I have a feeling I'll be all yours too."

❖

"Another early day?" Beau asked when after three hours of practice Parker started packing her stuff.

"A few days, Coach, and after that I'll stay out here until midnight if you want," Parker said before draining a bottle of water. "Thanks, Natasha. I'll see you both in the morning."

"Keep your eyes open," Beau yelled as she waved to them over her shoulder. Sydney was waiting for her on the back deck wearing another one of her T-shirts over her bathing suit.

"I'm planning on it," she whispered as she smiled at Sydney, "considering what's in my line of sight."

"Did you make up your mind about what you want to do today?" she asked when Sydney put her arms around her waist.

"I'm sure there's plenty, but I'd like to spend another day on the beach with you." Sydney kept her arms wrapped loosely around Parker, probably because she was soaked from her practice.

"Let me change and I'll be happy to take you." She dropped her bag in the kitchen and didn't say anything when Sydney followed her to the bedroom, where she sat on the bed while she showered and dressed.

Sydney most likely wouldn't stop her if she suggested they stay in and on the bed for the day, but rushing would ruin anything that would come afterward. And for once, what came after really getting to know someone sounded appealing to her.

"You told her about your fucked-up family and she's still here," she whispered as she stuck her head under the shower spray.

When she stepped out dressed like Sydney, she stopped to admire how good Sydney looked spread across her bed. "What?" Sydney asked when she didn't say anything.

"You're beautiful."

"Thank you," Sydney said after a long pause. "Considering some of the women you've dated, that's a surprising compliment."

"Everything about you is different from anyone I've ever known," she said as she sat close enough to lay her hand on Sydney's cheek. "That would've been enough to keep me curious about you, but you're a gorgeous woman."

"I'm not sure I understand what you mean."

"It means that I'm glad you're here," she kissed Sydney on the lips, "and I'm glad we've had this opportunity to be together." Sydney moved closer when she kissed her again. "But what first made me notice you was this beautiful face," she said, and laughed.

"Just the face?"

"We'll get to the extensive list eventually, but I don't want to start our afternoon with you mad at me."

They made a few stops before Parker headed down the road to Barnaby's secluded beach. It didn't take long to set up their chairs and umbrellas, so Sydney suggested a walk before lunch.

"It's going to be hard sitting in a cockpit for hours after this," Sydney said as they walked holding hands.

"Do you get a lot of vacation time?"

"More than I ever use." Sydney laughed as Abby ran around them in widening circles.

"You're welcome to come back whenever you like."

"I appreciate the offer, but with my upcoming move, it'll be a while before I get to take time off for fun." As they neared their starting point Sydney took them deeper into the water. "So I plan to get all my fun in now."

"Can I do anything to help you along those lines?"

Sydney didn't let go of her hand as they waded out. "There's only one thing I've never done on a beach vacation." Sydney didn't elaborate but blushed.

"Do tell," she said, holding Sydney from behind.

"That first day when I noticed you running," Sydney said as she laid her head back on her shoulder, but not far enough for Parker to see her face.

"You want to run with me?" She lifted Sydney a little higher so she could kiss her neck. "That's easy enough, but I could think of some other things that might be more fun even if there's sand involved."

"I'm not interested in a jog, Kong, and you didn't let me finish." Sydney tugged on her hair. "It's what happened when your sisters were still here."

"Ah," she said softly, her lips right up to Sydney's ear. "You've never been skinny-dipping, and you've spent your vacation peeking at me naked."

"No, I haven't, to the skinny-dipping, and you've made it really easy to catch a naked Parker sighting since you drop your pants constantly."

"Everyone should try it at least once." She held Sydney tighter when she tensed.

"It's really open out here, though."

"No one's around for miles, but don't worry. I'm not taking any chances with you."

"So you aren't interested?"

"Seeing you naked?" She bit Sydney's earlobe, which made her laugh. "You have no idea how much, but I've got some place other than here in mind. Don't sweat it. You won't be leaving a virgin."

"All that reading sure has given you a talent with words."

"I'm glad you think so, but that's not my greatest talent." She turned in the water so they were facing away from the shoreline.

"Is that the best you've got to let me know what I'm missing out on by not sleeping with you?"

"Such a busy mind, Captain." She kissed Sydney's temple. "I meant, I have a better command of tennis than I do of the English language."

"So you suck in bed?" Sydney turned and wrapped her legs around her waist.

"In ways that'll make you scream," she said, and winked. "Come on before I ravish you out here, whether you want me to or not."

They had lunch, then lay on the blanket instead of the chairs to be closer. It was late by the time they packed up, and she stopped to buy a couple of steaks for the grill and the ingredients for the side dish Sydney wanted to make. Their time together revolved around the simplest tasks, like grocery shopping, but it opened her mind to possibilities that had never registered on her radar, like a long-term relationship. Having someone like Sydney would mean years of these types of moments, ending the revolving door that had been the norm for her bedroom. But the permanency of one person didn't scare the shit out of her like it had up to now.

"You have everything you need?" Sydney asked when they reached the last aisle of the store.

Imagining someone like Alicia in Sydney's place for a fleeting moment made her shiver. "Yeah, I think I do," she said, and for once she felt her statement went way beyond groceries.

❖

"Tell me."

Eric and Ethan Prophet glanced at each other, then at the phone. The double beds in the old hotel sagged incredibly low and, like everything else in the room, hadn't been replaced or updated in years. The phone's speaker feature was the one modern oddity.

"We took pictures of her and her whore on the beach today," Eric said. He and Ethan were identical twins, but Ethan had been born three sandwiches short of a picnic, as their father loved to say about his shy but slow son. "They stayed for hours, but never suspected we were there."

"Did you send them?" Their father's voice boomed through the room and made them both sit straighter, even though he was a thousand miles away.

Eric nodded toward Ethan, giving him permission to speak. "We done did that an hour ago," Ethan said, his voice softer and higher than his brother's.

"Anything to confess?" They shared a long, guilty look between them, and both pressed their legs together. "Don't make me ask you again," their father hissed.

"Nothing, sir," Eric said with as much authority as he could. "All we did is what you asked us."

"Keep it that way, and call if there's anything else. Try to find out who this woman is that's staying with her, but don't get close enough to be noticed."

"Yes, sir," they said together before Eric disconnected the call.

"Do you think he believed us, brother?" Ethan asked, having to speak louder to be heard over the ancient air conditioner that made more noise than cool air.

Eric looked down at the stack of pictures, the top one of the blonde and Parker coming out of the water. The whore still had her legs around Parker's waist, and whatever she'd said had made Parker laugh. The photo had captured Parker in a moment of joy, but it'd be short-lived once she was sentenced to an eternity of misery in hell.

It was wrong, but the image and Parker's ease with women excited him, and no amount of prayer or fear of what his father would do to him if he saw the bulge in his pants was controlling his urges. Parker King and her sisters were an abomination to God, and even the sight of them made him weak enough to unleash Satan. That was something he'd try harder to fight against…tomorrow. Right now the evil in him needed release.

"Open your legs, Ethan, and let me see," he said, pointing at Ethan's crotch. "Don't make me ask you again, boy." He did his best to sound like Father.

"I'm sorry." Ethan moved his hands to cover his face as if he was ashamed to be in the same condition. "I didn't mean it, brother."

"You know what to do," he said, speaking softer in an effort to relax Ethan into cooperation. Father had preached how wrong this was when they were little and he bent them over the padded sawhorses he kept in the barn, and he said the pain of him penetrating them was meant to condition the urges away. That was his theory, but Eric had learned a different lesson. Only the weak were the ones holding their ankles in that hot smelly place. The strong were the ones standing behind them trying to teach righteousness.

"Pray for forgiveness while you're on your knees, sinner," he told Ethan as he unfastened his belt.

After their mission he'd start his own church with as many followers like Ethan as he could find, if only to prove to Father how strong he was. The Bible was right. Blessed were the weak because they would find salvation by serving him, and they would serve him as well as Ethan whenever it pleased him. It'd be his reward for being a faithful soldier of God.

CHAPTER NINE

Parker and Sydney didn't leave the island the next day, but spent their time in the water again after Parker's morning practice. Midday when the temperatures drove them inside, they relaxed in the library, content to sit and read.

After dinner, Parker walked Sydney to her room and pointed to the robe she'd laid on the bed. "You feel like celebrating your last day of vacation?"

Sydney looked at the robe and smiled. She'd spent most of the day staring at Parker and fighting the urge to spread her legs and beg Parker to do something to alleviate how hard and wet she was. "What did you have in mind?" She'd never considered herself a sexual person, but Parker made her want to be touched and quell the desire that flowed so freely. Not that she'd never orgasmed with Gene, but she'd never initiated sex.

"I want you to get naked, put that on, and meet me outside."

Parker caressed her cheek before leaving the room and closed the door behind her, which didn't surprise her since Parker had done everything to make her comfortable from the moment she'd come to stay. From an early age her mother had always said that life uncovered surprises in the strangest places, and the really good ones were gifts from heaven as a way of showing that God cared.

She was sure a hot tennis player wasn't what her mother meant, but at the moment she felt extremely cared for. The robe Parker had provided was similar to the one she wore every morning, only this one was her size. Thoughts of who it belonged to didn't get very far when she found a tag on the inside label, bearing the same store name as the bag Nick had dropped off earlier.

Parker was waiting for her in the hall when she opened the door, and she looked fantastic bathed in the candlelight from the hurricane lantern she held.

"Thanks for the great robe."

"Thanks for putting it on and coming out here." Parker held out her hand.

"Are we going somewhere?" she asked, already having an idea as to where they were headed.

"I noticed on the calendar that there's no moon tonight, and I took it as a sign that the Fates want me to grant your wish." When they stepped outside, Parker opened a small metal box close to the back door and flipped the switch inside it. In an instant the house went black and the quiet whirr of the air-conditioning system stopped. Aside from the light Parker was holding, the area around them was pitch black. "Want to go for a swim with me?"

"Is it safe?" She could hear the surf in the distance, which was choppier than usual from the wind blowing at a good clip.

"The only shark you'll find out there has already promised to behave, so you'll be fine. It smells like rain, so we won't see many stars with all these clouds, but I don't see any lightning."

Sydney held on to Parker as they made their way down the path to the beach and noticed the outside lights of the house she'd stayed in previously. Since they provided the only other illumination except Parker's lantern, she started to get excited about sharing this experience with her.

At the shoreline Parker smiled before blowing out the candle. Sydney could barely make out Parker's features because of the red dots the missing light left in her line of sight, and she stayed quiet as Parker pulled the tie of her robe open. When the night air hit her chest, her nipples tightened, and she almost moaned when Parker moved behind her to take off the robe and the material rubbed against them.

The breeze from the Gulf had cooled the temperature some, but thankfully the water wasn't cold. Parker held her hand as they entered it, and Sydney was surprised at how different it felt without her suit as it swirled around her thighs. It was sensual, and the deeper they got, the more all her inhibitions melted away in the waves.

"You okay?" Parker asked from an arm's length away.

"Thanks for this," she said, then dipped her head back to wet her hair so it wouldn't blow in her face. "I can see now why you like this so much."

Parker ran her hand down her arm to take her other hand but didn't move any closer. "The first time I came out here and stripped I thought I was a genius for buying here." She laughed. "I find it relaxing and freeing, but I don't know how relaxed I'd be with one of those gigantic condo buildings next door."

"Don't tell me you're modest?" Since Parker kept her distance, Sydney moved closer and had to fight to keep the quiver out of her voice when their bodies touched. "Your photo shoot says otherwise."

"I'm not modest per se, but I don't enjoy being hunted by every creep with a camera either. Every once in a while it'd be nice to go out when I'm on the road and not have it reported," Parker said as she took them deeper. Sydney had to hang on to her or tread water. "It was ridiculous in England this year, but I think Alicia's manager had the photographers on speed dial."

"You aren't going to see her anymore?"

"I've been enough of a publicity boost for her in this lifetime, so no. Alicia has a great voice, but her world revolves around Alicia. Everyone around her is there to fulfill every whim that pops into her head, and saying no is an invitation to being up front and center for a major meltdown tantrum."

"You don't look like flunky material to me, Kong."

Parker laughed before she kissed her. "The only time I'm overly aggressive is at the net, but that doesn't mean I enjoy the diva act all the time."

"If I promise to keep my diva-ness to a minimum, do you think it'd be okay if I came back to see you after I get settled and you're back from the tournament?"

"Only if you promise me something."

"What?" She moved behind Parker and put her arms around her neck.

"That we do this again." Parker peeled away one of her hands and kissed her palm. "Only we wait for a full moon. Don't you think I deserve a treat for being so good?"

"You're on."

She let go of Parker and took her hand as she started back to shore. Parker helped her put on her robe before she lit the lantern. "Your only problem will be turning me off, Captain."

❖

"You can drop me off if you want," Sydney said when Parker turned in to short-term parking.

"I plan to carry your bags in, so don't start complaining. You never know, I might need a reference from you one day."

It was interesting to walk next to someone who got as many double takes as Parker did when people spotted her. The brave ones waved, and Parker acknowledged each one.

"Aren't you worried being out alone, considering the kind of mail you get?"

"I try to stay vigilant, but so far crazed tennis haters have stuck to the mail." Parker followed her through security with the pass Sydney had gotten her at the counter. "As ridiculous as those things have been, something tells me the soldiers of God won't have the guts to carry out their threats."

"Let's hope you're right."

They sat away from the crowd at the gate since Sydney wanted to say good-bye properly. She was flying to Atlanta, where she'd board a flight to Miami. From there she'd pilot a flight to New York, since that was the deal she'd made when she'd rearranged her schedule to spend more time with Parker. She was about to continue their conversation when a little girl around seven walked up and just stood in front of Parker.

"Hi," Parker said, holding out her hand. She smiled as if she'd hold it out there until the hero worship wore off some and the girl noticed it. "What's your name?" Parker asked, and got the same frozen expression.

"Ms. King, we hate to bother you, but my daughter would love her picture taken with you," the woman standing next to the kid said. "And I'm sure if she remembered how to form words she'd ask you herself."

"What's your name?"

"Am…Am…Amber," the girl finally got out, and raised her hand to shake Parker's. Sydney smiled and enjoyed this sweet, patient side of Parker.

"How's your game?" Parker asked.

"I'm just learning." Amber was becoming more animated and was now shaking Parker's hand enthusiastically.

"Just remember, the more you practice, the easier it gets."

Sydney laughed when Parker stood and Amber clammed up again as she cocked her head back to keep eye contact. When Parker made a circle with her finger, Amber got the message and turned around to face her mom, who stood by with the camera.

They took four shots before Sydney dropped her purse and held her hand out for the camera. "Would you like to be in a couple?" she asked the woman.

After another five shots the two returned to their spots, leaving them alone. "You certainly made their day."

"The kids don't bother me. It's good to encourage them to keep playing if they're interested. There are worse vices than tennis."

"Captain Parish?" The flight attendant waited for her to answer.

"Can I help you?"

"Sorry to bother you, ma'am, but we confirmed you were flying with us today. Our pilot has a sudden bout of flu and we can't find his backup. We know you're flying on to Miami, then New York, but would you consider adding the short hop to Atlanta?" The woman put her hands up and smiled. "If you don't want to, don't shoot the messenger, okay?"

"Sure, call off the search for a backup. I'll be happy to help out."

"Great. We start boarding in three minutes."

Sydney groaned because of the quick good-bye she had to give Parker. "I have to go."

"Duty calls, Captain, no problem." Parker pulled something out of her back pocket and opened her mouth, getting ready to say something when the attendant started the preboarding set of instructions.

"I'm sorry, Parker, but I have to leave now." The required list of pre-flight checks assaulted her brain.

Like she had before they left for the airport, Parker kissed her gently on the lips; then she pressed a piece of paper into her hand before giving her the bag she'd carried in. "Good-bye, then," Parker said, and didn't leave until Sydney waved one last time before heading to the cockpit.

The crew took care of her bags, and after her checklist they were fifteen minutes late pulling away from the gate, only to get stuck behind a line of jets waiting for takeoff. During the lull she pulled what Parker had given her out of her pocket. Written neatly on the slip was Parker's contact information with a message on the other side.

If you need to—call me.

"Flight 1382, you are clear for takeoff on runway five," the tower informed her.

"Flight 1382 proceeding to runway five," she responded. With one last look at the note she put it away. "Good-bye, Parker." She pulled back on the controls to get the plane airborne.

"Did you say something, Captain?" her copilot asked.

"Probably not enough."

She didn't know what was waiting for her in Atlanta or with her career change, but her life had been perfect for the last few days. Perhaps the best thing was to leave it at that, because the bubble of bliss had popped the moment she walked away from Parker.

They both had to get back to their realities, and she couldn't see them ever meshing.

❖

The weather off the coast turned from blue skies to torrential storms halfway to New York, so Sydney had to veer more inland than she would've liked. Going so far off course had kept everyone safe, but put them two hours behind.

"The bitch in 2B wants you to personally reimburse her for the Broadway show she's missing," Nicole, the first-class attendant, said when she delivered the coffee Sydney had ordered. "She wants you," Nicole tapped her on the shoulder, "because you gave in to your fears over a small, insignificant patch of summer showers."

"Tell her I'll cut her a check when she tells me when and where she got her pilot's license," Lawrence, her copilot, said. "If the bitch doesn't have one, tell her to sit still and shut the fuck up, or I'll tie a flotation device around her fat ass and fling her out."

"I'm glad to see the anger-management and client-sensitivity classes are working for you." Sydney laughed. At least he'd said what she was thinking and saved her the trouble. All the tension Parker and the beach had taken out of her was short-lived. After she'd waited forever to take off in Mobile, her day had steadily gone downhill, and the large bedroom set she felt like she constantly carried around was back. "Thanks for the heads-up, Nicole. We'll get her with corporate as soon as we land."

"What show was it?" Lawrence asked.

"*Wicked*, I believe."

"Figures," he snorted. "A bitch going to see a show about a witch. That's appropriate." They all laughed again and Nicole went back to her post. "How was your vacation, Syd?"

"Not long enough." She couldn't bring herself to say any more.

It was true she'd left Parker sooner than she'd planned, so the explanation of whatever had happened between them and how it couldn't progress didn't take place. Even though her relationship with Gene was over, she felt guilty for the few intimacies she'd shared with Parker. What she'd done and how she'd acted were no different than what she'd accused Gene of.

That wasn't exactly true since she hadn't slept with Parker, but she wasn't truly free of her past either. As much as she didn't want to deal with Gene, she'd have to go back to Atlanta and meet with her one last time. Gene hadn't earned that kind of respect, but a final conversation would make it easier to start over with nothing left undone.

"Sorry to hear that, but we're glad to have you on this route," Lawrence said. "You saved our ass today. I love Miami, but I would've missed my anniversary. My wife and I owe you."

"Glad I was available, and congratulations."

They landed forty minutes later, and Sydney was thrilled that the management representatives waiting at the door whisked away the disgruntled passengers. It was raining in New York as well, and judging by all the late flights, finding a cab would be about as easy as finding the Holy Grail.

"Hey, Mom, I just landed but there's no way I'm getting there soon, so if Margo arrives you two go ahead and eat." She left the message, trying not to bump into anyone as she walked through the packed corridors. She wanted to see her family but would've been happy to head to one of the airport hotels and go to bed. Her exhaustion was numbing.

Sydney answered on the first ring without glancing to see who it was. "Did you get my message?"

"I haven't heard from you since your little tantrum, so I didn't look for any messages." Gene's voice was flat, her words a bit slurred. "Are you ready to talk now?"

"There isn't much to say. It's me, not you. We've grown apart, and we want different things. Did I leave any clichéd bullshit out?" The leather handle of her bag was slippery since her skin had become clammy from the sudden surge of anger. That was better than the nausea that extreme bouts of emotion usually caused. "I'm trying my best to keep up."

"Sarcasm isn't flattering coming from you, Syd."

"It's not sarcasm." Outside, she couldn't believe how short the cab line was, but not having to check bags had its perks. "You gave me every insulting line you could pull when I found out what all the late nights were about. I'm giving you the opportunity to juggle as many women as you want without having to hide it."

"You're willing to walk away from all the time we've invested in this?"

"Do you honestly think guilt will work for you? Even if I weren't moving, this wouldn't have worked." She muted the phone and told the driver her mom's address. "Individually we weren't ready for the happily-ever-after, and we won't find it together."

"You believe that now because you're pissed, but when the smog clears you'll see."

"That doesn't make sense, but if you mean I'll come to see I can't live without you, don't waste your time waiting. I'd like to end this before we can't stand each other."

"You can forgive everyone in the world but me?"

The conversation was uncomfortable with an eavesdropping driver, but the trip into the city reminded her of her birthday when she was a child. The buildup of anticipation and joy of seeing her mom and Margo was balancing her emotions. "I did forgive you. I just don't want to be with you or anyone who makes a habit of disrespecting me. If you want to believe that I haven't forgiven you, remember I didn't give the world my heart and trust. That gift went to you, and you treated both like used cat litter."

"It was the one time, and you can't let it go."

"You're right." "One time" was as big a lie as agreeing to it, but she was done wasting her time. "It was once and I won't ever let it go, so accept it."

"When are you coming home?" Gene's voice got softer, but Sydney knew better than to think the change had to do with remorse or compassion. The angrier Gene got in any situation, the softer her voice became. She'd used that form of intimidation in every fight they'd had, but Gene was someone else's problem now.

"I'm returning to Atlanta to close on the condo, period." This useless conversation had changed her mind about going back for that last talk. "I've arranged to have my stuff moved, and why am I repeating myself?" She yelled so loud the driver's eyebrows shot up. "We've been through this already. You have a month, so either move out or put a bid in with my Realtor."

Gene slammed something down. "You owe me at least one civil conversation, Sydney."

"No, I don't." She was having trouble holding the phone to her ear. "It wasn't one, Gene, so don't keep lying to me. There were actually about six, that I know of, but you didn't mean enough to me to fight about it. The truth is, I wasn't enough, and even if all of a sudden I were, I'd never trust you again. I tried to make it work, but I'm done."

"Why invite me to come this past week, then?"

"Because I'm an idiot. There's nothing between us to salvage. What we had is not only over, it doesn't matter to me anymore." She disconnected because she didn't have anything else to say or add. "What matters to me going forward is pasting together my faith in other people," she said softly against the back of her phone. "But you shredded so much in me I don't know if I can."

It'd been three days since Sydney left, and Parker sat at her kitchen table staring at the phone. "I'm not familiar with proper waiting periods to call someone, but this is driving me crazy," she said to Abby, who had his head next to the phone.

His eyes moved from her nervous fingers to the portable and he woofed, as if saying to get on with it. "I know she said she'd be busy, but dialing ten numbers can't take that much time." Abby whined at her whining.

"Of course, this is fate's way of saying 'fuck you' on behalf of the women you've left hanging pathetically in their kitchens waiting for your call. Only you were moving on," she scratched Abby's snout, "to sit like a ten-year-old with a crush watching the phone. All I need is tissue and a gallon of ice cream to become a member of the dumped club."

Abby barked and bumped her arm closer to the phone. "If I press redial on the numbers she dialed, I'll come across as either a stalker or clingy." Abby barked again, then whined.

She pressed the first number without overthinking anymore and hoped for the best. "Hello." It wasn't Sydney, but the person who answered was female.

"Sydney, please."

"Sure, hang on, she's in the shower."

What a strange thing to tell a stranger on the phone, but her throat closed a little at the implication. Maybe this woman had been in the shower too, and run out to answer the phone. If she was, why in the hell would she do that? Was she a moron? If she had Sydney naked in water she wouldn't run out to answer the goddamn phone. "I'm going to need Prozac or hard liquor before the summer's out."

"Hello, did you say something?"

"Hey, Sydney, it's Parker." She'd finished practice and still hadn't changed, but the silence that followed her introduction chilled her more than the air-conditioning on her sweat-slicked skin. "I wanted to make sure you made it okay."

"I'm sorry I haven't called, but I've been slammed since I got here. How are you?"

"Fine…practicing and running." She didn't have any aunts to call, but if she did, any phone conversations between them would be going pretty much like this, she thought.

"Parker." Sydney sounded as distant as the miles that separated them. "I owe you an apology for running out on you like I did."

"It's no biggie." *I am fucking crazy*, she thought as she pressed her hand hard into the tabletop.

"To me it was." The noise from the television in the background disappeared as if Sydney had either walked away or closed the door. "You were great and generous for everything you did." Sydney stopped talking, and Parker didn't help by adding any small talk. There was no use. "I didn't share it with you then, but I recently ended a long-time relationship, and you helped me through the worst of it."

"I'm sorry." She sounded like a moron, but nothing else came to mind. Were there condolence cards for breakups? "Can I do anything? You can come back and take some time to regroup, if you want." *Stop talking before you sound any more pathetic*, a voice screamed in her head.

"That's nice of you, but impossible right now." Sydney seemed ready to say something else but lapsed into silence again.

"Let me help you." After Sydney left, Parker had wanted more, so much so that Sydney hadn't left her thoughts. This was the first time outside her family that she'd shared so much because she needed Sydney to know her. That was the price of moving forward to something more permanent. Longing had never been a part of her vocabulary, and now she knew why. Her entire body hurt suddenly like the one time in her life she'd had the flu.

"You're sweet, but—"

"You don't need to explain, and you've got my numbers if you need to talk. Good luck."

"Wait," Sydney said loudly. "It's not you. I just need time alone, and that's not fair to you."

"Sure, take care of yourself." She disconnected and threw the phone at the wall, scaring Abby. "Lesson learned, boy." She hugged Abby and let her tears fall on his back. "You're my longest relationship and it's going to have to stay that way." Sydney Parish didn't want her, but she'd learn to live with it. After all, she wasn't the first person to think she wasn't worth the effort.

❖

The line went dead and Sydney blinked and tilted her head back. She'd looked at Parker's card numerous times but hadn't given in to the urge to call her. It wouldn't have been fair to Parker to give her false hope.

Since Sydney had gotten back, Gene had called three times a day, each call more demanding. It wasn't at all like what Parker was going through with her stalker, but this taste of unwanted attention was making her insane. However, the call Parker had just ended hurt more than all the ones from Gene.

She dialed and waited. After four rings she didn't think Parker would answer, but the click proved her wrong. "Please let me explain a few things before you hang up again."

"I'm sure you're dealing with enough without me piling on for explanations," Parker said, sounding like the liquid velvet she remembered. Parker's voice was like fine liquor that clung to a glass when you swirled it and warmed you from your mouth to your chest. "We had fun, but that's over. You had to get back to your life."

"I can't blame you for being upset, but don't trivialize the time we spent together. I consider you a friend."

"I am." Parker's tone didn't really change, but Sydney knew what having a friend meant to someone like Parker. It was the same with Gene. They didn't have girlfriends in the platonic sense. "If you ever need anything I'll be here for you, but that's not what you want, is it?"

"Are you angry with me?" There wasn't a problem with the connection, but Parker was drifting away. Sydney was tired of being hurt, though. She didn't relish giving her heart away again, only to be let down when the next bit of fluff with perky tits and an empty head came along. Once was enough.

"No, but I want you to be honest." Parker's cough sounded muffled, as if she'd moved the phone away. Parker was evidently too polite to curse directly into the receiver. "I'm sorry. That was uncalled for. I am your friend, Sydney, and I just wanted to make sure you were all right. You don't owe me anything, so take care of yourself."

"It really doesn't have anything to do with you." She was a jackass for reverting to the old clichés, but saying any more would leave her open and exposed to the possibilities of real pain. She'd thought the beginning with Gene had been hot, but compared to Parker that had been a dying matchstick. In a few short days Parker had left her like some Harlequin romance character that was a pile of quivering need.

"Sure, it does. It has everything to do with who I've been, but I'm used to karma dropping her calling card." Parker laughed, sounding more relaxed. "Now I understand the questions about my conquests, as you put it better. Do me a favor, okay?"

"Name it."

"When you do the comparison, and you will," Parker's sharp wit was back, but this time she seemed to be using it as a barrier to hide behind, "remember, I'm good at winning on and off the court, but the trophies I've collected came and went with no promises."

"What does that mean, and what's the favor?"

"The day someone gives me the chance to make a promise, I intend to honor it. This jackass who hurt you obviously didn't, but I'm not her."

"You sound so sure."

"It's not whether I'm sure, Syd. It's whether you believe me, and you don't. Don't feel bad, though. I wouldn't believe me either. Not with my track record."

"So that's it?" Sydney thought someone might jump from the closet and put police caution tape around her, she was so unstable and indecisive.

"As they say in the tennis world, the ball's in your court." Parker laughed again. "We don't really say that, but take your time and call me when you're ready. I promise not to screen my calls, and I'll understand if you never feel you can."

"Thanks." She wanted to believe that this was her chance at

happiness, that Parker was the attentive hostess who'd romanced her, but that's how Gene was in the beginning. "Take care."

"You too."

And she planned to do just that. She'd take care of herself for once, and learn from her mistakes. Parker King was a mistake, but it wouldn't take much of a push for Sydney to chance it. That alone made her steer clear.

CHAPTER TEN

W hat the hell are you doing?" Margo asked when she rejoined
Sydney with the iced coffee and hot chocolate she'd waited in
line for.

Sydney peeked over the sports section of the paper. "Waiting for
you and watching the hundred bags you've accumulated, why?" The
front and next couple of pages of the *Times* sports section had a long
article about the Open, which started the next month. The large half-
page color photo on the front showed Parker as her racquet hit the ball
in her last serve at Wimbledon. The sight of it brought the smell of salt
air to mind. It also left the taste of happiness on Sydney's tongue, and
she relished it.

"Since when do you read sports?" Margo carefully placed the hot
chocolate down and dropped into the chair across from her. They both
had the day off and had spent it together shopping. "And it's hot as hell
for hot chocolate."

"I like to peruse the whole paper to get my money's worth, and
I've acquired a taste for chocolate. It's no big deal." She folded the
paper so she didn't have to stare at Parker's image. No sense torturing
herself since she'd gotten what she asked for. Parker had left her alone
to figure out where she belonged. The answer so far seemed to be lost,
lonely, and confused.

"If you owned a bird you'd have lined its cage with that section,
so I don't believe you." Margo pushed her chair closer, careful not to
create an avalanche of boxes and bags between them. "What are you
now, a paper miser?"

"I was killing time waiting. Is that answer more to your liking?"

"I'm on your side, remember?" Margo stirred four sugar packets
into her coffee. "I thought we'd celebrate the sale of your condo tonight,

but you haven't cracked a smile today. Did Gene do or say something while you were in Atlanta that you didn't mention?"

"She bought the place, so I had to be civil, but it wasn't as bad as I thought. I could tell she's still pissed, but like I said, she was okay."

"Okay." Margo dragged out the word. "What's got you so down then?"

"I'm tired, not depressed, so please stop asking me that. I love you for worrying about me, but you don't have to. I'm fine." *And I'd be better if I knew how Parker was or who she was with.* Surely, though, Parker had moved on without wasting another thought on her. If she had, she had no one to blame but herself…well, and Parker, a little. It was childish to want someone to think about her and put a candle in the window, as it were, but she kind of wanted Parker to pine away for her just a bit. That was about the hundredth reason she needed therapy, because clearly that kind of thinking was borderline crazy.

"Have you heard back from the Realtor?"

"Not yet. When she filled out the paperwork for me, she told me she'd had a couple of other offers, so I'm still waiting. You're a pain in the ass at times, but the thing I love about this place is having you so close."

"This pain in the ass found you that great apartment, so watch it."

"There's a couple more near the one you found, in case this one doesn't pan out, which is good. Work has been crazy lately, so if it keeps up, it'll be nice if you can keep an eye on my place."

"Since you have been working nonstop, you haven't told me how your date with Annette from my office went. She couldn't stop talking about you."

Margo tried to hide behind her drink, but Sydney noticed her mischievous smile. "She was nice enough, but you failed to mention that her dog hears the voice of God."

"I'm so sorry, Syd. She's cute, but none of us realized she's a bit touched. Had you agreed to a second date, though, you would've found out her parakeet was the Dalai Lama in a previous life."

"How does she know?" She couldn't help but laugh. Since her move she'd agreed to four dates, and all of them proved the universe was screwing with her.

"He meditates in the morning, and she swears he can put the cat in a trance." Margo was laughing hysterically when she finished. "Our in-house counsel sends her thanks for flushing out Annette's peculiar home life before she asked her out."

"From my record lately, I might follow Annette's example and get a few pets of my own, holy or not."

"Come on, you just started dating again. True love takes time."

"What's your excuse, then?" She poked Margo on the shoulder.

"Every great guy I meet seems destined to end up with a guy named Larry. I'm beginning to think I channel Liza Minnelli when I agree to go out with someone. One date and I add to the numbers of great gay men."

"At least we have each other. We can eventually be known as the Parish sisters, who were unlucky in love but adored by our sixty cats that could purr in harmony."

"Bite your tongue." Margo downed the rest of her coffee and slapped her hands together. "If I can't find a good man who worships me for the goddess I am, I'll switch teams and find a nice butch who will."

"Trust me, sometimes women are no better than men."

"Stop looking at the world through Gene-colored glasses. You could be staring at your future love, but you'll miss the opportunity because of that frigging woman." Margo kissed the side of her head before she started gathering up her things. "Are you ready to move on?"

Sydney flipped the paper over and looked at Parker again. She'd never forget the days they'd spent together or the way Parker had made her feel, but it was time to let go of the fantasy completely. "Sure." She said it, but it wasn't heartfelt.

Those days on the beach had whizzed by as quickly as one of Parker's serves, but they sure had left a profound mark on her heart.

❖

Parker buried her face in her towel, the heat making the cloth almost uncomfortable against her skin. "You're ready, Boris. I think the other women at this tournament, they're in big trouble," Natasha said after she'd packed her racquets and joined her at the other end of the court.

Parker had used the month to work on all her shots and improve her stamina. Beau had planned for the higher-than-normal heat factor in New York through extra running time, but no matter how hot or exhausted she was, she couldn't rip Sydney Parish out of her head with pliers.

"Thanks, Natasha. I'm feeling good enough to envision the finals this go-round. You promise you'll come up and practice with me?" She shouldered her bag and took Natasha's as well. This would be her last practice at home in Alabama, since they were taking the next couple of days off to take care of last-minute details before heading to New York. Abby was leaving with Beau that afternoon to stay with Nick until he flew up to meet her and Beau in the city.

"I wouldn't miss it, especially since Gray will be there. If I can't have you, I'll make a play for that sister of yours." At least Parker's sisters would be there for the entire tournament. "If I'm lucky, I'll get to compare her ass to that billboard of yours you did a while back."

"Don't remind me, and I'll put in a good word for you with Gray. See you in two weeks. Beau set up some playing time for us once you arrive." Natasha kissed both of her cheeks before she left, with a promise she'd call when she arrived in the city.

Parker was anxious to get back to the one thing in her life she understood and excelled at. The only time tennis disappointed her was when she flubbed a shot. Clearly relationships weren't her forte. She was through mooning over a woman who obviously had no interest in her, so she did her best to wipe Sydney from her mind, which worked as well as serving left-handed.

Four days later she and Beau arrived in New York and checked into their hotel in Times Square. After they registered and unpacked, they headed to the Stage Deli for sandwiches and a slice of cheesecake. It was their first indulgence after settling in, and the next week was her second, since Beau wanted her to stay in and rest.

After her forced room time she walked over to Central Park for an early-morning run. As she took time to stretch she couldn't help but notice the woman staring at her as she went through her own stretching routine. The hate mail had started coming more regularly, and she found herself looking around for threats whenever she was out alone, which was making her crazier than the letters. The beautiful blonde close by didn't send up any red flags, though.

The woman broke her silence when she made eye contact, and when the stranger straightened she noticed the woman almost equaled her in height. "I'm sorry for staring. I just wanted to say good luck."

"Thanks, I appreciate it." Before they could get into an in-depth conversation she put the earpieces to her iPod in place and started down the path. At this time of the morning she missed the tranquility of the beach, since New York always seemed to be full of activity no matter the hour.

The next two weeks would be like all the others prior to any tournament, full of practice to acclimate to the weather and keep up her game. The worst part was the wait for play to begin, but she attributed her fast starts to her pent-up anxiety over each tournament.

One thing was biting into the boredom this time, though—her internal argument about whether she'd try to find Sydney. They were at least in the same city again, and finding her would answer why Sydney hadn't called. Had she found someone new and didn't want to hurt her feelings? Even if she had, Sydney owed her at least one more talk.

She finished her run, then took a cab to the practice facility Beau had booked to meet Natasha for two hours of tennis. The heat was brutal, but she still felt good after they were done and headed back to the hotel for another night of room service.

As soon as the sun set, Beau knocked on the door connecting their rooms before he came in, dressed for a night out, and dropped into the chair across from the one she sat in, reading a book.

He hated to disturb her since she appeared so relaxed in boxers and T-shirt, but it was time she got out of her funk. "Want to go out tonight?" He knocked her feet off his armrest.

"Aren't you supposed to keep me indoors eating healthy foods and drinking distilled water, or something along those lines?" Beau laughed at her sarcasm. "Surely you don't want to lead me astray in the big city?"

"I was thinking dinner, Parker, not a night of picking up hookers."

"I don't know. Hookers could be a new bonding experience for us. I promise not to tell Nick anything, if you're game."

"No, thanks. How about dinner at Bouley instead? I got us an eight o'clock reservation." He laughed as he poked her with his foot.

"How, pray tell, did you manage that, Coach Beau?" She snapped her book closed and gave him her full attention. He could tell she was kidding, but she was more reserved than usual.

After a summer full of unpleasant mail, he'd been thrilled she'd stayed home almost constantly, since he was afraid for her, but she'd become skittish every moment she wasn't on the court. He knew better than to think it was because some psychopath who'd found his calling in writing clever death threats. Captain Parish had left her mark, and it'd been like a slow poison working itself out of Parker's system.

"That's easy. I made the reservation in your name. It comes in handy to know the tennis god so well. Come on, you've looked a little flat lately, and this might be fun. You can get dressed up and hit the town with me." He pressed his hands together and stuck out his bottom lip.

"Sure, what could happen?"

The cab dropped them off in front of the restaurant fifteen minutes early, so they waited in the bar for their table. Enough celebrities were sprinkled throughout the eatery to take the pressure off Parker, so she was looking forward to trying the much-talked-about restaurant.

"Welcome, Ms. King, and thank you for joining us this evening. If you and your companion are ready, please follow me." The hostess led them to a table almost at the center of the restaurant. A few people nodded in her direction but otherwise left her alone, which was fine since she wasn't in a social mood.

She took the chair facing the door and accepted her menu from the waiter. When she glanced up she noticed the same woman from the park, only now she was wearing a light summer suit and her hair was pulled into a bun at her neck. She stepped into the bar and sat at one of the stools, glancing at her watch and the door. Seeing the woman made Parker's fingers twitch, but not from anticipation. It was more a sense of apprehension.

"What are the chances of seeing the same person twice in a city this size in different locations?" She put her menu down and reached for the wine list while Beau glanced around to see who she was talking about. "The Opus One, please," she told the waiter, who nodded and left.

"Who are you talking about?" Beau turned almost completely in his chair to get a better view of the patrons seated around them. Her mouth was open to compliment him on his superb table manners when an entourage walked through the door. Two she recognized right off.

"Holy shit." It was the best curse she could think of with this many people around. "What in the hell was I thinking when I asked what could happen? I should've stayed in and finished my book instead of flicking the Fates on the head for kicks."

"What?" Beau turned around again. "Holy shit," he echoed, and from his profile she could tell he was horrified.

❖

Sydney stood off to the side in her pilot's uniform, watching as the staff fell all over Alicia and the group with her. She spotted Bobbie Daly in the bar and walked over to meet her. Bobbie wrapped her in a hug and kissed her hello.

"How was your trip over from the airport?" Bobbie asked.

"Not too bad, it was a slow-traffic night. It's more crowded in here than on the street." She glanced around the restaurant from the circle of Bobbie's arms, but the crowd at the door kept her attention. Seeing Alicia made her think of Parker.

"If you want, we can go somewhere else. I wanted tonight to be relaxing for you since I have plans for you later."

She'd had enough of the sycophants surrounding Alicia, so she turned and kissed Bobbie's cheek again. "I hope it involves going home so I can get out of this monkey suit."

"You bet."

❖

Parker saw every moment of the touching reunion, and the tingle in her fingers she'd felt when she first saw Sydney's girlfriend was replaced by the white-hot rage that built behind her eyes. She curled her hands into fists. When in the hell had she become such a fucking moron? She'd been as wrong about Sydney Parish as she'd been about anything in her life. In her mind's eye she saw Sydney throwing away the card she'd given her with her numbers like it was a flavorless piece of gum.

"Park, heads up, man."

She looked away from the second kiss Sydney exchanged with the woman when Beau spoke. Alicia stood next to her with the bottle of wine they'd ordered, looking indecisive. It appeared as if she was trying to pick between cracking the bottle over Parker's head or drowning her when her bulging carotid exploded and took them both out.

"The fucking least you could have done was to blow me off yourself, asshole, and not have your flunky do it," Alicia muttered.

The wine that made it into Parker's mouth from the sudden shower was delicious, and despite the humiliation, she had to laugh at how many waiters descended on Alicia when she picked up the wine bottle from the next table. They carried her out of the place with her minions trailing behind like a tail on a kite. A loud kite that knew more curse words than a regiment of hardened marines.

"How about Chinese to go with all this good wine?" she asked Beau as she wiped her face calmly and pulled her collar away from her neck. The stench of alcohol was making her nauseous.

"I don't know how I'm going to make this up to you, and slap me silly the next time I have any grand plans to pull you out of a slump." Beau threw two hundred-dollar bills on the table and they got up to leave. The manager tried to give him his money back, but she waved him off. It wasn't the restaurant's fault that Alicia had exacted her pound of flesh in mini-diva fashion.

❖

Sydney almost pushed Bobbie down trying to get to Parker before they left. Parker didn't turn her head as she hurried out, and Sydney was surprised into inaction at the sight of her. Or, more accurately, the sight of Parker with Beau instead of a date.

For weeks she'd convinced herself Parker had forgotten her faster than she served a tennis ball. Her fear had deprived her of a good friend, as had her morose thoughts that Parker had treated the memory of her like sea foam, something there one moment, then gone with the next wave.

A couple was exiting a cab when she reached the door, and Beau and Parker stood laughing as they waited. Sydney saw the person run out of the shadows when Parker had her back turned, and she screamed in shock from inside the restaurant. Beau's distance from the hooded individual prevented him from doing anything, but his expression seemed to make Parker turn. Bobbie's hold on Sydney's shoulders kept her from going outside to help.

❖

A dark blue ski mask covered his face, but Parker focused on the large curved knife in his hand.

"Death to those who go against God."

The hoarse whisper held hints of garlic and the guy smelled sour, but despite the discomfort she held his hand by the wrist, using all her strength to keep him from hurting her again. Her side felt like a raging wildfire had broken out, burning away her belief that she was untouchable. Beau stood motionless for only a second longer, but before he reached her, the attacker ran back into the alleyway and out of sight.

The cut was almost in the middle of her chest, as if the religious fanatic had aimed for her heart. He'd missed but cut deep enough that blood ran through her fingers as she kept them pressed tightly to her chest. As the blood mixed with the wine stain, she stared at it and thought inanely that the colors definitely didn't match.

"I think I'm in the mood for some tapioca pudding from the hospital instead of spicy beef, and remind me never to accept a dinner invitation from you again. You're like a walking magnet for disaster," she said in a light tone, trying not to make Beau feel any worse than he probably already did.

"You'll be fine," Beau said, before he screamed at the driver to drive to the nearest hospital.

"Who are you trying to convince, me or you?" She closed her eyes and concentrated on her breathing. As much as her chest hurt, seeing Sydney in someone else's arms hurt worse.

❖

"It's not fatal, that's the good news. But I'm going to have to put in about seven stitches." The emergency room doctor had cleaned the wound and explained that the shots he'd administered were to deaden the area before he started working.

"Will it affect my play?"

"Well, Ms. King, I wouldn't recommend playing until these come out."

"You are kidding, right? I haven't busted my ass all summer to watch the US Open from my hotel room." She sat up and swung her legs over the gurney, ready to find another hospital. This was New York. Surely at least one hospital had a more reasonable doctor. Only Beau's strong grip on her shoulder kept her there.

"I'm sorry, but one pull from playing tennis and these could rip."

"And what? My lung and heart would fall out of the tiny hole?" She used the same insulting kindergarten voice he had.

"No, but it'll leave a hell of a scar."

"Parker, could you just lie there until the nice doctor is finished? The tournament doesn't start tomorrow, so don't worry about it." Beau studied the bulletin board across the room, most likely to keep his eyes off her bloody but naked chest.

Where the cut ended she had a wicked-looking scratch that continued down along her rib cage. Beau had talked to the police, but without a description of the attacker they'd been honest about the likelihood of catching the asshole. They did, though, tell him they'd file a report and talk to the police in Gulf Shores to compare notes.

"These are going to take longer than the start of play to come out," the doctor added as he probed the area with his fingers.

"Just start sewing and let's get this over with." She wasn't about to argue about her playing capabilities with some guy she'd just met who looked like the ink on his diploma was still wet.

"I really enjoyed your play at Wimbledon this year," he said as he started suturing.

"I don't mean to be rude, but could you please just finish? After being attacked by a religious zealot, I'm a little on edge and dying to lie down in my nice quiet hotel room." The guy smiled and nodded before he went to work. "Thanks."

It didn't take him long to place a neat row of stitches on her chest and bandage it. They shook hands, and he and Beau left so she could put her wine- and blood-stained shirt back on. She'd tossed her jacket in the trash as soon as they'd led her to a room. With the local the doctor had administered she wasn't in a lot of pain, so she tried to put the night out of her head. The one thing she couldn't forget was Sydney and her date.

The odds of sharing her morning run with the woman Sydney was sleeping with made winning the lottery twenty times in a row doable. If she'd had a long talk with the tall woman with model looks, would Sydney have come up in their conversation? Whoever the woman was, she and Sydney were having a good laugh at her expense, because she knew now Sydney probably only saw her as a kid with a crush.

"Ready?"

"What, I'm sorry?" Parker finished dressing and gazed up to a worried-appearing Beau.

"Are you ready?"

"Yeah, let's go. Doc, thanks for the great service. If you need tickets, just let Beau know and he'll set you up," she said, shaking hands and signing a few autographs for the nurses before she left.

"What do you think tomorrow will bring?" Beau asked when their taxi headed back to their hotel.

"With my luck lately, poison ivy and dysentery."

❖

The next morning Parker woke up with a dull pain in her chest and someone banging on the door of her room. "Beau, we're going to have to talk about these accommodations, man." She grumbled as she got up and opened the drapes so she could find her robe. With an impatient yank, she opened the door, pulling her stitches a bit. "What?"

"You royal bitch." More than one guest was standing at their door so they could watch Alicia scream at her, obviously their reward for having been awakened by the pounding. She smiled and waved to one young woman standing next door in a just-long-enough T-shirt.

"To what do I owe this pleasure to this morning, sweetheart?"

"Don't sweetheart me, you bitch. How could you?" Alicia slammed the paper she had rolled up in her hand into her chest before walking past her into the room. "Oh, my God, I'm sorry, Park," Alicia said when she turned around and she was bent over grimacing in pain. "Are you all right?"

"Yes, but if you insist on hitting me again, I'll be forced to ask you to leave." She accepted Alicia's help to the chairs by the windows and didn't say anything else to provoke her. She could understand why Alicia was upset, but after Alicia had doused her in wine she thought the temperamental artist had gotten it out of her system.

"I didn't mean to hurt you, but I saw that bullshit in the morning edition and got pissed." The newspaper she'd been hit with was lying by the door, so Alicia retrieved it and handed it to her. When she read the headline, she figured her pen pals were most likely in heaven. This was enough ammunition to justify their actions and make even her believe she was starting to piss God off.

LOVERS' QUARREL LANDS PLAYER IN HOSPITAL AND SINGER IN JAIL. The five-inch-high letters took up the entire first page. The small picture included in the bottom corner showed her and Beau leaving the ER. The photographer had gotten a great shot of her stained shirt as they stepped through the door.

"Anyone with an I.Q. higher than a squash won't believe this." She smiled and held her hand out to Alicia after dropping the fish wrap on the floor. She chuckled when all Alicia did was cross her arms over her chest and tap her foot.

"I am many things, Parker King, but easy ain't one of them." Despite her words, Alicia moved closer but stayed out of her reach.

"I don't think you're easy, just like I don't think you're a rabid ex-lover who stabbed me. Though, if it'd help you out, I'll give the paper an exclusive and tell them you couldn't help yourself." She held her hand out again, and this time Alicia took her up on the invitation and sat in her lap.

"You hurt my feelings."

"I'm sorry, and you're right. I'm a bitch."

"Royal bitch."

"Royal bitch, but my leaving without telling you was me doing you a favor. I was headed home for the summer and figured that's not how you wanted to spend yours, so I bailed. I'm just a tennis bum with a couple of good years left if I'm lucky, while you have years in the limelight." If her bullshit got any deeper she would have to wake Beau to start shoveling for her, she thought.

Alicia let out a laugh for the lame explanation before she stood, pulled the tie of her robe open, and dropped to her knees to place a gentle kiss on the swollen patch of skin around the white bandage. She slowly ran her hands up her legs before she spoke. "You know something, Parker?"

"What's that?"

"You're so full of shit." Alicia leaned forward again and bit down on her nipple, applying pressure until she moaned. "You know something else?"

It took her a moment to trigger the part of her brain that formed coherent speech before she could answer. "What?" She thought it was a safe bet that every guy and every lesbian who'd seen Alicia on stage would give their right arm to trade places with her right now.

"I happen to find that an adorable trait." Alicia rested her hands on her knees for balance as she rose to her feet. "You like what you see?"

She nodded as Alicia raised her arms over her head and waited. This was the part where the beautiful scorned woman usually said "too bad" and walked out as payment for her past sins. Alicia surprised her, though, by stripping off her tight pullover, followed by her jeans. With the slow, sexy walk that drove her fans into a frenzy when she did it in her show, Alicia moved to the bed and lay down.

"Then come on over here and see how much better it feels."

She hesitated. She wanted to appease Alicia, but this was only sex. The smell of the ocean and the feel of Sydney in her arms as they laughed in the surf came to mind as she stared at Alicia's body. The beautiful woman was there for the taking, but she wasn't sure it was something she'd ever want again. She was either becoming more discerning or a large tumor was pressing on the horndog part of her brain.

"No strings, lover, none at all. Call it pity sex since you're hurt," Alicia said, as if understanding her hesitancy.

"It's the least you can do since I just read you stabbed me. If it's in the *Post*, it must be true." Parker held her side and stood, allowing her robe to drop to the floor. When it did, Alicia sighed.

"You're a bitch, but goddamn if you aren't the best-looking one I've ever laid eyes on."

"How about we take this slow?" Parker couldn't believe what she was saying when she felt Alicia press into her body as soon as she lay down. Alicia was there, naked and ready, and she was bailing. And damn it if she wasn't in the mood. Alicia's perfect curves should've evoked something, but it was like her sex took a look and said nah.

"Slow's good." Alicia reached for her nipple again, frowning when Parker caught her wrist and stopped her.

"Slow as in no, and not as in sex."

"What in the hell is the matter with you now?" Alicia said as she sat up and let the sheet fall away.

Alicia was so intoxicating to look at that Parker was questioning her sanity, but the damn little voice in her head was screaming how wrong this was. She couldn't decide if the voice, or that she'd developed one at all, was more annoying. "Nothing. I just don't want you to think I'm taking advantage of you after everything's that's happened."

"You're not kidding?" Alicia looked at her like she was indeed insane but didn't move to touch her again.

"Ah…" The pink nipples on high alert almost did her in. "No, I'm not."

"Then just lie here with me and take a nap. I've been out all night avoiding the press, and you owe me at least that."

She couldn't find a good reason not to give in to that request, so she clicked her mouth closed and sighed when Alicia immediately cuddled up to her. Alicia's nipples were still hard as they pressed into her side, and she tried to ignore them since they were attached to the most perfect, and definitely real, breasts she'd ever had the pleasure of laying eyes on. She'd lose her playgirl reputation over this one for sure if anyone ever found out, but she was okay with that since it felt right not going through with what her body wanted.

It didn't matter that Sydney was with someone else. She still felt guilty being with Alicia, or anyone, if all it was going to turn into was sex. Release was one thing, but it was time for something else that would bring more permanence and peace into her life.

❖

"You can't have been sleeping all this time?" Beau's phone call woke her up out of an exhausted sleep. For a minute, Parker wondered who the naked body pressed up against her back was, until she became fully conscious and remembered how she'd spent her morning.

"Not exactly," she said, and kept her voice low.

"Open the door, it's locked."

"Give me an hour, and then you can come over." She pulled out of the tangle of limbs behind her and sat up.

"Why?" Beau sounded incredibly suspicious.

"You can wait, or you can come over now and see a naked Alicia in my bed—your choice."

"Maybe if we beat you a couple of times a day with a tightly strung racquet, you'd start learning from your mistakes."

"Yeah, well, when Brad Pitt shows up in your room and lies down on the bed naked with a come-hither look, we'll talk about your stronger-than-steel willpower, Coach. Until then, give me a chance to take a shower."

"This might be good. The papers have been calling all morning after you and I made the headlines. Take her out to lunch and let the press see you together, but I'm coming with you after what happened. Showing the world Alicia wasn't the one who stabbed you is the least you can do for the girl. But if you want me to dump her again for you, I'm quitting."

"I'll keep that in mind if I want new representation."

"Where are you going?" Alicia asked, her voice sounding rough.

"To shower, then I'm taking you out to lunch, if you're free. It might help out to have the sharks snap some pictures of us together so your fans won't think you're a homicidal maniac." The ramifications of the morning became as bright as the light streaming through the window when she looked at the bed.

For once the infamous Kong had gone against her instincts and hadn't followed through on a sure thing. After a few kisses she'd held Alicia until they went to sleep. For some reason she felt like she'd led Alicia on more than if she'd given in to her wishes, because allowing her to stay implied there was more to come, and Alicia wasn't getting anything else from her.

"Can I join you?" Alicia sat up and combed back her hair with both hands, which arched her back, enhancing her view.

"Huh?" She smacked her lips together and tried to get back to her thoughts before Alicia's body smashed her reasoning with a big two-by-four.

"You know, help keep your stitches dry and all." Alicia pointed to Parker's chest and waited.

"Nah. Relax, and I'll be out in a minute." Alicia appeared extremely tense at the brush-off, but she didn't say anything. That was a relief, and in a couple of hours she'd be done.

Alicia walked out toward the waiting car first while Parker flipped through her messages. They made it out of the room without any major meltdowns, and she wasn't shocked to see the paparazzi, since Alicia's management team was standing nearby. While she read the slips in her hand she mentally reviewed everything she'd said from Alicia's arrival until now and was sure nothing sounded remotely like a promise.

"Come on, lover, we have reservations and I'm starved." Alicia slid in first after she opened the door. "Then I have plans for you."

She stared at the slip in her hand, prompting Alicia to repeat herself. Why the hell had she agreed to eat with this woman or put the room phone on mute when they'd gone to sleep? Sydney had called and she'd have to shake Alicia before she could call back.

"Did you hear me? Get in here so we can eat. Then I have plans for you."

"Not if I can help it," she whispered to herself as the doorman closed the door behind her. When it shut she started a countdown. She was only a few hours away from getting Alicia out of her life for good.

❖

Sydney wanted to hit something after she finished the morning edition of the paper, especially after Parker's name had been linked to Alicia's—again. She didn't remember ever being this jealous ever before, but after seeing Alicia up close last night, she couldn't find a flaw on the perfect body. And with the skimpy outfit the singer was wearing, she'd had a lot to study. Or maybe she was overreacting to the story because she was tired and close to burning out, having worked nonstop since her arrival. Whatever it was, it was driving her mad.

After she'd moved so she could have a more predictable workday, the airline had had a rash of retirements. Her last day off was the day she'd spent with Margo, and she was grateful she and her mom had taken over her move for her. The place Margo had found was an affordable, fantastic two-bedroom place as big as her condo in Atlanta, so she wouldn't have to downsize.

She stared out over the park from Bobbie's balcony in an effort to peel her eyes from the picture of Parker, who, despite being covered in blood and wine, still looked fantastic. Bobbie had really made her feel welcome, but she was looking forward to her own space. She'd miss the view and Bobbie, though.

"You want me to take the day off and help?" Bobbie asked when she joined her, dressed for work. Before Bobbie sat she kissed her on the forehead.

"Absolutely not." She took Bobbie's hand. "I've got the movers lined up for the end of this week, so I'm going to enjoy the next couple of days with my mom. With any luck I can get you and Margo out of the bank long enough to treat you to dinner."

"I'm not as stubborn as Margo, so name a time and it's a date." Bobbie laughed. "What I will fight you for is the bill, so you might as well concede the battle now."

"I'm lucky to have you." She squeezed Bobbie's hand before releasing it. "Have a good day at work and I'll see you tonight."

Bobbie kissed her again before she left, and she finished her coffee and the article about Parker before her shower. When she'd left the beach she'd promised herself to find something or someone to be happy with and forget the past. She'd been on the few dates Margo had set her up on when she had the time, but her past was so littered with disasters she wanted to carry a machete when she went out.

As she stepped under the spray she thought of what Margo always said: *If you do what you've always done, you'll get what you've always gotten.* Up until then she'd thrown herself into the people she'd been with, and after a time she'd felt clingy and needy since it seemed like she was doing all the work. Parker had been the first one to really go out of her way to romance her, but she had the dating record of Gene on steroids.

The picture of Parker leaving the hospital had softened her hard stance on just forgetting about her, though. Even if the story about Alicia was fictitious, the blood on Parker's shirt wasn't. She flipped through the papers again after she dressed to look for the hotel the photographer had followed Parker to. The fact that they were allowed to include that kind of information pissed her off too when she remembered the letter Parker had allowed her to read.

She dressed casually and decided to walk, since Bobbie didn't live that far from where Parker was staying. One of the convenience stores a few blocks from her destination had buckets of beautiful roses outside, so she figured the front desk would more likely connect her to Parker's room if she came with a delivery. She'd tried the cell number Parker had given her and had left a message with the front desk, with no luck. Parker might be in town but she wasn't taking any calls.

The corner before the hotel was crowded with people leaving the M&M's store, and she smiled at all the children with their bright yellow shopping bags. They were slowing her pace by peering at their treats as they walked, but their laughter took away her impatience.

A limo was parked by the entrance to the hotel, and a little boy bumped her when she stopped walking. Alicia walked out and spoke over her shoulder to someone still inside, but with the crowd the only word Sydney heard was "lover." A few seconds later Parker followed Alicia into the car, with her head down and flipping through a stack of papers. Parker's hands stopped and she hesitated, staring at one of the slips for a moment. Sydney thought about calling out to her, but what was the use? She'd been right about taking a chance on Parker. It would've ended in disaster.

She dropped the arm she'd cradled the flowers in so they hung loosely in her hand and muttered, "You've been busy, Kong."

The driver closed the door and hustled to the other side of the car. Sydney wanted to fling the bouquet at the vehicle but gave it to a homeless woman pushing a cart in the direction of Times Square instead. She was grateful Parker hadn't spotted her. "How pathetic would that have been?" she murmured. She turned and headed back toward the park, her chest aching as if someone had dumped a load of sand on her, only she really couldn't blame it all on Parker. She'd had a chance and she'd passed. Parker wasn't hers to mourn or suffer over the loss of.

"How about lunch at the Plaza?" she asked her mom on the phone.

"What's wrong?"

"Nothing, just thinking of my to-do list." Mentally she added, *Put the womanizing scum, Parker King, at the top of the list.* "I just checked off the first item and felt like celebrating."

"Must've been big if we're going to the Plaza."

"Actually it wasn't all that important, so I'll see you in an hour."

❖

"Have they installed some sort of jungle drums since the last time I was in town?" Sydney asked Margo when she walked into the Plaza and Margo was already seated at her table. "Or does Mom have you on speed dial?"

"Did you retire from flying to become a detective?" Margo stirred sweetener into the iced tea she'd ordered and smiled at her. "You're getting grumpier by the minute, and it's not becoming."

"Are you channeling a Southern debutante again?" She pointed to Margo's drink when the waiter came up. "I'm not in a bad mood, I'm just having a bad day."

"Well, you've been having the same bad day since you got to New York. Every time I see you it feels like someone ran over your cat, and you don't have a damn cat."

Margo's innocent comment made her think of Abby running down the beach with her shirt in his mouth. So few days, but such blissful memories. In that one moment, she'd belonged. She hadn't felt any pressure to contrive conversation. She'd been at peace not only with herself but with another person like she'd never experienced with anyone outside her family. But Parker seemed incapable of really considering someone else's feelings.

"Don't sign me up for happy pills yet." This wasn't a setback, only a reality check that made her realize her search wasn't over.

"I catch you taking pills and I'll put you over my knee," Lucia said as she sat down across from Margo. "If you need happy, a cosmo's much cheaper and less trouble."

"Maybe a cat would be less mind-altering." Sydney kissed her mom's cheek.

"Think of all the vacuuming, though," Lucia said as she reached for them. "Have I told you how much I love having you both in the same city?"

Sydney wished she had her mom's outlook on life. Her sunny disposition and humorous streak made her one of those people others wanted to be around. Her dad had agreed and added that her classic beauty wasn't bad either.

Margo had taken more after their mom, with her soft red hair and high cheekbones, and Sydney guessed she would age well too. Neither of them had been as lucky as their parents when it came to love, but they'd had the ideal role models. At least she had that over Parker, who she needed to stop wasting her time thinking about.

"It's good to be back."

"Maybe now that we have you captive for the next hour you'll tell us how you spent your vacation," Margo said, and Sydney didn't miss the look Margo and their mom exchanged.

The last few months had been like waiting for Christmas when you were four and woke up to a naked tree. Disappointment was at times more depressing than failure. She'd told Parker she'd call when she was ready, but a small part of her wished Parker had disregarded that comment. "I didn't do anything special. Next time we can make it a family trip, and we can rent a house and drink cosmos all day."

"You're going to have to tell us eventually, or we'll have to sedate your sister every time we get together," Lucia joked. "Either that or get it over with and tell us to go to hell."

"I went on vacation expecting something, got something else at first, then something else again, and it ended too soon. By the time I left, I ended up with the something else entirely from what I expected when Gene bailed on me."

Margo flagged the waiter and ordered them all a drink. "What do you think, Mom, is there an answer buried in all that code? Could you try explaining again since I'm at a total loss, Syd?"

"You know, you're sitting at home watching something mindless and you get the urge to color your hair or something equally out of your norm. You do it, and when the towel comes off, instead of the pretty blond locks the box promised, your hair is pink. It's stupid but not permanent, so you try to forget about it and move on."

Margo still appeared confused, but Lucia took her hand and laughed. "Honey, that was the longest way possible you could've picked to tell us to go to hell and mind our own business." Lucia kissed the back of Sydney's hand, then leaned back so the waiter could deliver their drinks. "To stupid mistakes, pink hair, and learning to laugh at them all."

"Thanks, Mom."

CHAPTER ELEVEN

Practice was slower paced for the next few weeks as Parker played to compensate for her somewhat limited mobility. It probably would've been better to take a week off, but she insisted, so Beau wrapped her chest every morning so she wouldn't tear the wound open again and to minimize the pain so she could keep loose. The tournament started the next day, and she realized her sets would last longer since she'd lost some of the power in her first serve, but hopefully the strength of the rest of her play would balance out that weakness.

"You want me to go with you?" Beau packed all her racquets and picked up the bag so she wouldn't have to strain herself. "Maybe a change in tradition will be lucky for you this time."

"I know Nick has theater tickets for tonight, big guy, so no, I'll be fine. My tradition got me to the finals last year, and if that's where I end up this time, I'll be happy. It won't get me any of Kimmie's chicken soup, but I'm sure we have a trophy in that front room she can use if I ask nicely enough." She scratched her chest and wanted nothing more than to take a shower. As the cut healed, it itched more, and she hoped she wouldn't look like she was feeling herself up in front of the cameras in the morning.

"Okay, but we'll come with you if you want."

"Beau, hand me that bag and get the hell out of here." She held her hand out and glared at him.

"No, I'll carry it for another twelve hours, thank you. It'll be waiting in your room when you get back, don't worry. Have fun tonight and I'll see you in the morning. Call me if you need anything. And don't worry about the family. Nick's picking them up and bringing them over from the airport." They took a cab back to the hotel and went their separate ways.

In the two weeks since the attack, she'd worked on getting stronger and tried to live down the headlines in the local papers that covered the story of her and Alicia getting back together. Alicia didn't seem to be denying it, though she was trying to forget about it. A nap and lunch didn't constitute a joyous reunion. She'd turned off her cell, so now Alicia wouldn't stop calling Beau. It was crazy that she'd arrived in the city with a crazy stalker who loved sending her threatening letters and had picked up another nuisance—Alicia.

That chance encounter had also cost her the opportunity to talk to Sydney. She'd returned her call numerous times but got her voice mail every time. It was as if she'd had one sliver of time to reconnect, and because of the bizarre circumstances she'd experienced, it had closed permanently, or at least until Sydney got back from whatever rock she'd crawled under.

After her shower Parker dressed and called down for a cab. Every tournament and its outcome were always different, but her routine before she started play never varied. It was crazy to be so superstitious, but after the luck she'd been having lately, she didn't want to chance it.

"Where to?"

"The River Café in Brooklyn," she said, and sat back to enjoy the trip across the bridge. She'd found the restaurant by chance, and it had one of the most spectacular views of the city's skyline she'd found in all the years she'd been coming here. It was geared more for a romantic date than eating alone, but she liked to sit by the windows and stare at the one city where she hadn't triumphed yet.

The place was torturous, really, since not only was it filled with couples sharing intimate conversations, but it reminded her that in tennis, at least, New York had kicked her ass in spectacular fashion. This year that humiliation seemed to be magnified. But tradition was hard to part with, so she went in determined to enjoy the beautiful surroundings.

Her table was ready when she arrived, and most of the conversations in the main dining room stopped when she followed the host down the center of the room. She held a thin book of Robert Frost's poetry under her arm and placed it on the table when the waiter handed her a menu.

"Welcome back, Ms. King. Would you like the usual?"

"Thank you, Barry," she said, glancing at his name tag, "and yes, the usual would be fine." Her waiter moved off to get her drink, so she perused the selections in the menu even though she always ordered the same thing.

She'd never minded eating alone, even with the whispering and the covert looks around her. The solitude she found in a crowded restaurant and a good book let her forget about tennis for a couple of hours. In the morning she'd think about nothing but it for days to come. The next opponent, the mistakes she'd made, the aches after a couple of grueling afternoons on center court, and all the other things Beau would want to cover once play began. A tournament was all-consuming, but this time she'd welcome the distraction.

Thinking only about tennis would be like pouring sand in a bottle. Eventually it would be so full nothing else would fit in and she wouldn't have the energy to waste her thoughts on her past mistakes.

Barry put the mug down and took her order, and when he left, she opened her book. Perhaps her road was long, and if she had to travel it alone, she'd have to make the most of it because she didn't want to jump back on the same merry-go-round of women. It was time for her to take the other road.

Who knew, maybe the frustration alone would hone her talent on the court.

❖

"You're staring," Bobbie said before she took a sip of her mixed drink. "And I'm glad I was able to surprise you. I read she always comes here before the start of play. This is as close as I'm going to come this year to seeing her, since I couldn't get tickets."

"I'm sorry, what?" Sydney answered, but kept her eyes glued to Parker drinking hot chocolate three tables away. The mug wasn't clear glass, but she was sure that was what it was.

"I said you're staring. I didn't take you for a star-struck tennis fan, Syd. The precocious Ms. King and I met not that long ago, so if you want I can introduce you." Bobbie lifted her glass and aimed it in Parker's direction.

"You know Parker?" Sydney finally stopped looking at Parker and faced forward.

"Parker? My, I may have overemphasized my relationship with the pinup girl of tennis. Do *you* know her?" Bobbie put her drink down and reached over to hold her hand. "I'm glad you said yes, so I wouldn't look like some crazed groupie when I came in here alone. I love her style of play, and it would be a dream come true to meet her. So, do you?"

Sydney had been sulking the entire day but had accepted Bobbie's invitation to try a new place that might hold a surprise. Leave it to Bobbie to deliver Parker. All that was missing was a bow on her head and someone to scream "Stop being an asshole" in her ear. "Yes, we've met. How do you know her?"

"I couldn't believe my luck, but I spotted her in the park before a run. I wished her luck while she stretched. She thanked me, then took off like the mob had put a hit out on her. Ms. King actually gave me the run of my life when I tried to keep pace with her. After I was done, I was amazed I was still conscious, but ended up having to take a week off to recover. If she does that every morning, no wonder three sets of tennis seem to be a breeze for her."

"Yeah, Parker seems to take on everything in her life with the same type of vengeance." Sydney returned her attention to Parker, who surprisingly appeared lonely.

"I saw her staring at us the night Alicia made the scene. It seemed weird to run into her again after spotting her that morning. As intently as she was looking, I chalked it up to her thinking the same thing, but if you know her, maybe she had her eyes on you."

"What do you mean, she was looking at us?" All she could remember from that night was the guy who'd stabbed Parker and the blood on her shirt when she went to get into the cab.

"I was looking at her when you walked in and her eyes followed you to the bar. She was watching us say hello before Alicia gave her a wine bath. You know you read about stuff like that, but you never think you'll actually ever see it play out. Don't you think—" Bobbie was still talking when Sydney stood up and walked to Parker's table.

"I'm sorry I didn't call you back," Sydney said in a soft voice as she stood next to the empty chair across from Parker.

"No problem, I see you've been busy." Parker gazed past Sydney to the tall blonde who seemed to be her constant companion, raised her mug of hot chocolate, and saluted her.

"I could say the same thing about you." Sydney played with the napkin in her hand that she'd brought with her and took deep breaths, as if trying to keep her emotions in check.

"You're right, but no more than usual. I've been trying to get ready for tomorrow, but it's been slow going."

"I read about what happened." Sydney twisted her napkin into a knot.

"It wasn't as bad as they made it out to be. The cut slowed me down, but it's too long a summer to sit home alone," she said, and placed her hands on her book after she put it gently on the table.

She was so mad she was talking through her teeth with her jaw clenched. After a slew of messages she'd left, she couldn't still give Sydney the benefit of the doubt since she was here with someone else. It shouldn't matter to her, but it did. Perhaps this was fate's payback, considering the number of women who'd probably felt betrayed by her. "It was great seeing you again." She lowered her head and glued her eyes to the backs of her hands.

"If you wanted to get rid of me, just say so."

"I'm not trying to ditch you, but I don't want to keep your date waiting. It really was nice seeing you again."

"That's it?"

"I'm sorry, but I'm confused. You left me a message, and I apologize for missing your call, but I returned it…numerous times. You never picked up the phone again, so I finally got the message you didn't want to hear from me, which makes no sense to me since I was returning *your* call. What's different now?" She spoke softly and realized she sounded like an ass, but this whole exercise was stupid.

"Besides, I see you're getting on just fine with your life, so there's no reason for us to talk unless you just want to gloat, which seems a little beneath you." She lifted her mug again in the blonde's direction, but the woman just sat with her chin resting on her palm, her eyes moving from her to Sydney as if she were watching a tennis match.

"What in the hell is that supposed to mean?" Sydney asked in a menacing tone as she leaned forward. "And why are you being so obnoxious?"

"Your date's getting lonely."

"I'm sure my friend doesn't mind sitting alone for a minute. Not that I'm sure why I bothered to come to talk to you, since you evidently have some sort of bug up your ass about something. I've been staying with Bobbie, and she's not my date. Well, not technically."

"Is there a problem, Ms. King?" Barry returned with her appetizer, and it seemed he and everyone around them was riveted.

"No problem, just an acquaintance who wanted to wish me luck." She smiled up at him then at Sydney. "Thank you, Sydney, you've done your duty, so don't let me keep you."

"Why, is Alicia going to be here any minute?" Sydney asked

so loud the people sitting closest to them cocked their heads in their direction. It was almost comical how red Sydney turned after she said it, but they were past funny.

"If you're dying to know something, then ask me, not that you have any right to. I'm a dog, but honesty isn't my problem," she said in a heated whisper.

"Did you sleep with her since I've seen you last?"

Parker hesitated. Sydney must have recently gotten her own reality show and they needed a juicy opener for ratings. Either that or she'd been heavily medicated when she'd stayed at her house. Either way Parker wasn't eager to find out, so she looked up at Barry before she returned Sydney's volley. If this ended fast enough she could get the hell out of here before it got any worse. "Did you need to ask me something else?" *I so do not need this shit tonight*, she thought as Barry opened and closed his mouth a few times.

"I'm sorry, please excuse me," he said, appearing disappointed he'd been dismissed.

"Now to answer your question, yes, I have."

The one good thing, she thought as soon as the words left her mouth, was that what was left of the hot chocolate had reached room temperature. This wasn't exactly how she imagined her life getting worse, so with as much dignity as she could, she took her napkin and wiped off her face.

She quickly added up her tab mentally and left enough for the meal she wasn't sticking around to eat, plus a tip. Sydney didn't say anything when she got up and left without a glance in her direction.

"You know, Parker, one of these days you'll have to learn that honesty isn't always the best policy, because people don't give a shit about the truth," she said out loud as she waited for a cab. It wasn't like Sydney had the right to be mad at her. After all, she hadn't even cared enough to pick up a damn phone. "No," she said stretching out the word, "you spent weeks moping like an idiot while Captain Sydney got over you."

"You're an idiot if that's what you think," she heard Sydney say from behind her. "I didn't call you back because I saw you with Alicia outside your hotel the morning after you'd been attacked. I should've given you the benefit of the doubt, but after one bad relationship I felt like I couldn't chance it." She crossed her arms when Sydney stood before her. "I missed you, and you haven't left my thoughts since I had to run out on you."

"That's not the impression you left me with after our call. You wanted me to leave you alone and I did. When I didn't hear from you, I thought I had my answer. That's not important now, since I really don't know you at all."

"You can't mean that?"

"I hate to disappoint you, but I do. In all those days you never mentioned anyone in your life. I talked to you and you never said a word about your friend in there, so I'm curious as to what else you left out while you were busy judging me."

"How was your summer?" Sydney asked, in a strange change of subject.

"The days before this tournament bleed one into the other, so you can picture how I spent my summer. You really should get back in there. It was great seeing you again, but it would be rude to keep your date waiting."

"You really are eager to get rid of me, aren't you? And I told you she's only a friend."

"No, Sydney, I'm really not, but I don't know what the hell is going on. If you were in town, why not return one of my calls? Right now as much as I want to rekindle our friendship, I can't afford to play games. I need to go back to my room and order a sandwich or something and let you go back to your evening. Tomorrow I have to be able to concentrate on why I'm here and not on whatever opinion or thought you're going to run amok with."

"Please, Parker, I was wrong this summer for not giving in to my urge to stay longer. I was also wrong not to call you back. You haven't left my thoughts since I had to leave, but my ex has left me a little skittish." When the cab pulled up, Sydney started talking faster, as if she had a slim chance of getting everything out before she left.

Parker handed the driver a twenty and walked away from the cab line. "You're all I thought about too, but I'm smart enough to know when I'm too late." She kept her distance and crossed her arms over her chest again.

"It's good to know you didn't forget me immediately, even though I'm not as smart as I thought. I can't blame you for being mad, but you're not too late. Hearing you slept with that narcissistic bimbo, though, is making me question why I'm out here," Sydney said, mirroring her pose.

"It's not what you think, and even if it was, you don't have a right to complain," she said softly, not wanting to hear that Sydney didn't want her in her life, but afraid of scaring her away. "I missed you and you left me wanting, but this isn't the time to get into it. When you're ready, give me a call and I promise we'll talk as long as you care to."

"You forgot your book," Sydney said when she didn't move, and held it just out of reach.

"Not the way to treat a first-edition Frost." The leather was splattered with chocolate. It wasn't ruined, but the damage would remind her how things had ended or started between them. She still hadn't made up her mind how this would go.

"I'm sorry for ruining it. I don't know what came over me."

"I know exactly what came over you. Call it experience."

"It isn't one I'd like to repeat again."

Parker looked down at herself and smiled. For what little had been left in the cup, Sydney had gotten good coverage. "You have good aim, but why doesn't just one woman ever go for the water glass?"

"I'll ask at the next support group meeting I attend."

They were joking, but she hadn't moved from her spot and neither had Sydney. She was still marginally pissed but couldn't deny that the attraction was still there. "What are you hoping for here, Sydney?"

"Just to spend time with you, if you still want to after my display of immaturity in there. This past summer we started something special, and because of my fear I robbed myself of your company. If you really have to go I'll understand, but even though I don't deserve it, could you give me a few minutes?" Sydney made the first move and reached for her hand.

"I want more than a few minutes, so did you kiss your date good night?" She pointed to the restaurant's entrance.

"Again, not my date, but against my better judgment, I admit that I did."

"You're not hiding any other beverages, are you?"

"No." Sydney laughed. "I actually owe my friend a drink for being the crazed tennis fan she is. She's not dangerous, but she read that you like coming here before the Open, only she didn't tell me before we got here."

"And if she had?"

"Just because I'm dumb every so often doesn't mean I like to repeat my mistakes. I would've come even if you hadn't spoken a word to me."

"Protecting yourself from hurt isn't dumb." She led them closer to the parking lot for more privacy. "How are you holding up? Long-term relationships aren't my forte, but I know what it's like to mourn the loss of important people. You should've said something this summer. I wouldn't have been so flirty."

"I'm fine as long as I don't psychoanalyze myself too much, and you were perfect this summer. After the humiliation of all her cheating, it was nice to know someone found me attractive. That the someone was you was an extra bonus, but I'm sure you're not interested in talking about my tragic love life."

"Actually I'm really interested in talking about your love life, but my take on it isn't tragic…from my perspective anyway. Only you haven't been open to the conversation until now." She laughed and cupped Sydney's cheek. "Are you going to clobber me with your purse if I kiss you?"

"No, but we should wait."

"Oh." She let Sydney go and took a step back. "I thought—"

"You thought right, Kong." Sydney grabbed her by the lapels of her jacket to stop her retreat. "I want you to, but this is a new dress and I don't want to get chocolate on it." Parker's smile reminded her of the predatory look she got before she served, and Sydney didn't stop her when she hugged her hard enough for her feet to come off the ground.

"You've kept me waiting long enough."

The kiss surprised her because it made her realize how much she missed Parker. She could feel the calluses on Parker's hands as they came up and framed her face, but as rough as she was on the court, Parker was always gentle with her.

"I think the people inside have gotten enough pictures to post on Facebook. Would you like a ride back into the city?" Parker asked, letting her down as she kissed her again.

"Sure."

As they walked back to the cab stand, Parker told her about her pre-tournament tradition of eating alone.

Sydney couldn't believe she was getting dumped at Bobbie's covered in chocolate. She might've been afraid of taking this chance, but now she was impatient. "Can I see you tomorrow?"

"I thought we'd have dinner, but tomorrow's good if you're tired."

"I'm not tired, so pick a place and it'll be my treat."

"I told you I usually eat alone, but since this is the only place in the world where that tradition of mine doesn't work, I thought I'd come up with some new superstition to follow like it's my religion." Parker opened the door for her and bent down to talk to her. "If we share a meal and I win, you'll have to commit to the same thing next year, even if you decide to ditch me."

"If I treat and you win, do I get to keep the trophy?"

"How about I pay, and you come along for the ride?"

They arrived at Parker's hotel, and while Parker stripped out of her soiled clothes in the bathroom, Sydney stood at the window overlooking Times Square. She'd glanced at the bed briefly, and the image of Parker rolling around on it with Alicia made her prefer the neon outside. No way in hell could she compete with someone like that, or any other girl Parker had been associated with over the past couple of years.

In a way she was shocked she was here since, compared to the women Parker usually went for, she was like the one picked last for a school-yard game. It wasn't because the team leader wanted you, but more like you were better than the dorky kid who always wore his pants too short and had an ink blot on his shirt.

"My dress is stained." It was a poor excuse to get out of the room, but she didn't want to be there anymore. She wanted to be back in the library at Parker's beach house with Parker reading her something from the hundreds of books that lined the shelves. No one was there in all that solitude competing with her for Parker's attention.

"I thought we could stop at your place and you could change and maybe drop that in cold water or something, so the stain won't set." Parker pointed to her dress. "I feel bad for doing that."

"You don't mind?"

"Mind what?"

"Leaving here." She waved around the room, not knowing what else to say.

"I want to have dinner with you, and I don't care where we go to do that. Abby and I have been pining away for you, so don't disappoint me now that I have you back," Parker said as she held out her hand and waited.

They took another cab to Sydney's new apartment, which was finally hers after weeks of back-and-forth with the owners. She'd only had a chance to move one piece of furniture and the bulk of the clothes she didn't need at Bobbie's. She left Parker to walk around the space while she changed.

When she emerged Parker was holding the book Barnaby had given her. Every time she looked at it, she smiled. It was a collection of love poems and sonnets by Shakespeare, and she'd appreciated and enjoyed it that much more since Barnaby had thought enough of her to part with the treasure by his favorite author. With any luck she could convince Parker to read some selections from it tonight.

"How about takeout, and we'll come back here and eat?" She wasn't ready to share Parker with the adoring tennis fans they were sure to meet, no matter how out of the way the restaurant.

"Sure." Parker pointed to the Chinese place down the street.

They spread the cartons of food between them on the oak floors of her living room since she hadn't wanted to eat on the bed, which she'd had delivered only because it was at her mother's instead of in storage. She'd slept in it from the time she was ten, and it was as comfortable as their conversation was becoming as they put their separation behind them.

When Parker looked at her watch and grimaced, Sydney asked, "Am I boring you?" The night had ended no matter how great things were going, when a date looked at the time.

"No, but it's close to midnight. I need to get going if I want to stay awake on the court tomorrow. The networks hate it when players nap during the matches on center court. Tell me I can see you again and I'll go away happy."

"You can see me again, but why don't you stay here and take a cab back early?"

"Because I doubt I'd be able to serve or lift my arms over my head if I slept on the floor. Come on, I'll walk you home, and if you behave, I'll give you and the blond bombshell some tickets for tomorrow's match."

"You don't have to sleep on the floor. I have a bed, and I was planning to stay here anyway." She walked Parker to the bedroom and showed her the neatly made bed pushed up against the back wall. "I wanted to get reacquainted with my bed, and if you're here it'll make it more special."

"It's a double bed." Parker stood in the doorway with her hands crammed into her pockets, looking at it like it was a bed of nails.

"Yes, but I've had it for years. I promise it's great."

"Where are you going to sleep? I don't want to make you uncomfortable."

"Come on, Kong, we'll make the best of it." She stripped her pants off and pulled her bra through one of her sleeves before she lay on the side of the bed closest to the wall. She hoped Parker understood this wasn't about sex, but about getting to know each other and building trust. One more headline hinting at Parker and Alicia or any other hot girl together in bed, and she'd kill Parker in her sleep.

She's leaving, she thought when Parker turned and walked down the hall, but she started breathing again when the light switch in the bathroom clicked on. Parker came back in her underwear and the T-shirt she'd worn under her shirt. She displayed the same chivalry she had at the beach as she sat on the other side of the bed and fluffed up the pillow before she stretched out for the night.

"Good night," Parker said, and touched the side of her face.

"Aren't you going to kiss me?"

"We can move slow until you trust me and you understand I'm not going anywhere."

"I want *you* to understand something. I was with my ex for two years, and I never felt anything close to what I do with you. Please don't think you have to prove yourself to me. From our first meeting you've been nothing but considerate. I'm tired of hiding behind what someone else did to me."

Parker rolled over a bit and pressed her lips to Sydney's, then lengthened the kiss when Sydney put her hands on her shoulders and tugged her closer.

An electric current ran through Sydney, strengthening as Parker kissed her. Two pieces of a difficult puzzle seemed to click together. She didn't have to force the need to belong to Parker. It was just there waiting for her to accept and build on.

Parker pulled back first and rolled Sydney onto her side and spooned behind her. "You're going to get hate mail for ruining my reputation," she said, and kissed the top of Sydney's head.

Sydney held Parker's hand and closed her eyes. "I can live with that, Kong. Thanks for taking a chance tonight instead of calling security."

The next morning Sydney panicked when she found the space next to her empty. She thought Parker had left until she saw her jeans still folded and hanging over the footboard. She found Parker on the floor in the living room with her eyes closed and her legs folded under her in a meditation pose.

The silence and the early-morning light streaming through the naked windows made the empty room seem almost like a temple, so she stayed quiet. Not even the light knock on the door made Parker open her eyes.

"Good morning, Sydney." Beau stood in the hallway with two large black bags.

"Good morning. She's in there if you're here for Parker."

"I am, but why don't we let her finish before we barge in." He set the bags down inside the door, unzipped one, and took out a smaller bag. Sydney couldn't help but see the tennis outfit dotted with sponsor logos folded neatly right on top. Even the socks had something sewn on them.

Beau smiled. "Her talent gets all those companies to use her as a walking billboard, but that's her reward for proving she can play."

"Does seeing Parker wear this on her sleeve really make someone want to drive this car?" She pointed to one sleeve before touching the material.

"No more than watching car racing makes me want to try Viagra, but you got to give the guy credit for driving around the track in that thing. That takes gumption, as my mama used to say."

She laughed at his analogy and knew he probably answered this question often. "What's she doing?"

"Going over every shot in her head. Reviewing every possibility so she won't have any surprises or allow herself any weaknesses. Parker's the real deal, Sydney. She gives the folks what they pay big money to see. For her it's all about straightforward power tennis that takes no prisoners and makes the shelf life of the balls next to nil."

"Is that on and off the court?"

"I don't know. You spent the night with her. Did she force you?" Beau asked with an edge in his voice.

"You know better than that. I'm sorry. I shouldn't have said anything."

"Nonsense. Beau loves to cause me trouble whenever he gets the chance." Parker stepped behind her and placed her hands on her shoulders and a kiss on the top of her head. "Are you working today?" Parker had obviously gotten up and walked quietly on bare feet to where they were talking.

"No, I'm not. I was planning to watch you on television, if you must know my deep, dark secret."

Beau handed Parker an envelope that she then handed to her. "How about you and your friend join Beau and my sisters at today's match?"

She took it, then kissed Parker on the cheek. "Bobbie's going to be thrilled."

"Yeah, well, tell her to be thrilled all she wants as long as she keeps her lips to herself," Parker said as she took her shirt off.

Beau changed Parker's dressing and wrapped her chest tight enough to cover the wound but still let her breathe. When he was done Parker slipped into a pair of comfortable sweats and sandals.

"I want you to be careful today, but have fun." Sydney stayed away from the bandaged area, but the sight of Parker's chest made her hurt. "And when you're done, I want you to come back here." She placed her hands behind Parker's neck and brought her head down so she could kiss her. She wanted Parker to taste the passion she'd awoken in her.

Parker turned before getting into the car and looked up to the windows. Sydney stood there and watched as she brought her fingers to her lips, appearing a little dazed from the kiss they'd shared. She waved and smiled before Parker disappeared into the car. It had taken only a night for the fear of the unknown to disappear.

CHAPTER TWELVE

The stands around center court were filling up, and down on the court the line judges and ball retrievers were taking their places. Beau seemed riveted to Parker's warm-up, and he explained that he wanted to make sure she showed no signs of pain. From the way her younger opponent was studying Parker's serve, so was she. The story of the attack outside the restaurant had died down considerably, but everyone Parker played would try to find a crack in her game.

Sydney and Bobbie sat and people watched as the crowd around them grew. "How's she doing?" Sydney asked.

"She doesn't look like she's sucking on a lemon when she serves like she did after this first happened. The grimace was involuntary and a good indicator of her pain level, but I've never met anyone who can kick the shit out of a bad situation like Parker." He took his hat off and combed his hair back. "Sorry about the language."

"Don't worry about it. Bobbie and I aren't that fragile."

"Then you think you'll be all right alone for a bit? I want to go check on her one last time before the match starts." He stood but hesitated before he left. "Anything you want me to tell her? I mean anything that doesn't require me to kiss her on the lips or touch her inappropriately."

"Tell her it might not make a difference, but she's upped her rooting section by two."

"I sure as hell think it makes a difference, so hang tight and I'll be right back."

"I hope she'll be okay. That cut on her chest looks like it must've hurt, and it's not fully healed yet," she said, just loud enough for Bobbie to hear, so she was surprised when someone else answered.

"It'll take more than some nut to slow Park down. Mendela will be eating fuzz by the end of the match."

She had to tilt her head back to see the woman's face, as did

Bobbie. Actually, there were two women, tall enough to block the sun when they stood shoulder to shoulder.

"When she was ten, she played in a tournament with a broken arm. Hell if the tadpole didn't come in third," the other woman said.

"You must be Parker's sisters." Sydney moved to stand, but the King closest to her put her hand on her shoulder to keep her in her seat.

"I'm Kimmie, and this is Gray." Gray stuck her hand out after her sister's introduction and smiled as if the people around them weren't shouting their names and pointing.

"Nice to meet you. I'm Sydney Parish and this is my friend Bobbie Daley. Parker's thrilled you two could make it up for this. The last time I saw her, you two were headed to south Florida for a tournament. How'd it go?"

Bobbie spoke up. "Are you kidding, Sydney? They kicked ass. The Viper and the Terminator took the title and the cash pot without breaking a sweat. I saw it all on ESPN2." Bobbie was obviously having a hard time keeping herself in check and trying not to borrow a pen from someone to ask Kimmie and Gray to autograph her forehead.

Sydney laughed at Bobbie's expression of rapture and was glad Parker had thought to give her a ticket too. It had taken her ten minutes to convince Bobbie she wasn't joking about the center court seats, and now they were sharing them with two more of her idols. She wasn't a huge sports fan, but to someone like Bobbie today was like winning the sports lottery.

"I suggest you breathe at regular intervals throughout the day. If not, you'll miss the match when you pass out." She whispered the warning as a joke to get Bobbie to calm down. When she did, she noticed Natasha heading in their direction. The last of her jealousy melted away when she saw how Gray's eyes stayed glued to her advance.

"Kimmie, why don't you slide in here next to Bobbie and let Natasha have your seat?"

Gray turned to her and smiled. "Thanks, Sydney. I see that my little sister's starting to wise up." The announcer introducing Parker and Mendela helped take the attention away from her flushed face.

The crowd jumped up and cheered when the two players stood from their places on opposite sides of the judge's chair. Parker's tan appeared even darker against the tight white shirt she wore, and she seemed anxious to begin as she took out a racquet and bounced its head against her palm.

Sydney crossed her fingers and held them under her chin when Parker and Mendela walked to their end of the court and nodded to the judge. *You can do it, Park*, she thought as Parker bounced on her feet a few times.

"Quiet, please," the announcer said as he pointed to Parker when the crowd quieted.

The ball girl threw Parker two new balls, and she bounced them both on her racquet before selecting one and throwing the other one back. She squared her shoulders and let out a long breath, as if blowing out any pain. After four bounces she threw the ball up and connected with it dead center on her racquet. It flew past her opponent so fast, Mendela didn't bother to move her racquet from the ready position and only got out of her stance when "fifteen-love" was announced from the chair.

"If you were hoping for a slower-paced game from Parker King, sports fans, you have come to the wrong place," the radio announcer said into the earpieces Gray had brought for everyone. He was somewhere above them, and Gray had explained that they loved to listen to gather information to tease Parker with later. "I think she was giving Mendela a warning shot across the bow with that one. Parker's recent misfortunes will not do the Spaniard any favors today."

"Quiet, please." Parker waited for the crowd to cooperate before setting up for her next shot. This one nicked the net on the way over, so she had to serve again. The second serve was a little slower paced and Mendela hit it back to the baseline, then ran to the net to establish an early aggressive game. But Parker placed a two-handed backhand shot just inside the line.

"Since she's such a power player, folks often forget she has a finesse game," the guy said. "If Mendela's smart, she'll stay away from the net, because while Parker was great in England, statistically she's better on this surface. Play the net, Mendela, and watch those shots drop all day."

"She's got a finesse game all right," Sydney joked.

For two sets she watched Parker almost surgically remove every aspect of Mendela's game, all while barely breaking a sweat. When Mendela rushed the net, Parker sent some blistering heat toward the baseline with deadly precision. When Mendela took the hint and moved to the baseline, Parker dropped the ball right over the net, making her almost lose skin when she dove after the shots.

Watching the game at the USTA Tennis Center was an experience for both Sydney and Bobbie. The small screen of her television couldn't capture the atmosphere and energy of center court live, and she was still smiling at the "Kong" chant the crowd was still shouting as Parker finished the match, dropping only three games. Her tennis bag repacked and shouldered, Parker took a few minutes on her way out to sign autographs for the fans hanging down from the stands.

The King sisters high-fived each other before they hugged Beau and Nick. Beau was so caught up in celebrating he didn't notice the attendant in the aisle standing next to him until he turned from hugging Bobbie. When the guy handed him a note, his shoulders drooped and he cringed. Sydney was afraid that whoever had been harassing Parker had struck again, but Beau read it and smiled.

"Let's go take a tour of the locker rooms, girls." Beau and Nick had moved into the aisle to let them pass when someone else tapped him hard on the shoulder. She was glad he was standing between them since she had the sudden urge to rip out a chunk of Alicia's hair.

"Beau, could you tell Parker I'll wait for her outside? I figured we could share a limo back into Manhattan," Alicia said, her eyes never leaving Sydney's. "I gave a few interviews on the way in, so we need to talk before we head out. That way we'll have the same answers about getting back together."

"Parker's got a ride back into the city. I'll tell her you came to watch the match, so thanks from both of us. After all, as you know, dedicated fans are what it's all about," Beau said sweetly, but he tried to hurry them up the stairs before Alicia blew up, she guessed.

"Maybe Kong can make it through one meal without getting soaked," Beau said when Alicia was out of earshot, and they all laughed.

"Maybe," she said, "but if last night was a typical Kong evening for her, I doubt it. Let's hope chocolate comes out easier than wine."

They were all still laughing when Beau escorted them into the locker room, and Sydney and Bobbie stood back so the sisters could have a moment to talk. Bobbie was quiet, but her head appeared ready to pop off, judging by the way she was looking around. She'd delivered such a thorough commentary on every player they'd seen, Sydney knew Bobbie would give that guy on the radio a fit if they handed her the mike.

"You think if you slept with her, we can come back this weekend?" Bobbie asked in a whisper.

"I slept with her last night and you got court-side box seats out of it, so don't push your luck."

Bobbie opened her mouth, but Parker called them over before she could say anything.

"Congratulations, you were awesome," Sydney said.

Parker accepted her hug and kept her arm over Sydney's shoulders as she stared at Bobbie.

Bobbie gushed as she pumped Parker's hand. "Yeah, great game, Ms. King. Thank you so much for the tickets. That was a once-in-a-lifetime experience."

"Bobbie, honey, she'll need that hand to play this week," she said, and smiled up at Parker, hoping she didn't mind overexuberant admirers. "Parker, this is my friend Bobbie Daly, and in case you haven't caught on, she's a big fan of women's tennis."

"Ah, my running partner's identity revealed. You kept up pretty good until the last two miles," Parker said with a smile as Sydney held her closer. "How about I treat you two to dinner?"

"Don't you want to invite your sisters?"

"They've got an interview with one of the local sports channels tonight, so they can't make it. If you two have plans we'll try for some other time."

"I'd love to. I just didn't want you to leave out Kimmie and Gray to take us. How about it, Bobbie, hungry?" Sydney snuggled closer into Parker and wrapped an arm around her waist.

"I don't want to get in the way," Bobbie said hesitantly.

Parker patted Bobbie on the shoulder as her hand slid farther down her back to the top of her butt. "I want you to go in case the mad bomber here throws some more hot chocolate on me. She does that and I can use you as a shield."

"Then I'd love to. Take your time and I'll wait over there." Bobbie moved to the wall of photos.

"Thanks again for the tickets. I loved watching you play." Having Parker this near reminded Sydney of waking up that morning with Parker cuddled up against her back. She'd felt so peaceful she'd drifted back to sleep with a complete sense of happiness.

"Will you still be in town day after tomorrow?" Parker asked as she tied one shoe.

"Yeah, I have a flight tomorrow at noon, but I'll be back tomorrow night. I'm on a light schedule until I get settled."

"Good, you can make the next match, then. If you want, that is." Parker held her other shoe as if waiting for her to answer.

"I'd love to." She leaned closer, even more drawn to Parker and what she could bring to her life, and what they could be together. Parker moved the rest of the way and kissed her.

"Do you think she'd survive another match?" Parker pointed to Bobbie, who was studying the wall like it was a fascinating piece of art, apparently trying to give them a little privacy.

"Do you know CPR?" She looked at Parker with a serious face.

"I'm more of a mouth-to-mouth kind of girl."

"I'll bet. Come on, Kong, your groupies are taking you out to dinner." She stole another kiss before Parker bent down to put on her shoe, then called across the room. "Clear your schedule on Saturday, Daly. We've been invited back." The happy dance Bobbie did almost made Parker fall off the bench from laughing so hard.

Bobbie took a cab home after they ate, leaving Parker and Sydney alone for the walk to Sydney's apartment. They'd decided on a small Chinese restaurant, where Parker's presence had caused pandemonium with the staff. Sydney was sure their picture would be framed and hanging on the wall the next time she went in for takeout.

"Will you come up for a little while?"

"You aren't getting tired of me yet?" Parker picked up their joined hands and kissed the back of Sydney's.

"I was thinking that you'd be the one who's bored by now." She wanted to sound confident, but Alicia had messed with her head. "I'm sure you're used to a faster crowd."

"For someone who's taken up a lot of my thinking time since this summer, you aren't very bright."

Sydney laughed at the insult, ready to say something back when Parker lowered her head and kissed her. The passion in Parker's soft lips erased her doubts. Parker King was young, but she was the person she'd been waiting for, and only she stood in the way of accepting this gift.

"Good night, Sydney." Parker kissed her again before letting her go.

"Please stay." Letting Parker out of her sight terrified her. Time and trust would temper that reaction, but right now she wasn't sure enough—not about Parker, but herself.

"Take some time and think about what you want. I'm not in a hurry, but for once I'm not playing around either."

Sydney couldn't accept the distance between them, even though it was less than three feet. "I think too much," she said as she took Parker's hand.

"That might be a better course than not thinking at all." Parker laughed in a way that sounded like she wasn't trying to joke. "I can totally understand your reluctance."

"I'm not reluctant."

Parker shook her head. "I won't freak out if you're honest, and I sure don't have the right to get mad if you are. Before I saw you in that café the first morning we had coffee, I never thought about the next day or the next woman I'd be with."

Sydney tugged Parker to her stoop and sat on the steps. "You've always been up front about all that, so why rehash it now?"

"Because when your vacation was over and you left, you probably thought we'd just had a fling and once you were gone, that'd be it. For me, though, it was a reality check."

"What do you mean?"

Parker let go of her and faced away as if she was embarrassed. "All those nights I concerned myself with how good the sex was happened because there weren't any strings attached, and I never considered how that attitude handicapped my future. How would any woman completely trust me when she took my past into account?"

"That works both ways, you know," Sydney said, and reached over to try to get Parker to look at her.

"You mean there's a benefit to being a player?"

"Not exactly a benefit, so don't puff your chest out just yet for being the ultimate lady killer," she said, placing her hand on Parker's chest. She smiled so Parker wouldn't think this was about judging her. "How do you think it makes me feel to know you want to be with me when you can have anyone?"

"Is this some sort of trick question?" Parker laughed. This time she sounded more relaxed. "You don't have a can of Coke you've shaken up in your purse, do you?"

The joke and Parker's demeanor showed the sudden tension had dissolved without her having to put a lot of effort into it. "You're safe from me, as well as with me," Sydney said before she moved to Parker's lap and kissed her. "You make me feel so alive, and I love the way you look at me. It's a gift to be so desired, and as a woman, I thank you."

"You're right about the desire," Parker said as she ran her finger along her jawline. "You don't have any reason to believe me, but you don't have to worry about anyone else."

"Then don't leave." She kissed Parker again, only longer, until Parker held her tighter. "Stay and hold me." She laughed when Parker stood without letting her go. "Put me down before you hurt yourself more than you already are."

"Start hunting for your keys and enjoy the ride. You're stuck with me until tomorrow morning."

"Hopefully longer than that."

❖

The cab driver stopped when Eric told him to, and the guy turned around when Eric and his fellow passengers didn't get out. The meter was at fifteen bucks when Parker and Sydney went upstairs.

"Keep the change." He held a twenty through the partition. "Out," he said to Ethan, elbowing him in the ribs.

He and Ethan stood back to allow their brother a chance to stare up at the apartment Sydney had rented. The lights had come on in the bedroom, but didn't stay on long. Eric knew it was the bedroom because he'd walked through the unit above Sydney's, and the building super had said the first three floors of the five had the same layout.

"It's the same woman from before?" Abel Prophet asked, his eyes on the dark window.

"Found each other like a fly finds shit," Eric said, and Ethan laughed. "She spent one night with the other bitch in heat, then took up with this one again."

"It's different, brother," Ethan said.

"What do you mean?"

The way Abel was looking at Ethan made Eric want to cut him; he didn't like anyone dismissing his twin as a halfwit, even if he was. "The pilot up there spreading her legs as easy as peanut butter on toast is older than Parker usually goes for. Compared to the others we've seen, Sydney Parish seems like a dried-up chunk of wood," Eric answered for Ethan.

"What went wrong the night outside the restaurant?" Abel asked.

"You come here to judge, brother?" He put his hand on the knife in his pocket with Parker's blood still on the blade. "I did Father's bidding."

"She's still alive, so obviously something went wrong." Abel started to walk back toward their hotel. "The world will never know the war we're fighting for God if you don't start killing every serpent you find."

Eric grabbed Abel by the back of the collar and yanked him to a stop. "Who done gave you the idea you're in charge?"

"I'm not, but Father was specific in what needed to be done."

"I'm not the retarded one, Abel," he hissed, but from Ethan's hurt expression he'd heard the comment. "He thought you couldn't handle her at full strength, so I did you a favor, but you're going to be the one who kills her."

"That's not my role."

"Your part is what Father says it is, so don't start whining," Eric said, and yanked harder on Abel's collar. "Or do you want me to call him and tell him you're nothing but an abomination like those bitches up there. You're either in or out, and if you can't do it, I'm sure he'll tell me to gut you, and I'll smile doing it."

"Shut up, you don't scare me."

"Think about it and we'll meet you back at the room." Abel stumbled when Eric let him go, and Ethan laughed again. "Come on, brother, I'll take you to the park." They started walking, but Abel stayed behind to stare at the darkened window again. "Pray for strength, Abel, you weak son of a bitch. You're gonna need it."

CHAPTER THIRTEEN

"Hello," Sydney said, surprised someone was still on the line after she'd dropped the phone twice.

"You're still sleeping at nine?"

"It's my day off, so I thought I'd indulge myself." She lifted Parker's hand from her stomach and kissed her palm.

"Good for you, baby, but it's time to get up and open the door for your sister and me," Lucia Parish said.

"You're here?"

"We talked about this last week. We brought you some stuff for the new place and got all the kitchen boxes out of storage, so press the buzzer."

"Tell her to put on a robe so she can help us carry this stuff up," Margo said, loud enough for Sydney to hear her in the background.

She clenched Parker's hand so hard it woke her. "Give me a couple of minutes, okay?" She hung up before her mother could argue.

"Problem?" Parker asked.

"How would you like to meet my mother?" The panicked way she'd blurted it out made Parker laugh. "I'm sorry to spring this on you, and if you don't want to stay, I'll understand, but she's downstairs." Her insecurities rearing up like gophers on a golf course hadn't scared Parker away, but springing her family on her wasn't a wise move, she thought as she looked at Parker's sleep-tousled hair.

"Breathe, Syd, and relax. Mothers love me, don't worry."

"How many mothers have you met?"

"Do you mean in general, or mothers of the women I've dated?" Parker kissed the tip of her nose.

"I'm not sure what that means, but I'll go with the option that mothers love you." Sydney laughed, only it sounded to her like someone strangling a chicken. She loved her mother and sister, but they were about as subtle as construction workers at high tea.

"Is there something you're not telling me?" Parker put her free arm around her and ignored the buzzer. "I thought you and your mom had a good relationship."

"We do. My mom and Margo are important to me, so I want you all to get along. I know it's stupid to worry about, but I don't want there to be tension whenever we're around them." She could have slapped herself at how presumptuous that sounded, but she didn't have time to analyze it now.

"Don't sweat it. I'll be on my best behavior."

"If you say not to worry, I won't."

"Great." Parker smiled. "Could you let go of my hand, then? If you squeeze any harder those backhands are going to be a bitch." Parker kissed her before she headed to the bathroom with her pants thrown over her shoulder. She was still laughing when the phone rang again as she closed the door.

Instead of answering it, Sydney moved to the window and waved to let her family know she was coming. Her mom stood on the sidewalk with a box at her feet and waved back when she noticed her. Behind her, Margo was busy taking more boxes out of the trunk of her car. With a deep breath Sydney pressed the release buzzer, opened her front door, and waited for them to climb the sixteen steps to her place.

"Hello, sweetie." Lucia put her box down inside the door and gave her a hug. "Sorry to cut into your sleep time."

As her mouth opened, so did the bathroom door, making everyone peer to where Parker stood with her hand on the knob and appeared to be mentally ticking through her options. It took only a second for her to take a deep breath and smile before she moved closer with her hand out.

"Mrs. Parish, nice to meet you, ma'am. Sydney's told me almost nothing about you except that you like gardening and were a teacher." The joke made Sydney glare, but Parker's smile never faded and Lucia didn't let go of her hand. She held it like she was trying to convince herself she was shaking hands with Parker King.

"Sydney, aren't you going to make introductions?" Margo asked. She'd walked in while Parker was talking, and she'd shaken her head like she was seeing things. "Or better yet, why not tell us why the number one tennis player in the world is standing in your living room? Did you win a contest on ESPN?"

"Margo, don't be rude," Lucia said out of the side of her mouth, without losing eye contact with Parker. "Though I'm curious about that myself. If someone had asked me to guess who I might find in Sydney's apartment, I would've gone with a monkey playing the banjo before you would've come to mind."

Sydney pulled the tie to her robe tighter, wishing she was still in bed like she'd planned. Before she could say anything, Parker put an arm around her shoulder and kissed the top of her head. "Do you train circus animals when you're not flying?" Parker asked softly while still smiling at Lucia. "I was wondering what was making all that noise in the closet last night."

"Not that there's anything wrong with you being here, but I'm at a loss for words as to why," Lucia said.

"Sydney was nice enough to put me up for the night."

"Just for the night?" Lucia dropped Parker's hand like it'd turned into a two-week-old dead fish and crossed her arms over her chest. The way she cocked her head slightly forward made it look like she was about to head-butt her. Parker's casual answer had erased any need not to be rude. "My daughter isn't a one-night-stand kind of girl. At least that's not how she was raised." Lucia stopped glaring at Parker to glare at Sydney momentarily as she spoke.

"Mom." Sydney dragged out the word and pinched Parker for laughing. "We met this summer. Parker was the friend I told you put me up after the fiasco with the plumbing."

"And the friend the *Post* just tied to Alicia," Margo added, in a way that sounded too gleeful.

"Take a nap with a woman and the world never lets you forget," Parker said.

"I thought you said you slept with her," Sydney said, more interested in Parker's answer than in getting her family to cool it.

"I did, as in closed my eyes and slept. Some maniac had just stabbed me, remember?"

"I remember, Kong, but with you I can't help but follow up on the facts. Want to run out for bagels while I talk my family into liking you?"

After quick directions on where to go, Parker finished dressing and left, but not before she carried in the rest of the boxes from the car. She had Margo laughing by the second trip up and winked at Sydney when they were done and she left to pick up breakfast.

"A tennis pro," Margo said when it was just the three of them. "Who knew you were such a sports fan? Did she swim up and seduce you with the ass I've been seeing in Times Square? I personally would've lasted two seconds before memorizing it with my tongue."

"You need serious help, Margo, serious."

"Are you sure about this?" Lucia asked.

"I know for sure that I'm happy. Does Parker have anything to do with that?" Sydney turned to the door Parker had just walked out of as if it would conjure her back. "Have you ever spent time with someone who hears you?"

"Your father, but we're not talking about him."

"Just be happy for me, Mom. Trust me, she isn't at all like people portray her."

Lucia laughed. "Of course she isn't. The papers live to print malicious lies about people all the time."

"Gee, thanks," Sydney said.

"You know what I mean. It's that whole leopard-spot thing. I'm your mother, and it's my job to warn you about these things." She put her arms around Sydney's waist and squeezed. "I just don't want to see you hurt by a tennis Romeo whose hobby is chasing women. I love you too much for that."

"I know you do, but I really like her."

"Enough to forgive her the occasional indiscretion?" Lucia asked. "I believe you're right about the occasional fish tale, but when you read so many stories, all on the same topic, you suspect that where there's smoke there's fire. Gene wasn't newsworthy, but she should've taught you a valuable lesson on commitment-phobic people."

"The tabloids also write stories about finding Bigfoot, only their pictures are never in focus." This wasn't what she had in mind when her family finally got to meet Parker. "And she's nothing like Gene. Their only common trait is they're both female."

"Is she why you've been in such a bad mood lately?"

"Mom, why don't you go put on a pot of coffee," Margo said, handing her a box with the supplies she'd need. When Lucia was out of range she moved closer to Sydney. "Quick, tell me about the sex, even though it'll make me insanely jealous. Is it fabulous? I hope on all that's holy the papers didn't lie about that part, for your sake."

"Margo, you need to follow your own advice and forget about high finance for a little while. Next time you meet someone, ask how many show tunes they know by heart, and if it's less than two, go for it."

"I don't have time. Besides, I can live vicariously through you. So come on, spill it."

"We haven't progressed that far yet." She dropped her head to her sister's shoulder and groaned. "Why in the hell do I admit these things to you?"

"Because you love me and want to dispel media myths whenever you get the opportunity, especially when the subject is this hot." The buzzer interrupted Margo and she aimed Sydney toward the bathroom. "You should've sent her to the place across town so we could finish this conversation. Obviously Ms. King is back, and after your confession, I think her reputation has been a bit overblown."

"If the press has gotten two things right, it's her skill on the court and off." She pressed the button to unlock the front door and smirked at her sister. "I just don't want to give in too easily. Parker seems like the type you should make work for it."

"Uh-huh." Margo pointed to the bathroom again. "Go freshen up and we'll take care of her for you."

"Be nice or there'll be hell to pay." She pointed at Margo and her mother, who'd just come back in.

When Parker walked in with a large bag of assorted bagels and breakfast pastries, Lucia and Margo were waiting for her in the front room. Sydney's absence made her nervous, and she was determined not to show it.

"That was fast," Lucia said.

"The place Sydney likes is on the corner and there wasn't a line."

"Would you like some coffee?" Lucia asked.

"No, thank you, but please feel free to pour yourselves a cup."

Margo put her hand on Parker's arm and led her toward the kitchen. "Are you a health nut who hates coffee?"

"I'm a health nut who loves cinnamon rolls, but not coffee." The way to go here was the same advice they gave prisoners of war—use short, succinct answers and she wouldn't get into too much trouble.

"Are you a womanizer?" Lucia asked, and Margo choked on the sip she'd taken.

"I see you're a gossip fan." Parker propped herself against the counter and shot both women a winning smile.

"Word of advice, sweetheart. Margo and I aren't interested in sleeping with you, so cut the flirting."

"Speak for yourself, Mom. If Sydney decides to go insane and move on, I'm a huge tennis fan." Margo smiled at her and waved.

"I've dated a lot in the past, Mrs. Parish, but I'm quickly learning the joys of a committed relationship. It just took the right woman."

Sydney appeared and pushed Margo aside before sliding her arms around Parker's waist. "Good answer, Kong. Just repeat it constantly when the groupies start coming out of the woodwork."

"Will do, baby." She grabbed a bagel from the platter Lucia had placed them on. "And feel free to talk about me while I'm gone. You can submit any further questions in writing," she teased, looking at Lucia. "Sorry to run out on you, ladies, but I have a practice scheduled in forty minutes. It was a pleasure meeting you both."

"You lie well, so you can see why I'm worried," Lucia said.

"If I lied well, I'd still have my favorite shirt, and my cleaning bill would be half what it is now."

"Is that some sort of code for 'stay out of my business, you old busybody'?"

"No, ma'am, but I'll let Sydney explain. I really do have to run."

"Will I see you tonight? My flight isn't scheduled to arrive until after seven," Sydney said as they walked to the door.

"I'll move my workouts today so we can have a late dinner. Be careful and call me if you need anything like fingerprints and a DNA sample." She held up Sydney's cell phone she'd grabbed from the kitchen counter. "I put my number into your memory just in case."

"Just in case, huh?"

"You never know when you'll have an overwhelming case of missing me and need to call. Or you might want me to meet some of your other family members on short notice so they can question my motives where you're concerned."

Sydney dropped her head to her chest and sighed. "I'm sorry about that. Were they horrible while I was getting dressed?"

"They love you, and they're devoted to you enough to be overprotective. That's nothing to apologize for, Syd. You should love being so well cared for. Besides, you weren't gone long enough for them to put me under the kitchen faucet so they could drip water onto my head to make me talk." She lowered her head so she could whisper in Sydney's ear. "Have a fun morning and a good day at work. And if you run into any single tennis players on your flight today, tell them you're taken."

"The same goes for you and the groupies, Kong. Be careful too and I'll see you tonight." Sydney acted as if she'd forgotten her mother and sister were in the other room and enjoyed the kiss Parker initiated.

"She does seem really sweet," Margo said when Sydney pressed her forehead to the closed door. "Of course, if you compare her to the loser you dated and the one before that, anyone would seem sweet. Did the police ever find your television and dishes? At least Gene only cheated on you and kept the theft to a minimum."

"Thank you for the recap. I know I haven't had the greatest luck when it comes to relationships, but this one's different."

Lucia poured her a cup of coffee and handed it to her over the counter when they joined her in the kitchen. She had a clear view of the front door, so hopefully the explanation of her and Parker's relationship would be short.

"So tell us how you met the charming Parker," Lucia said as she put things away in the small kitchen.

After the story, Margo was beating the side of her leg she was laughing so hard, and Lucia just shook her head. "She didn't start off on the best of terms, but hell if she doesn't know how to make it up to you," Margo finally said.

"I think it's from all the practice, dear. I wasn't kidding when I brought up her past women. When you see someone with a beautiful woman on her arm every single time, and they're all different in each picture, there has to be some truth to the gossip." Lucia put her hand over Sydney's and kept her voice light. "Just be careful and don't get too caught up in the swirl of being the new girl in Parker's life."

"What I'm planning on, Mom, is being the last girl in Parker's life," Sydney said, and Margo gave her a healthy slap on the back as a sign of approval.

❖

"Don't forget to pick up flowers. Women love that," Gray shouted from the bed. Kimmie was in the bathroom with Parker, busy straightening Parker's collar and combing her hair into place.

"Anything to get the girl to want to see me again, Viper," Parker said as she put her bare feet into a pair of soft leather loafers.

"She's seen you plenty and the thrill isn't gone, so you must be doing something right. You should warn her, though, because I think the cameras caught sight of her yesterday when they panned the box a couple of times," Gray said as she rested her shoulder against the doorjamb of the bathroom. "What's Captain Sydney going to do when the story breaks that she's Alicia's replacement?"

"Hopefully not kick me to the curb after telling me to stay the hell away from her." She shrugged and tried to put her past mistakes out of her head. All those beautiful women could become something so potentially ugly that they'd sink her future. "I don't want to lose her before I even have the chance to prove myself."

"No chance of that, kiddo." Kimmie held her jacket for her. "Go impress your girl with an early dinner and the King charm, but don't forget it's a school night. Tomorrow Marsha Cooper would love nothing better than to cram some tennis balls down your throat and knock you out early, so don't stay out late."

Before the doorman opened the limo door for Parker, he handed her the flowers she'd ordered. Aside from her morning practice session with Natasha, she hadn't left the room until now. She'd talked to Sydney prior to her flight to Miami, then took a nap. Sydney's return had been pushed back until eight, so they'd made plans to meet in the city for dinner.

They'd see each other again after her match tomorrow, since both Bobbie and Sydney planned to attend. Parker laughed as she thought of Bobbie and her offer to give her a kidney or anything else she needed to win. Sydney's friend had turned out to be funny and caring, two reasons Kimmie had asked questions about her availability more than once since they'd gotten to her room.

"Should I wait here, Ms. King?" the driver asked when they arrived at JFK.

"This is a good spot if security doesn't run you off. If they do, we'll wait for you here. She won't have any luggage, so it shouldn't take long."

Since Nick had called and made arrangements, an airline representative met Parker at security with a pass so she could meet Sydney at her gate. The guy told her a bad storm off the Georgia coast had delayed the flight, but she wouldn't have to wait more than fifteen or twenty minutes.

Passengers started to file through the exit, all seeming to be in a rush to collect their luggage or grab a cab into the city, so thankfully none of them noticed her sitting in the back corner. She stood only after the gate area was quiet for a few minutes. To her it was a sign that the last of the stragglers had deplaned and the crew would be out shortly.

The first one to appear was Willy, the flight attendant she'd met on her way back from London. He came and shook her hand and smiled. "For me?" he said, and pointed to the flowers. "You shouldn't have."

"I didn't, so keep your hands to yourself."

He laughed and signaled his coworkers to stop. "Then you must be the reason our boss was in a fantastic mood the entire day."

"She's inspired my mood as well, so you all don't do anything to change that," she said, but kept her eyes on the door.

Sydney stepped out after she'd powered down the engines and gathered her things. Seeing Parker again had been a priority all day, and her wish now was not to have to deal with a ton of traffic. Margo had promised to take care of a surprise for her, and she hoped she'd pulled it off. She didn't remember the correct quote, but she knew tonight would be pivotal to the future of their relationship. She'd come to a decision in Miami, and after studying it from every conceivable angle, as was her habit, she couldn't believe she'd waited this long.

"Excuse me, stewardess, could I bother you for some hot chocolate?" The question made Sydney snap her head up and turn around to look toward the waiting-area seats. Dressed for dinner, Parker stood there holding a large bouquet of roses. The sight made Sydney's heart melt. She hadn't been on the receiving end of romantic notions often in her dating history. Without thought for where she was or for Parker's injury, she ran the short distance, rushed into Parker's open arms, and gave her a scorching kiss. Only the applause of her crew made her lift her head.

"Welcome back, Captain. How'd you like to have dinner with me?"

Once her feet hit the ground Sydney ran her hands under the jacket and up the crisp pale yellow shirt Parker wore. The outfit was similar to the one she'd noticed while flipping through one of Willy's magazines during her break in Miami. Parker was right that she had a lot more gigs than tennis; with her height and great physique, she made a great model.

"You think I'm one of those easy fly girls who'll be swayed by flowers and a handsome younger woman?" She pulled her hands out of the jacket and slid them up to Parker's neck.

"You're not?"

"What else you got to offer, tennis pro?" She laced her fingers behind Parker's head and applied pressure as a hint for Parker to bend down.

"Just a limo and a reservation, but I'm open to suggestion, if that's not enough."

"That you're here is enough," she said, and kissed her again.

"Have fun, kids," Willy said as he shooed the others away.

They held hands through the terminal, and Sydney was content to listen as Parker answered Willy's questions about the Open as he walked with them. Being this happy was the strangest sensation, and she didn't realize she was crying until the tears wet her cheeks.

"Good luck tomorrow, Parker," Willy said before he split off. Sydney just waved and accepted Parker's help to get into the car.

"Are you all right?" Parker watched as Sydney took a rose out of the bunch and brought it to her nose.

"Did you know that pink roses are some of the only ones left that still have a fragrance?" She gazed at Parker's face in an effort to hold on to the magic she'd brought to her heart.

Parker nodded. "Red is more popular, so they're bred for bloom quality and lasting value. When you make something conform, I guess you have to sacrifice something. The pink and yellow ones smell sweet, but they die faster."

Sydney was surprised Parker knew the answer, but then thought of all the time she spent reading at home and in hotel rooms. At least, she read in hotel rooms whenever she wasn't entertaining some adoring fan or other famous woman who wanted her attention. It didn't seem possible Parker was knowledgeable and experienced in so many areas, considering her age.

"Sometimes life's like that." She relinquished the flower to Parker. "Don't you think?"

"Do you mean the best parts are sweet but fleeting?" Parker asked, and Sydney knew she understood her point.

"Maybe. The age-old question should be whether to cut them and take possession of them to enjoy their beauty for that fleeting moment, or leave them and just admire them from afar." She looked up to Parker's face finally and into the eyes that appeared sky blue against the yellow shirt. The thought of not being able to be this close to Parker again sent a real pain through her chest.

"Stick to the ones that are bred to look good but hold no pleasure for you, huh?" The corners of Parker's eyes crinkled when she smiled. "They're more reliable for the long haul, but that's not what'll make you happy, because for all their beauty, they're not whole."

"I guess that's what I mean."

"Maybe you should think of it this way. The red ones have been cultivated for endurance—that's their fate, so to speak, but these are complete." Parker held up the pink bloom.

"What do you mean?" Sydney needed to be convinced. Her earlier promises to herself to ignore her fears came roaring back.

"Until their time is up, these make you happy because they give you everything they have and don't hold anything back. They don't know how much time they have before they wither and die. They just want you to be happy until that time comes." Parker handed the rose back to her with a smile. "The experiences good and bad they've had up to now are what made them unique and whole. They'll never try to change what they are because that would cheat you as well as the bloom when they try to be something they're not."

"What happens when other people covet the same flower?" She put the flower down and took Parker's hand.

"You can't covet something that belongs to someone else, sweetheart. If you harvest it, it belongs to you, but only if you want it." Sydney looked at Parker's long tapered fingers as she took the flower back. "Too much, too soon?"

"Doesn't the flower have some say?" she asked, close to giddy at the turn the conversation had taken.

"The flower just feels lucky."

"How so?"

"Look at the beautiful vase it's found to stick her stem in."

Sydney's laugh started small, but she couldn't hold it in, and as she fell against Parker's chest she fought to catch her breath. "I'd have to love you, because you're obviously losing your touch."

"What do you mean?" Parker tried to sound indignant.

"Honey, that's the worst pickup line I've ever heard. Who else would fall for that? Wait, don't answer that. You look and smell so good, I'm sure people like Alicia don't care what comes out of your mouth."

"I love you, Sydney, and I don't want to talk about anyone else tonight."

"Say it again."

"I love you," Parker said as she put a hand in Sydney's hair and turned her head so she could kiss her.

With her eyes still closed, Sydney confessed more of her feelings. "The minute you turned the corner to step onto my plane all those months ago, I knew you would change my life, and I was right. I love you too."

That was all the conversation necessary, so she enjoyed the trip with Parker's arms around her. They'd eventually have to talk about the logistics of their relationship, but the details could wait. They could deal with things like past lovers and how many states separated their addresses because they'd cleared a significant hurdle.

The most important thing was that Parker loved her, and because she felt the same, anything was possible.

❖

Sydney took Parker's hand when the limo drove away from her apartment. The evening had been interesting so far, since about twenty people had felt compelled to stop at their table with well wishes and advice for Parker. She'd never felt so invisible in her life and would've been upset had Parker not paid for their drinks and left before they ordered. Their romantic dinner had gone from the nice restaurant to a pizza place, where they'd stood under harsh fluorescent lights talking over paper plates and napkins.

"Close your eyes," she said to Parker when they reached the front door.

"It's okay, Syd. I already know you don't have any furniture." Parker laughed as she searched for her keys at the bottom of her purse. "Or do you have your mother and sister stashed in there and you don't want to scare me? I can't be sure, but your mother looked like she had a few more things she needed to ask under harsh lighting and using a cattle prod."

"You're not getting in until you close your eyes, so shut them please," she said as she unlocked the door. "I have a surprise for you." She walked backward as she led Parker to her bedroom and hoped Margo had done as she'd asked. "Sit," she said when they were next to the new bed she'd ordered.

"There's something behind me, right?" Parker said, but kept her eyes closed. "It's not like I took the numbers any of those women offered."

"Let me help you with your backhand." Sydney mimicked a rail-thin woman's high pitch as she pushed Parker to sit. "Slut."

Parker kept her hands on her hips and bit her bottom lip as if not to laugh. "My slutty days are over, so you have nothing to worry about."

"I know, and I'm sorry. I don't mean to sound like a bitch."

"It's flattering, baby," Parker said. "The only bitch I saw tonight was the one you're talking about. As if I would've been interested in anyone else when the most beautiful woman in the place was already sitting next to me."

"I'm trying not to think about how lucky you are when it comes to women, but it's hard when you say things like that. You have a talent for words." Sydney wet the tip of her finger and traced Parker's lips. "You make me feel so much."

"I always want you to know how special you are," Parker said before she sucked her finger into her mouth to the knuckle.

"Lie back," Sydney said—reluctantly, because Parker would have to release her finger to comply.

"You got a new bed?" Parker stretched her arms up over her head. "Thanks, but you didn't need to go to all that trouble." When Parker's hand landed on a bag, she opened her eyes and stared at the luggage scattered around the room, all of which belonged to her.

"Too presumptuous?" Sydney asked, her fingers crossed behind her back. Margo had taken care of the bed, but Kimmie and Beau had brought the bags over.

Parker sat back up and put her hand back on her hips to bring her closer. "Abby's not hiding in the bathroom, is he?"

"I could fly him up if that'll seal the deal."

"I'm sure he's having a blast at doggie camp, so we'll leave him to it."

Sydney placed her fingers on Parker's cheeks and ran them along the curve until she skimmed underneath her jaw. "I want you to know something." Parker stayed quiet as she kissed just above her right eyebrow. "When I stayed with you, I wasn't playing you to try to get something from you."

"You don't have to tell me that." Parker's wide-open expression made her want to finish what she had to say.

In all the time she'd shared with Gene or anyone, she'd dreaded intimate moments, not because she disliked sex, but because the women appeared shuttered off from her. They hid their true selves because they had too many secrets, and letting her in would expose them. "For all the missteps I made with you, you never made me feel unwelcome. You gave me more in those few days than the woman I shared two years of my life with. That's one of the many reasons I couldn't get you out of my mind. Can you forgive me for ignoring you so long?"

"Taking time to decide what's best for you isn't a sin you need to ask forgiveness for. Maybe if we'd rushed it, all this would've been

was the summer fling we both worried about when it ended abruptly."
Parker kissed her again and Sydney's heart rate went up, causing her
pulse to spike. "I'm enjoying taking our time to figure out what comes
next. The only certainty I want is that you'll be with me, but the rest
we'll work out together."

"Do you want me?" The need for Parker to put her hands on her
was becoming a deep craving. The sensation both shocked and surprised
Sydney, since up to that point in her life that hadn't been the case. Sex
had been good, or at least that'd been her description of it because she
had nothing to compare it to. Now she knew that if making love to
someone was like a meal, she'd only had appetizers. With Parker she
wanted to feast until she sat back full and lethargic.

"More than anything I've wanted in my entire life, but I'll wait
until you're sure." Parker placed her hand under her throat and ran it
down between her breasts. There were too many clothes in the way, but
the sensation caused goose bumps on her scalp. "When you are, I'm
going to make love to you."

Sydney opened her eyes at the statement she was sure Parker
hadn't made to anyone before. There in Parker's eyes was the same
openness as before. The words weren't intended to break down her
defenses. Parker meant them. "Give me what I wanted that last night
we spent together. I wasn't truly free then, but now I'm yours."

Her permission unshackled Parker's hands and she squeezed her
left breast. She sucked in a breath and let out a moan. Parker smiled as
she reached behind Sydney. "The first time I saw you in this uniform I
didn't think it was the right time to tell you how fantastic you look in
this skirt." The humor let her relax a bit.

The zipper sounded loud in the mostly empty apartment as Parker
brought the tab down slowly. "I promise not to smack you if you
mention anything about it now."

"I've never really given much thought to the kind of woman I'd
want to be with when my playing days were over." Parker tugged the
blouse from the loosened waistband of Sydney's skirt. Sydney stayed
quiet, knowing in her gut that Parker wasn't talking about tennis. "But
now I realize I did have a wish list," Parker said as she started on the
buttons of her blouse.

"Is it a secret, or do you want to share?"

"I want," Parker said, and stopped when she opened the silk
garment and saw her bra. "Matching set?" Parker asked as she pushed
Sydney's jacket off.

"Not my usual choice when I'm working, but you inspired me." Sydney smiled as her skirt pooled around her feet and Parker ran her finger along the top of the black silk bikinis she was wearing. "The way you look at me—I never thought it'd turn me on this much, but it does."

"I'm glad you don't mind," Parker said as she stood, "because I can't help myself. You're so perfect, and you're so hot in this." Parker brought her hands up until her index fingers were under her bra straps.

"It's my gift to you." Sydney almost laughed at how quickly Parker was able to unhook her bra. If Parker's looks during dinner had been enough to turn her on, the way her eyes focused on her naked chest made her wet. She was clumsy as she undid Parker's belt, but blamed it on the sexual haze overtaking her. No one had ever made her throb like this, and it made her impatient.

"We have all night, baby," Parker said as she unbuttoned her pants and let them fall.

"I don't mean to rush." She pulled Parker's underwear down before removing her own. "I've been thinking about you all day, and now I need to feel you." She pushed Parker to sit back on the bed and straddled her legs. All she needed was a small touch to ground her, so she rubbed herself on Parker's thigh to calm the frenzy.

"Tell me what you want," Parker whispered as she held her with her hands on her hips.

"Kiss me," Sydney said, not able to stop her hips when the linen of Parker's shirt rubbed against her nipples, making them incredibly sensitive.

She moaned and came close to orgasm when Parker sucked her tongue into her mouth, but the contact between her legs was gone and it took her a minute to realize Parker had stood up and was holding her. "I'm so close."

"We're not stopping," Parker said as she laid her across the bed and hovered over her. "I'll take care of you." Parker's voice sounded so soothing but sexy before she took her nipple between her teeth.

It felt so good she lifted her hips and tried to make contact with any part of Parker. She needed to come so bad she was about to cry. "Please, I need you," she said, not caring that she sounded desperate.

"Not as much as I need you," Parker said as she moved down Sydney's body. She went slowly, wanting to savor every inch of Sydney as she reached her sex. The thought that this was so new sounded absurd to her, but it was. Never before had she wanted to please someone, but it was important to go slow.

"I need you here," Sydney said, putting her hand between her legs as if to give her a hint.

To Parker she looked lush, a word she'd read often but never used to describe anyone. "Then you should get what you want."

She parted the slick lips of Sydney's sex and simply looked for a long, intimate moment. Sydney's clit was so hard, and she was so wet, she felt like puffing her chest out a little in pride that Sydney wanted her this much. It was her goal to please so that her touch would be the only one she'd need from this night on.

Sydney clutched at the sheet but simply moaned when Parker lowered her tongue and pressed it to the wet opening. One taste and she was addicted as she slid her hands under Sydney's butt. She sucked on the diamond-hard clit long enough to make Sydney grab hold of her head to keep her in place, but she raised up, wanting it to last.

"No, don't stop," Sydney said as she spread her legs farther apart. "Oh, God," she said when Parker circled her clit with just the tip of her tongue.

"I'm not going anywhere." Parker moved one hand down Sydney's leg and back again, then slid two fingers down the length of her sex to get them wet. "I want you."

"Then take me," Sydney demanded, then screamed loud enough for the building to hear her when Parker lowered her head again and entered her completely. "Oh, please," Sydney said, her voice tight and choked off.

Parker thrust only three times and felt the walls of Sydney's sex clamp as tight around her fingers as her legs had around her head. She kept her hand still, enjoying the pulsing aftershocks until she realized Sydney was crying. It took her by surprise and she moved quickly to put her arms around her, hoping more than anything that they weren't tears of regret.

"It's okay, Syd, I've got you." She moved to her back so Sydney would be comfortable. "Did I hurt you?"

Sydney shook her head and clung to her like she'd disappear if she let go. "I hate to admit this." Sydney's words were filled with so much apprehension it was as if someone had punched her in the gut. Only regret made a woman sound so fearful.

"You can tell me anything." *But please don't let it be good-bye,* she thought.

"No one has ever wanted me this much. I was beginning to think I'd have to settle because I'd never be enough."

Sydney buried her head under Parker's chin as if she were embarrassed to admit what she saw were her shortcomings. "I can't make up for whoever came before me, but you have to realize how beautiful you are to me."

"Beauty really doesn't have anything to do with it." Sydney took a deep breath, apparently trying to suck in a bit of courage before she pulled back and faced her. "No one's ever treated me like a woman who's desirable enough that you just have to have her. I've never needed anyone to touch me like that, and I've never craved it the way you made me want it."

"We shouldn't waste tonight talking about nuts." Parker wiped Sydney's face with her fingertips and hoped she believed the sincerity of her words.

"We have so much to learn about each other, but before you I always viewed this aspect of any relationship as an obligation, so much so that I was starting to believe the ice-queen comments."

"If that's what the world wants to believe, let them." Sydney's expression went from sadness to shock in an instant. "I never want to share you, so if I'm the only one who knows how hot you are, I won't shed any tears over that."

"You are a gift, Kong," Sydney said, sounding as if a weight had been lifted off her chest. "You can pat yourself on the back for melting away any inhibitions I had in the bedroom, but you might never find my off switch. What will ESPN talk about if you're never seen again because you're trying to keep me satisfied?" Sydney leaned back even farther and simply stared at the length of her naked body.

"Off switch?" Parker laughed. "No way in hell—" Sydney placed her hand between her legs.

"Do you have any idea how bad I want you right now?" Sydney moved her hand through Parker's wetness.

"You don't have to ask for something we both want." She smiled as Sydney took her time exploring. Sydney seemed to be trying to make her feel the same desperation for her touch.

"I must be doing something right if you're this wet." Sydney kept her touch soft and her movements slow, making Parker curl her hands into fists.

"Christ," Parker said when her strokes got firmer and her back came off the bed a little.

Their eyes met as Sydney knelt between Parker's legs and tried to match the rhythm of Parker's hips. Seeing Parker like this made it easy to understand all the drink baths that spurned women had treated her to. Once you'd experienced Parker's touch, it'd be hellish to let it go.

Parker was quieter than she'd been as her orgasm started, and she tried not to lose concentration when the muscles in Parker's legs tightened as she came. They were definitely getting naked every chance they had, she thought as Parker fell back on the bed as if someone had drugged her.

"Remind me to donate all our pajamas to charity in the morning," she said as she snuggled next to Parker, then smiled when she felt Parker laugh before she kissed her forehead. "And thank you for not treating me like I'm crazy. Tonight was a gift."

"It was more than that. This is our beginning."

"That it is."

"Good night, my love," Parker said in a whisper, and the endearment floated in Sydney's head before settling in her heart.

She was on a path she'd never traveled, but she looked forward to the long journey in Parker's embrace.

CHAPTER FOURTEEN

Y our legs looked a little weak in that last game. Is something
bothering you?" Beau asked as Parker packed her gear after
changing. Her latest win had earned her a slot in the semifinals, but it'd
lasted longer than any of her previous matches in the tournament.

"Nothing's wrong, so stop stressing. Maybe I just wanted to give
the crowd their money's worth this time."

"Sure, you did. Could it be some good-looking blonde who's
keeping you up nights?" She glared at him, so he smiled as if to show
he was kidding.

"Does this mean she's not allowed to come over and play
anymore?" Sydney asked from behind them.

"Did you enjoy the match?" she asked. "Or did you chew through
your nails like nervous Nelly over there?"

Sydney stood by the bag she was shoving stuff into and kissed her.
"When Marsha broke your serve twice at the start, Bobbie squeezed my
hand so hard I thought I'd have to sedate her."

"At least someone has faith in me." Parker stuck her tongue out
at Beau.

"You, cute stuff, know how to show a girl an exciting time. Bobbie
may need counseling later, but I loved it. Can I get you anything?"
Sydney rhythmically ran her fingers through Parker's wet hair.

"A nap would be nice," Parker said.

"Done. Come on, unless you have something else to talk to her
about, Beau?"

He shook his head and kissed them both on the cheek before
leaving. Parker slipped on some sandals and a pair of light sweatpants
and was ready to go. Her new greatest fan, Bobbie, had offered them a
ride back to Sydney's apartment, which was good since she wouldn't
feel the need to make small talk.

When they stepped outside a number of fans were waiting for her with pens and programs for her autograph, so she plastered on a smile and started signing. Sydney had stepped to the side to allow some kids who were trying to attract her attention to move closer. Parker smiled at Sydney's expression as she looked at the young little tennis fans. It was the glimmer of metal catching sunlight that made them both look to the right where the crowd was the thinnest. As she caught the last motion of the ski mask being pulled into place, the attacker was already moving toward them. Only this time the knife seemed to be aimed at Sydney. She didn't hesitate to put herself between Sydney and the danger.

Sydney's scream made the rest of the crowd back up, and Parker swiveled her hip to bring her bag around as the knife sliced in to the hilt. It happened so fast she thought it would take a second more to feel the pain. "No," Sydney yelled as their attacker tried to pull back to free the knife, but she grabbed his hand and squeezed.

"You're going to die for this," Parker said when she figured out what had stopped the knife from reaching skin.

Her outrage made the attacker look down at her bag. She had no idea how long the knife was, but one or two fewer racquets, and at least part of the blade would've cut into her hip. While still holding on to the guy's wrist, she flung the bag down, disarming him and leaving her hand free to swing at his face. She connected with the bottom of his jaw, but she didn't have a chance to try again before security arrived and took over. Whoever it was had crumpled under her fist like a sandcastle in a high tide.

"Are you hurt?" Sydney asked through her tears, running her hands over her body as if checking for wounds.

"I'm fine, but I can't say the same for that asshole if security gives me a few minutes alone with him." She pointed to the masked idiot locked in a struggle not to be cuffed.

Once he'd been subdued, one of the officers ripped the mask off to see if she could identify him. The face was recognizable even with the split lip from her punch, and both she and Sydney said the name at the same time.

"Alicia?"

❖

"Ma'am, please, you can't attack a person in handcuffs," one of the security personnel said as he looked at Parker in a way that begged her to help him pry Sydney off Alicia. The second the ski mask had come off, everyone had been surprised when Sydney had gone after her with the intent to cause major pain and had actually gotten in a few blows before the security personnel caught her.

"Why the hell not? She just tried to kill Parker. I'd think that gives me the right to punch her," Sydney said as she kept her fists up.

"Come on, slugger, before they drag you off to the pokey too," Parker said, and the security guards had to hold Alicia back when she hugged Sydney. The taller man knocked Alicia to the ground and pressed his knee between her shoulders to keep her down.

A police unit and another car arrived, and the guy in plain clothes pointed to Alicia, which prompted the men with him to pick her up and put her into the back of one of the units. "Hi, I'm Logan Sully with NYPD, and I've been assigned to your case. Do you know this woman, Ms. King?" Logan flashed his badge before shaking hands with them.

"That's not a hard one, Officer, since she's got the number one single out right now," she said, keeping her arm around Sydney.

"I accessed the report filed the night you were attacked," Logan said as he flipped through his notes. "Do you think Alicia had anything to do with that?"

"Not unless she hired someone." She closed her eyes for a moment from fatigue. "She made a scene right after arriving, which is why I left that night."

"Gives her a good alibi," Logan said, as if talking more to himself.

"I guess, but…" She went on to explain what the attacker had said before cutting her, and the letters she'd been receiving. "All that started before Alicia and I got together in England, so this feels different."

"Either way, we'll look into it and get back with you."

"Are you sure you're okay?" Sydney asked once they were standing alone, away from the crowd that had gathered.

"I'm fine, I swear." Parker held Sydney against her as she stared at Alicia sitting in the back of the cruiser. Alicia was glaring at them, and she almost didn't recognize her with her expression of pure hatred.

"I wanted to die when I saw that knife go in."

She picked up her bag and showed it to Sydney. "She didn't touch me, but like I said, I wish security hadn't been so quick to respond."

"Why?"

"Because…" She unzipped the bag and removed some racquets. "She cut though all of them, and my stringer's back home." After a quick check she determined that every single racquet was ruined. "At least you got in a shot before they took her away."

"I'm sure someone here can restring them," Sydney said, with a look on her face that she could only define as part worry and part amusement. "Considering what could've happened had you not been hauling all that stuff, it's worth the sacrifice."

Beau, Kimmie, Gray, Natasha, and Nick walked up, and both men put their hands on their heads when they saw what she held. "All of them?" Beau asked, and she nodded. That prompted Nick to start dialing. "And Gunter's back home."

"But she's okay, Beau," Sydney said with a little heat, which made Parker and her sisters laugh.

"Sorry, you know I love Parker, but the tournament's not over."

"I guess on the way home you'll explain the great tragedy to me," Sydney said to her as Natasha and Beau emptied the bag.

"My game is about three-fourths talent and power, but the other fourth is equipment. How I hit and direct the ball is tied up in those strings, so Alicia's little stunt comes at a bad time. It's like you trying to fly a plane with wings that are bolted on loosely. It might be possible to do it, but I'm guessing you'd rather those suckers not be flapping in the wind."

"Horrible analogy, baby, but I understand what you're getting at."

Bobbie arrived with the car and they made plans to all meet up later in the city. They rode back to Sydney's apartment in silence, with Bobbie glancing in the rearview mirror a couple of times when the traffic slowed. As their eyes met, Sydney held up crossed fingers and smiled. She said a prayer of thanks Parker hadn't been hurt.

They held hands as they climbed the stairs to the apartment, and she kissed Parker before closing the bathroom door so she could shower in peace. Then she turned down the bed and guided Parker in for the nap she'd promised.

"I'm going to ignore the fact that you're naked." Parker smiled, pulled her down, and kissed her. "Oh, no, you don't. Get some sleep."

"I promise I'll make it up to you later, but that heat today was brutal."

Parker's eyes shut after she kissed her one more time, and her breathing evened out almost immediately.

After Parker had been asleep for a while, Sydney and Bobbie walked up the street to pick up their order at the restaurant three blocks away. The King sisters and the others had accepted her invitation after they swore eating on the floor wouldn't be a problem. They were on their way back when Sydney noticed a car stop in front of her building and two men get out.

Both of the athletic guys retrieved large black bags from the trunk after they looked at a slip of paper one had dug out of his pocket.

"Can I help you?" Sydney shifted the bag of food in her arms and kept a good distance from the two strangers.

"Please, if you could tell me where this address is?" The tall blond man had a heavy German accent and held the paper in his hand for Sydney to take.

"That's an easy one, since it's mine. Do you want something?"

"We have a delivery for Parker King, and Beau said we could find her here." Sydney recognized the shape of the bags as similar to the one Parker carried her gear in and smiled.

"Racquets, I'm guessing?"

"Yes, ma'am. A few that were cut today and some extras our boss thought she'd like to try. The company is flying Gunter in on a special flight to take care of everything, so hopefully he'll finish the rest of them tonight." The front door of the building opened and Parker came out wearing the sweatpants and T-shirt Sydney had left on the bed that morning. Looking better rested and wearing shoes, she stopped beside Sydney and gave her a kiss.

Sydney pointed to the two men dressed similar to Parker. "Who's their boss?"

"One of the vice presidents for the company that makes Head racquets. They're the top sponsor on my right sleeve, so let me make nice," Parker answered before moving to shake hands with the two delivery guys. With their greetings out of the way, one of the blonds started opening cans of balls and dropping them into a practice basket he'd pulled from the trunk. She was about to ask what he was doing when Parker unzipped one of the bags on the sidewalk and pulled out a slew of racquets.

For the next hour Sydney and the guests she'd invited sat on the steps of her building watching Parker play tennis in the street. Methodically, Parker took each racquet out of the bags and tried it until six stood against Sydney's legs.

Parker picked up one of the new ones her sponsor had sent over that she'd rejected and popped open the last can of balls. With a smile on her face she called out to Bobbie, "Want to play with me?"

"Ooh, Bobbie, I'd be careful," Natasha said. "I'm familiar with that look she gets. You may be in trouble." She laughed when Bobbie gulped.

"Try to remember I don't do this for a living. Okay?"

"I'll do my best." Parker winked at Sydney before she tossed up the first ball. Some of the little boys who'd been watching ran after the ball when Bobbie swung at it and missed. Sydney's new neighbors along the block had gotten a kick out of watching a more personal Open played right outside their windows and cheered whenever Parker hit a good shot.

Gray snorted some beer out of her nose when an elderly woman told Sydney that if she planned to date Cappie Pondexter from the New York Liberty basketball team next, she should let her know so she could make it down to the playground to watch.

Parker slowed her game a lot, from what Sydney could see, giving Bobbie a chance to hit a few back. They'd known each other for years and she'd never seen such happiness on her friend's face. After twenty more minutes Beau called it quits, but told Bobbie to keep the racquet to make up for stopping her fun.

"Thanks, guys, tell your boss I appreciate the prompt service," Parker said as the delivery guys packed the equipment she wasn't interested in.

"I'm going to have to buy a book so I can understand what all the fuss over racquets is about," Sydney told Parker as she retrieved the racquets she'd picked. Beau and Nick grabbed them from her and headed in.

"It's probably all in my head, so find one with a chapter on paranoia and craziness."

Upstairs, Sydney and Natasha worked in the kitchen heating the food that had sat forgotten on the stoop, and she judged how much to order the next time she invited a pack of ravenous athletes to her house for dinner. After the kisses and hugs good-bye, Kimmie and Gray offered to get Bobbie and Natasha back to their doorsteps for the night, and the guys flagged a passing cab, so Sydney took Parker in for a hot bath.

"You must've sweated off five pounds out there, and picked up another six in dirt." Parker smiled as if she didn't take her fussing too seriously since she was standing next to the tub naked and ready to join her. She stepped in and knelt between Parker's legs so she could wash her hair. "Move one leg up for me, sweetheart."

Parker draped half of her left leg out of the tub to give her room to get closer. When she did, Parker sucked her nipple in, making her forget what she was doing for a moment.

"You taste so good," Parker said from around her now-perky nipple.

"Oh, no, you can stop right there. I know you don't have to play tomorrow, but I'm bathing you and putting you to bed. As much as I love watching your cute butt run around the court, I like those short matches much better, and I have a feeling you do too." She heard and felt Parker release her with a pop.

"You're no fun."

"I'm plenty fun, but I want to take care of you." She rinsed the suds out of Parker's hair and finished the task with a kiss.

"And I thank you for it," Parker said with a smile.

When she was dry and in another T-shirt and shorts, Sydney propped her up against the headboard and fed her fruit for dessert.

Parker could hear Sydney cleaning the dishes they'd used, but Sydney had given her strict orders to stay in bed and out of the kitchen. She hoped Sydney really did want her to rest. Or did she not know what to say after what'd happened earlier in the afternoon?

A little later, Sydney slipped into a short nightgown, turned out the lights, and cuddled up next to her.

"Thanks for coming out for all my games so far. It means a lot to me to look up and see you sitting in the stands." She spoke softly and pulled Sydney closer, and she couldn't help but let her hands roam a little. Sydney's beauty surprised her at times. That thought ran through her mind as her hand came to rest on Sydney's backside.

"Not more than it means to me to be there. In a way it's kind of strange," Sydney said, making her laugh.

"Strange?"

"Not strange as in bizarre, sweetie. Strange as in seeing someone who does something for a living that other people want to go see and cheer. Does that make sense?"

"I've never thought of it that way."

"It's nice looking down and watching you excel at something you love. I love flying, but I don't have a fan club, and my naked butt isn't on a billboard over Times Square." Sydney kissed the patch of skin under her lips.

"Don't be so sure about that. I'm a big fan of yours, and if you want, I can have Nick talk to Nike." She stopped and laughed. "Wow, say that five times fast. Anyway, I've seen your butt, and it definitely beats mine any day."

"I don't want to keep you from doing what you love, but after today I wouldn't mind having you all to myself. It's still hard to believe that crazy bitch tried to kill you." Sydney laid her head on her chest, and from the way she was breathing, Parker could tell she was crying again. "I think about what could've happened and it makes me crazy," Sydney got out before she started to sob.

"Don't get lost in what could've happened." She held Sydney like she'd lose her if she let go. "The only thing you should concentrate on is how much I love you." Sydney felt hot wherever their skin made contact, but she was starting to calm. "My fear today had nothing to do with that knife slicing through me, but that I'd die without getting the chance to tell you how much you mean to me."

"I thought the same thing," Sydney said, her voice rough with emotion. "It's like everyone I know was impatient to build a life with someone, and some of them settled. They all felt sorry for me because I settled more than anyone, but I never thought I'd find someone who fills every part of me." Her eyes were bloodshot when she lifted her head, but she still looked beautiful. "I finally did and almost lost you just as fast."

"But you didn't," she said, and smiled as she framed Sydney's face with her hands. "You didn't, and you weren't hurt, so it's all good." Sydney nodded. "Want to hear what I figured out today?" Sydney nodded again and groaned when she started to hiccup.

"Marsha was kicking my ass, gloating the whole time, and for a while I was thinking I might lose to America's sweetheart." Sydney gazed up from her chest as if interested in where this story was going. "Last year, that thought would have pissed me off because of the work that goes into preparing for a tournament like the Open, but this year I figured you wouldn't think any less of me if I lost, so it didn't matter as much. I looked up there and saw you biting your thumbnail, and it hit me."

"What did?"

"I love you, Sydney. Don't get me wrong. I don't think of you as a trophy, but after winning your heart, I could never win another game of tennis and it wouldn't matter." *In books after someone confesses love and the girl gives her a huge kiss, she doesn't break down like her dog just died.* She held Sydney as she sobbed into her chest again.

"You could tell me that a million times a day and I'll never get tired of hearing it." She used the bottom of her T-shirt to wipe Sydney's face dry after she choked her confession out through her tears.

"Enough tears for one night, cute stuff. Let's get some sleep so you won't be tired at work tomorrow. Where're you headed in the morning?"

"A morning flight to Houston then Dallas, where I'll get to cool my jets for three hours before heading back. I took the shitty schedule this time so I could get off to watch the rest of your matches."

Parker rolled them over so she could tuck the blanket around Sydney's body. After a gentle kiss, she spooned around behind her and relaxed.

"How am I going to sleep when you go back to Alabama?" Sydney covered the hand she'd rested on her abdomen under her nightgown.

"That's easy, I'm not going back. At least not without you." Sydney didn't say anything and pulled her hand up between her breasts. Parker stayed silent as well, certain that her answer had put some of the demons in Sydney's mind to rest.

❖

"Sir, we found this in one of the drawers in the desk in the bedroom. We also bagged numerous newspaper articles on Ms. King and her playing schedule." The uniformed policeman handed Logan Sully a bag with a letter in it. The note in the plastic sheaf was like many of the others Parker had received, explaining her death because she was an abomination to God.

"This doesn't make any sense," Logan muttered in a low voice after reading the note for the third time. He'd listened to Parker's explanation of how she knew the pop sensation who'd attacked her.

"Why not, sir?" one of the officers who'd accompanied Logan to search the apartment asked.

"She attacked Parker King because she couldn't have her. Don't you think that'd make Alicia an abomination to God as well? And this time there was no threat during the attack." Logan continued when the two policemen looked like they weren't following what he was saying. "Outside the restaurant, the unknown perp runs up to Parker King and stabs her. But before he does, he says, 'Death to those who go against God,' or something like that. Three weeks later Alicia does the same thing, only this time in broad daylight dressed the same, using the same weapon. Obviously the same person didn't do this, but where did Alicia get this note? If you compare it to all the others the Alabama police faxed over, I'd bet my paycheck they match."

"I'm thinking the bitch is crazy, boss. The head-shrinkers call that spiraling mental illness," another policeman said. "I bet she got the idea from the note and the first attack and thought she could get away with it and blame it on someone else."

"All right, Sigmund, collect the rest of the stuff and let's head back to the precinct. I'm sure Ms. King would like to know that the nut that sent all the notes is still out there, since Alicia couldn't have done the first attack. Unless she had an accomplice. The sooner we find out the truth, the better, since I have money riding on the outcome of the Open this year. This dope Alicia could have cost me a fortune if she'd knocked Parker out of the tournament."

CHAPTER FIFTEEN

D o you have some lunch money?" Parker asked as she helped
Sydney put her jacket on.

The question made Sydney laugh and turn around as soon as her arms had cleared the sleeves. "Yes, but I don't need any. The airline feeds us wherever we land, or in the air, depending on the flight. What are you doing today?"

Parker pulled her closer and kissed her forehead. She appeared worried after she'd had to wake her from a nightmare three times during the night.

"Play tennis, watch some television, then wait for you to get back. I'm going to miss you today, Captain."

"Come down here, Stretch." She tugged on the back of Parker's head and stood on the tips of her toes. "I'm going to miss you too. Promise you'll be careful and stay away from maniacs carrying knives until I get back?"

"I promise. You stay away from low-flying birds and frisky air attendants. I'm the jealous type, so keep that in mind, Sparky."

"I'm not the one that keeps making the cover of the tabloids." She kissed Parker again before heading out to flag down a cab. With any luck she'd get favorable tailwinds and be back in time for them to go out to dinner.

She was almost at the gates at JFK when her cell phone rang and she came close to dumping her purse to find it. "Hello," she said, out of breath.

"Hey, Captain."

"What, you miss me so much already, you're calling me at work?" She waved to one of the ticket agents who was walking into the building beside her. She almost sighed in relief when she felt the air-conditioning the moment the doors slid open. How Parker could run around in this weather was a mystery to her.

"It's true I miss you, but that's not why I'm calling. Remember when you said something about me making headlines every time the papers are printed?"

"Yes, I'm dating a chick magnet. What can I tell you?"

"Are you at the airport?"

"Walking down to collect my crew and plane as we speak." She dropped her purse for the security scan and showed the agent her ID.

"Before you go flying off into the wild blue yonder, stop at one of the newsstands, if one's nearby."

"Are you kidding me?" She looked at the front page of one of the national rags and saw herself staring back under a headline that read WOMAN WHO BAGGED KONG.

The photographer had captured her in an unguarded moment, her hands pressed together and standing on her feet like she was cheering something Parker had done on the court. Despite her FDNY ball cap and sunglasses, anyone who knew her would recognize her.

"I wanted to give you a heads-up before you get teased about it."

"Thanks." She continued to stare at the photo, and her immobility started to make the customers around her stare as well.

"Are you mad?"

"No, honey, just surprised that anyone would do this. I'm nobody."

"You're kidding, right? You're the woman who bagged Kong. I think the mayor may honor you with a medal this afternoon when you get back," Parker said, then sighed.

"What's wrong?"

"I'll tell you about it this afternoon. Fly safe and I love you."

She wanted to call Parker back and find out why she suddenly sounded so frustrated, but she was running late for her preflight checks. Surprisingly no one stood behind the desk at the gate when she got there, so she walked down the Jetway to the plane to meet the crew.

Turning the corner, she could feel the heat in her face when every single employee in the vicinity stood by the door holding a newspaper and pen. The heat of her blush only increased when they started to clap and chant the mantra that had reverberated through center court the day before: "Kong."

"Way to go, Killer. We didn't know you had it in you," Willy teased before he hugged her.

"I'm not going to be able to greet passengers, am I?"

"Captain, you're in love and I'm happy for you. You are in love, aren't you?"

"Blissfully."

"Then don't sweat it. We did that because we like you, not to embarrass you. If by some wild chance some uptight passenger recognizes you and gives you a hard time over this picture, they'll find something extra in their coffee, so don't give up your routine. Besides, you were just too tempting to pass up, considering what you were wearing. No wonder they put you on the cover."

"I thought Parker would get a kick out of it, so I wore it as a joke." She looked at the T-shirt in the picture and laughed. When she'd dressed, her top selection had seemed right. Hanging off the Empire State Building was King Kong trying to knock some planes out of the sky, the bottom caption asking, *Who's Your Monkey?*

"So?" Willy asked.

"What?" She folded the paper and stored it with her bag.

"What's the answer?"

"William, at times like this it's important to remember how young Parker King is compared to us." She paused and Willy leaned closer and nodded. "It truly boggles the mind how many slang off-color expressions Park knows with the word *monkey* in them. So the simplest way to answer that question is, no comment."

"Any with spanking involved?" Willy's question made her ears hot.

"Out."

"Can you sign this for me before I go?"

"Out." She pointed to the door but laughed at him.

❖

"What can I do for you, Officer?" Parker asked as he pointed to the spot next to her. She'd watched him walk across the practice court with an unhappy expression, but she didn't want to burden Sydney before her flight.

"Good morning, Ms. King." Logan put his hands on his knees.

"Please call me Parker. Do you have more questions? If you do, I'm not sure how much more I can help you except maybe refer you to Alicia's agent. She's a handful he's been able to keep under wraps for a while now, but she's more known for excessive partying than violence."

"I came by to tell you that Alicia made bail and was released this morning."

"How much?"

"How much what?" Logan seemed confused.

"How much was her bail?"

She could feel Logan's eyes on her but she kept hers on Natasha and Beau as they entered the facility. "That's an interesting question, I believe it was $150,000. Why do you ask?"

"I'm figuring that when Sydney gets home and tries to kill her, it's nice to know that it'll only cost me fifteen grand to get her out of jail. It's only ten percent of the total, right?"

Logan laughed and nodded. "That's right. I wanted to ask you, though, who do you think it was outside the restaurant when you first got to town? Do you think Alicia had someone working for her?"

"Detective Sully, this is my coach Beau and my practice partner Natasha." She waved to them when they stopped in front of the bench. "To answer your question, I don't know. I've been receiving those threats for months now, but my pen pal hasn't acted on any of his promises."

"So no idea who the first assailant might have been?"

"None. All we have are the letters the bozo keeps sending, talking about God and sin. I guess you get extra heaven credit for killing the lesbian who he's fixated on. Then again it could've been a crime of opportunity. Crazy person with knife and ski mask whose hobby it is to hang around nice restaurants on the off chance I have reservations."

Logan shook his head and laughed along with Beau and Natasha. "Good theory, but I'm thinking no. I want to concentrate on that crime, since we already know who committed the second attack. And please, call me Logan." He handed her a card with his information on it but didn't stand. "Alicia was probably copying the first crime and got the idea from the note we found in her apartment. It was a photocopy. Any idea how she got that?"

"Alicia spent some time with my coach and me this summer, so she probably took one of the copies Beau carries with him in case we get more fan mail."

"Makes sense. We'll be in touch if we find anything else."

"Thanks. It'll be nice having someone watch my back aside from

Beau and everyone else who loves me. I don't like having to put them in danger as well, so it's a relief you're armed. Do you play?" She handed Beau the card so she could grab a racquet.

"Just enough to know how bad I am."

"Stick around, then, and see if we can show you some new tricks."

"I first saw you play in the French Open a couple of years ago, and I've been a fan ever since," Logan said.

"Thanks." She stood and stretched. "I remember that match and the heat."

"Remember, I'm a phone call away if you need something."

She nodded before jogging out to the court. "Hopefully all we'll have to talk about is tennis," she called back to him, but that was unlikely until her number one fan was caught.

❖

"Ladies and gentleman, if you would, please pick up your trays and bring your seats to their full and upright positions. We'll be on the ground shortly. The temperature in New York is a balmy eighty-six degrees and the local time is nine fifteen. Any of the personnel on board will be happy to help you with any connecting flight information. On behalf of myself and the crew, we want to thank you for flying with us today, and we hope to serve you with all your future flying needs." Sydney turned off the microphone and concentrated on the landing lights into JFK.

"Good job, guys. I'm glad this day's finally over." She checked her position again and made some minor adjustments for their final approach. The layover in Dallas had been extended by forty-five minutes because of an idiot who'd tried to get through security with a loaded gun. That and the newspaper coverage of her were running a close race to trample on her last nerve.

"Anytime, Syd. Any chance we'll get to meet Kong at the airport? We heard we missed out a couple of days ago," her navigator kidded her, ignoring her quick glare.

She stood at the door with the rest of the crew to bid farewell to the last passengers. If she hurried she might be able to get home before eleven and Parker wouldn't be asleep. When the crew slowed in front of her, she wondered why the waiting area was still crowded, considering the hour. The sight confirmed that if Parker was the person she was going to spend the rest of her life with, and she fully planned on it, their time together would never be boring or lack practical jokes.

Parker, wearing an animal tag from her ear and a leash around her neck, was signing autographs for some laughing fans. Not until she turned and faced the crew could they read the T-shirt that answered the question Sydney's had asked. The *Bagged and Tagged* caption had all of them wiping tears from their eyes and her shaking her head.

Yep, definitely not boring, she thought, and laughed when Parker handed her the leash when she got close enough. "And don't you forget it, Kong. I have witnesses," she said before she kissed Parker hello. "What are you doing here? You're supposed to be home resting for tomorrow."

"I have good news and not-so-good news, but we'll talk about that later. Why don't you introduce me to all these good-looking uniformed people milling around behind you?"

She turned in Parker's arms and introduced her crew, feeling the bicep resting against her shoulder flex every time Parker shook hands with someone new. The urge to give some of them bathroom-cleaning duty crossed her mind when they flirted outright with Parker.

"This might come in handy," she said as she pulled lightly on the leash before unbuckling it from Parker's neck. They held hands as they walked to where Bobbie stood waiting. Along the way Parker told her about Logan's visit and why.

"They let her out? She tried to kill you."

"She did, and a lot of cat gut made the ultimate sacrifice for me," Parker joked.

"This isn't funny. People who do that don't deserve to be walking around. She's probably planning her next strike now."

"I'm sure Alicia's trying to find a good attorney, not another way to kill me. I just wanted to come down here and tell you so you wouldn't be pissed when you heard it from someone else, but I see that's wishful thinking," Parker said as she opened the back door of the car.

"I'm not mad at you. It's just not fair that you have to worry about this the night before your match."

Parker kissed her again as she ran her fingers through her hair. "I'm not worried, and I don't want you to be either."

"Yeah, why's that?" Parker's touch and her lips so close to her ear were a turn-on. It amazed her that lust beat out concern.

"You should be more worried about what Bobbie's going to think of you when you don't talk to her because you're making out with me in the backseat. But just in case she's listening, she should keep her eyes on the road instead of the rearview mirror. If she gets into a wreck trying to get some new pointers, we'll give her name and address to the papers and tell them she's the one that knocked me out of the Open. Bookies everywhere would be happy to come over for a visit," Parker said, loud enough for Bobbie to hear her, then laughed in a way that made it sound as if it came from deep in her belly.

By the time they got to the apartment, Bobbie probably needed a cold shower, and Sydney needed to be carried up the stairs because her legs refused to move except to come apart.

"Hurry with the key, honey," she demanded. Parker had put her down and propped her against the wall to get the door open. "I need you."

Parker carried her to the bedroom. When she laid her on the bed and had her skirt halfway off, Sydney stopped any further advance.

"We have to stop, Parker."

"Stop? I don't think so," Parker said as she peeled her T-shirt off.

"Yes, we do. You've got a match tomorrow, and remember what happened the last time. I don't want Beau to make you stay at the hotel because I can't control myself."

"That's the point, I don't want you to control yourself." Parker threw her skirt over her shoulder and got her panties off with no problem. When she started on the buttons of her blouse, Sydney tried to squirm farther up the bed and out of Parker's reach.

"I mean it, you have to stop."

Parker knelt on the bed and moved closer until she was beside her. "You want me to stop?"

"Yes, I do," she said, her eyes on Parker's naked chest. "I don't want to, but we have to be good."

Parker ran her fingers through her drenched sex, and she couldn't help but moan at how good it felt and how badly she needed Parker to make her come. "You want me to stop doing this?"

"No. I mean yes! Don't do that."

Parker withdrew her fingers and brought them up to paint a wet spot on her blouse over a hard nipple. "How about this? Should I stop doing this too?" Parker asked before she bit down gently over the material.

With frantic movements, Sydney came close to ripping the material when she pawed at it to get it off. Once she had, Parker rolled on top of her and sucked hard on her nipple, almost making her climax. When Parker put her hand between her legs, she exercised the last of her willpower and grabbed her wrist. "We really shouldn't."

"Come on, Syd, you know you want this. I can feel you want this," Parker said, and wiggled her fingers surrounded in wet heat to make her point.

That snapped the last of her hesitation. "Take off your clothes before you get too caught up, baby," she said, and watched Parker take her sweatpants off.

Naked, Parker covered Sydney with her body and took a second to enjoy the feel of soft skin. Sydney's short nails dragging up her back made her roll over until Sydney was on top, which made it easy to touch her.

When Sydney's hips started to move, taking her fingers all the way in with each downward stroke, Parker stopped her. "Not yet, honey, I'm not there yet," Sydney protested.

"Kneel down for me," she said, which made Sydney blush for some reason, but she nodded.

Sydney grabbed the headboard and glanced down at the first touch of her tongue. "You taste so good," Parker said as she snaked her hand up between Sydney's legs. "You're so wet." She ran her tongue the length of Sydney's sex, swirling it around Sydney's clitoris. "You want me, baby?"

"So much," Sydney said, and released one hand and pulled Parker's hair to make her put her mouth back on her.

She didn't make Sydney wait any longer and sucked her clit against the roof of her mouth before slipping two fingers in.

"Oh, God," Sydney said, sounding restless, and her hips bucked so hard Parker had a rough time keeping her lips wrapped around her pulsing clit. She hung on, though, and the moment the orgasm hit Sydney full force she held her up with her free hand so she wouldn't smash her head against the bed.

Sydney lay on her like a wet noodle and Parker held her until her breathing calmed.

"You okay?"

"I'm doing great, thanks to you," Sydney said, the words muffled because her mouth was pressed to the curve of her breast.

"I love you, and I'm glad."

"I love you too, and I want you." Sydney moved down until she was kneeling again, only this time between her legs.

"The shirt wasn't a joke, baby. I'm all yours." Sydney was about to kiss her when the phone rang. "Ignore it, they'll call back."

"It might be about your case." Sydney didn't move off her as she answered. "Hello." Sydney paused to listen. "Hey, Beau, yeah. Hang on, she's right here." Sydney handed over the receiver, then straddled her. She stared as Parker pressed the receiver to her ear and Sydney's nipples got painfully hard. When she squeezed one gently, Sydney's hips jerked forward, leaving a wet trail on her abdomen. By reflex her legs pressed together.

"Parker, are you having sex?" Beau asked as soon she grunted.

"Not that it's any of your business, but no, so whatever you want, make it snappy."

"Could you put Sydney back on the phone for me, please?"

"Yes?" Sydney asked, concentrating on Parker's eyes. When Parker put her fingers back inside she was ravenous, instantly ready again.

"Sydney, have you ever heard of Della Sanchez?"

"Should I recognize the name?" She shimmied forward at Parker's request and closed her eyes when Parker's thumb pressed against her hard clit.

"Maybe a subscription to a tennis magazine would do you good. Della Sanchez is the number five player in the world, and she knocked Parker on her ass last year during this tournament."

"Uh-huh," she said, losing track of the conversation when Parker pinched her nipple with her free hand.

"Just a few more minutes, Sydney, I promise." Beau spoke faster. "Think about how much better Park would play tomorrow if she's lacking a little something from you."

"Do you know what you're asking?" Her hips stopped at what Beau was saying.

"Do you want to live with the world's biggest whiny baby if she loses?" Beau hung up, and her sex clenched at the thought of what she had to do.

"Honey, how about a shower?" Sydney rolled off the bed.

"Now? You want to take a shower now?"

"Come on, please."

Parker got up and followed her into the bathroom. As a reward for getting out of bed she kissed Parker and turned her around and faced her away from the tub.

"I've been thinking about this since you left for work," Parker said, and kissed her again when she leaned in to turn on the water. Parker put her hand between Sydney's legs, and she almost forgot her unspoken promise to Beau. Her need to come was so great it would cause physical pain if they stopped abruptly.

"There you go." She felt guilty as she said it, but it was the only way.

The second the spray hit Parker, she blinked rapidly. Sydney stepped back in case she had to start running as Parker shut off the cold water.

"I didn't want to do it, baby. You have to believe me."

Parker calmly took a towel off the rack and started to dry her hair. "I realize that. Beau, on the other hand, is going to die the next time I see him."

Wanting to have sex again in her lifetime, Sydney just nodded. The word "behave" became her new chant as she watched Parker's butt move back toward the bed. Tomorrow afternoon couldn't come soon enough.

CHAPTER SIXTEEN

Beau, I wouldn't do it if I were you. She's still pissed, and thanks to you, I think it spilled over to me. I can't tell you how much I appreciate that." Sydney took her seat in the box and stopped Beau from heading down to the locker room and getting the short end of Parker's temper.

"It was for her own good. She'll thank me later. Hopefully she'll take out her bad mood on Della."

Sydney smoothed out the linen shirt she wore over a tank she'd pressed that morning in an effort to stay neat. Her mother had called and informed her that if she planned to appear on the cover of any more magazines she'd have to look at in the grocery checkout line, the least she could do was dress nicer. "If she doesn't, I'm taking the phone off the hook from now on."

"She's really mad?"

"Let's just say that when you called last night, I was one happy camper, and you interrupted us before I was able to, well, you know."

"Return the favor?" He laughed.

"Keep it up, and I'll let you foolishly wander into the lion's den down there." She pointed toward the court, surprised to find Parker staring up at them with a muscular shorter woman standing next to her. "That's a really big girl."

"Yeah, and as powerful as I know Parker is, Della scares the shit out of me. She beat Parker last year in straight sets. That was bad enough, but the bitch taunted her throughout the whole match. She made Park mad enough to throw off her whole game, including her serve." Beau greeted the rest of their group, who'd arrived with drinks and snacks.

"What do you mean she taunted her?"

Gray cracked open her water as she too looked toward her sister's warm-up. She answered her before Beau had a chance. "You'll see once this match starts. I can't imagine Della's changed her style that much. She pushed too far this year and was disqualified in England, that's why she didn't play. The bitch's started the shit already, telling the papers that's the only reason Parker walked away with the title."

Parker was warming up with some serves, and from her detached expression it seemed she was trying to ignore the asshole across the net. Della smirked when Parker's first practice ball flew by her and just walked to her chair and sat down, not giving Parker the courtesy of hitting it back. The ball boy waved his hand, as if in pain from catching the ball. Della looked up into the stands, searching until she locked eyes with Sydney.

She watched Della reach into her bag and pull out the paper with her picture on it, then kiss it before blowing another kiss up at her. Della just laughed when Sydney stood up and put her hands on her hips.

"Beau, get me down there now," she said, her anger building. She'd spoken loud enough to attract some of the photographers who'd aimed their lens in her direction.

"Calm down, slugger. She's trying to get to Parker through you. Don't let that happen right before the match." Beau tugged on her hand.

"I don't want to see that overgrown adolescent. I want to see Parker before this thing starts."

Parker glanced up into the stands for Sydney before heading back down the tunnel to change her shirt before the match, surprised to find her and Beau standing where the spectators wouldn't see them. "Hey, what're you doing here?"

"Waiting to wish you luck and to tell you a few things."

"Hey, Beau, would you grab me a fresh shirt?" Beau nodded, but Della simply leaned against the tunnel wall opposite them and stared.

"Parker, if I asked you to do something for me, would you?"

"Sure, baby, if I can. What do you want?"

"Go out there and beat the crap out of that asshole over there." Sydney pointed to Della and aimed her middle finger at her when the woman blew her another kiss.

Parker smiled at Sydney before putting her arms around her. "And what do I get if I pull that off? You know she's the one that beat the crap out of *me* last year?"

Sydney peeled Parker's shirt off for her when they heard Beau behind them and draped it over her shoulder. She accepted a towel from Beau and dried her off before helping her put on a fresh top. When she'd tucked in the new billboard, as she called Parker's shirts, she dragged Parker's head down and kissed her.

"You want to know what you get?" She nodded, and Sydney pulled her back down and whispered in her ear. The little speech was hot enough to make Parker so weak in the knees she had to prop her back against the wall. Sydney kissed her ear and looked up at her when she finished.

"Really?"

"Yes, more than once if you want, and I'll even take the phone off the hook, but only if I get to come back here Saturday to watch you play in the finals."

"You should give motivational classes," Parker said as she and Della watched Sydney unbutton her own shirt.

"For luck." Sydney tucked it into Parker's bag and put on the shirt Parker had taken off. "I have to admit these look a lot better on you," Sydney said as she glanced down at the loose-fitting garment.

"You look good in my clothes, baby, and as soon as I'm finished kicking Della's ass, you'll look even better out of them," she whispered before shouldering her bag. "See you soon."

The opponents had been introduced and had taken their places by the time Beau and Sydney made it back to their seats. Della was serving first, and while Parker jumped on every ball that came over the net, the level of Della's play held and she won the game. When the network cut to commercial and Parker had a few minutes' reprieve, she noticed the paparazzi had their lenses aimed at Sydney, who was biting her thumbnail when Della broke her serve and went up by two games to none.

It amazed Parker less than an hour later as she sat toweling off her face that she'd lost the first set without winning a game. She looked toward Della, watching the last of the water she was drinking slide down her throat. She didn't even look all that winded.

"Do you think she'll deliver all the stuff she promised you if I win? Tell her I'm staying at the Hilton if she's only interested in sleeping with the winner. All that delicious skin looked mighty inviting."

Obviously Della was trying to shatter what was left of her concentration. "She's not your type, Della." She sounded calm despite wanting to get up and smash every racquet in her bag over the woman's head.

"Blond, beautiful, and sexy. What about all that isn't my type?"

"She's all that, but she's not into assholes. I could recommend a good charm school for the off season."

"Laugh it up, King. Forty minutes to go before you get to go home to the little bitch so she can lick your wounds. I'm about to knock Kong off her perch."

"What Sydney licks on me is really not any of your business."

"Quiet, please."

She waited for the crowd to follow the official's instructions before she turned around and asked for some balls. It was time to give Della Sanchez a taste of what she loved to dish out.

"Fifteen-love." The score got the crowd into the game and the announcer to scream into every pair of radio headphones in the stadium. She'd woken up from the nap she'd been taking during the first set with an ace to start the second.

She felt good and looked forward to the next two sets, because hell if she was losing this match. To get Della even madder than she was from swinging and missing the serve, she winked at her before she served again. This time the ball came over the net with the same intensity and Della got a piece of it, only to have it skitter off into the stands. The crowd went wild when Parker twirled her racquet and pretended to holster it after "thirty-love" came over the loud speakers.

The crowd was squarely in her corner, but Della should've been grateful since the cheering drowned her out. Her colorful outburst would've gotten her thrown out if the chair had heard all the curse words.

The next hour full of long, blistering volleys started to cause wear on Della's face. As a power player she wasn't used to this amount of running, and with each sprint from one end of the court to the other, Della's face got redder.

In the middle of the third set, Della stopped play for at least five minutes to have an argument with the line judge over what she deemed to be a questionable call. Parker just bounced the ball and looked up into the stands, waving back to Sydney, who'd stood and blown her a kiss.

"Game, set, and match, Miss King." The announcement came after she'd broken Della's serve for the third time in the third match. She shook hands with Della at the net and tried to ignore the quick "Fuck you" Della offered when she turned and waved toward the crowd. The win put her that much closer to the only title she didn't have.

As in all her other matches, she stopped at the entrance to the tunnel and took time to sign autographs. She picked randomly from the pieces of paper that were being held over the side, along with pens. In an automatic move she grabbed the one closest to her hand when she'd finished signing the program a kid had passed her. It wasn't until she had it in her hand that she noticed her name on it written with the same calligraphy as the others. When she looked back into the crowd, she couldn't tell who it belonged to in the sea of faces. Waving quickly, she turned and walked back into the tunnel, leaving a horde of disappointed fans clutching unsigned programs.

"Honey, that was brilliant," Sydney yelled when they made it down to the locker room after the match. Parker was pumped by the win but tired. The heat was starting to drain her, the hard court surface only intensifying the temperature.

"I aim to please," she said, before grabbing her stuff to go.

"You aimed for the baselines and kicked the shit out of Della," Beau said.

"You, I'm not talking to, and if you put your fingers anywhere near a phone to call Sydney's apartment, New York City won't be big enough to hide you."

"Parker, apologize to Beau."

"I help you win and this is the thanks I get?" Beau tried to sound wounded.

"It's nice to know that you attribute all my skill to sexual frustration, Coach."

"If that's the case, you ain't getting any until after Saturday." Sydney squealed when Parker picked her up, threw her over her shoulder, and started for the door. "Parker, my mother has seen me on the cover of the *Enquirer* once this week. You make it two and there'll be hell to pay."

She put Sydney down and tried to maintain her good mood. It was hard, considering the love note she'd been handed before coming down the tunnel. She was kicking herself now for not paying attention to who'd handed her the envelope. Whoever it was wasn't content with the courier service anymore. She'd recognized the fanciful handwriting the moment she'd opened it. Her decision not to tell Sydney, she convinced herself, was to protect her from worry.

Later when they got to the apartment, Sydney enlightened her with what seemed to be an important lesson in relationships, centering on an open-dialogue lecture after she let her read the note. It was just one of the many ways she figured Sydney would change her life, but getting to share her days with her made a lecture on anything worthwhile.

❖

"Call him right now."

"Let's go take a shower, then I will. Come on, Syd. It's not like the stalker's going to burst in here and kill me," she reasoned. Their argument had started at the front door when she had made the mistake of showing Sydney the letter.

The nut who sent it had attached the picture of Sydney that'd been in the paper, promising to save her from Parker's evil influence, which strangely made her feel good that the threat hadn't spilled over to Sydney. The more she looked at it, the more it niggled her that she should recognize something about the letters and the way they were written. It was odd for someone who wanted to kill you to use old-fashioned calligraphy to pen the death notice. Instead of a simple overt threat, it was almost like a polite invitation for you to die at the time they decided.

Sydney picked up the phone and handed it to her, along with the card Logan had given her when he dropped by her practice.

"This is serious, Parker. Some crazy person out there wants to send you to the big tennis court in the sky, and it's time for you to start treating that threat with some degree of respect." Sydney put the phone down for a moment, walked to where she was sitting on the bed, and stood between her legs. "I love you, Kong, and I want you around for years to come. Please do it for me?"

"For you, anything," she said, and accepted the phone. It didn't take a lot of arm-twisting to get Logan to agree to meet them at Sydney's apartment.

At Sydney's urging she lay down and didn't wake until Sydney came to tell her Logan was there. He was already reading the letter through the clear evidence bag he'd placed it in when she joined him in the kitchen.

"I'm sure this will be like the others, no prints or DNA, but I'll have it tested," he said as he stripped his gloves off. "I'll call you once I know for sure."

"Thanks." She propped herself against the counter and tried not to yawn. Even after a nap she still felt fatigued. "We'll be here, I guess."

"It'll make me feel better if you stay inside for now. The stalker actually handed this note to you, so try not to put yourself in harm's way."

"So I hide until this asshole finds a new hobby?" She crossed her arms over her chest.

"I can understand how frustrating you find the situation, Parker, but you have to be careful. This guy, he's trying to make a point or a name for himself, and you don't want to give him the satisfaction."

"Don't worry. She's not going out until we can keep her safe," Sydney said, and from her tone Parker didn't see any sense in arguing.

❖

Eric and Ethan Prophet stood in the alley a block away from Sydney's front door and pointed when Logan stepped outside with a large envelope under his arm. Their brother Abel stood close by on the sidewalk, propped against a tree with his eyes closed, working through the rosary in his hand.

"Look," Ethan said in a loud whisper, as if Logan might hear him if he raised his voice, even though Logan had gotten in his car.

Abel opened his eyes in time to see Logan pull away, and he squeezed the cross so hard it cut into his hand. They'd watched Parker and Sydney arrive earlier and had decided to watch the house to see if they'd go out for the night. Not that Abel planned to hurt Parker yet, but if he had the chance to get close to Sydney before that, he would. While he waited he'd methodically moved from bead to bead as he prayed for the opportunity to rid the world of Parker King. She would be the first of the King sisters to receive salvation through death.

"Are you sure you got the stomach for this, Abel?" Eric asked. He still clutched the rosary in his hand, the beads wrapped around his wrist. "You've been away from us so long," Eric said, to taunt him as they walked. "Your pretty beads and fancy clothes make you look like a faggot. You sure you don't want to go back there and hang around with your queer friends?"

"What's your problem?" Abel turned suddenly, grabbed Eric by the throat, and slammed him against the nearest building. Eric didn't move when he pressed the cross to the side of his neck, as if sensing how sharp it was. Next to them Ethan bounced on the tips of his toes with his hands on his head. "You tell me now or get the hell away from me until this is over."

"Abel, please," Ethan said as his tears fell fast.

"Well?" he asked, and pressed harder against Eric's throat until drops of blood ran into his collar. "It don't matter how long I been gone. I'm back, and I'm gonna cleanse the evil out of that bitch or die trying. You either help me or get away from me."

"Sorry," Eric said as soon as he let him go. "You found that girl and forgot about us."

Abel didn't need any other explanation. His brothers had been ten when he'd left, and he shuddered when he imagined how their father must've acted out his frustrations once he'd cleared out.

He'd run for what he thought was love, but his father's teachings got louder in his head as his fake life started to unravel. "You can't outrun the Lord," his father had always said, and he'd been right. Besides, he was tired of hiding behind the façade he'd meticulously built because he was ashamed of his past. It was time to go back to what he knew best, and killing Parker and her sisters was the price to get his father to accept him again.

"I'm sorry too, but when we're done here I won't be leaving you again."

"You swear," Ethan said.

"I swear, so let's go get ready."

They took a cab back to their hotel and nodded to the clerk behind the metal mesh. They'd paid for three weeks in cash, and another hundred to the maid to stay out of their room. The Do Not Disturb sign hung permanently from their knob, and the small slip of paper was still wedged close to the top, a sign no one had entered after their morning out.

He had to jiggle the key in the lock to make the mechanism work, and his brothers stood close behind even though they were alone in the hallway. Their collection of knives was still perfectly lined on the dresser, so shiny the sunlight that made it through the grimy window made them sparkle. They had wrapped one of them in heavy linen since it was special. It still had the blood of the beast on it from their failed attempt outside the restaurant.

"Let's pray," he said, and all three of them fell to their knees around the small inflatable pool with chicken wire over it, sitting between the beds. "I'm the alpha and the omega, the beginning and the end. He who believes in me shall know the kingdom of heaven."

"Yes, brother," Eric said.

"Lord, I need you to guide my hand in defeating the beast." Abel lifted the chicken wire slowly. "The crowds who don't know no better love her." He reached inside and provoked a warning rattle, but it didn't stop him. God was on the side of the righteous and protected his warriors from the serpents.

"Send me a sign that I'm on the right path." The thick powerful body of the diamondback rattlesnake coiled tightly around his arm but was still able to shake its tail. Once it was firmly in place he reached for another one, and it wrapped around his other arm. Both snakes were agitated, their tails shaking vigorously, but he lifted them until they were at eye level. Their heads were pulled back in strike position and he placed them close to his face to give them the opportunity to attack him.

"I've lived my life serving you," he whispered. Sweat covered his face. "You strike down the unbeliever and those who go against your word, using the soldiers brave enough to do Your bidding. We know you have no compassion or mercy for those who live outside your word. There's no room for indecency or sin."

Eric and Ethan nodded but stayed quiet. The larger snake opened its mouth, its rattle moving furiously, but didn't strike. A drop of venom dripped from its fangs, though, and dropped to his arm as if in baptism. "Thank you, Lord. I'm ready to do your work, and the time to rid the world of my sins is at hand."

He lowered his arms and held his breath as the snakes released him and slithered back to the others in the pool. Eric covered them again and stared at him as if in awe.

"I've only seen Pa do that."

"Leaving you was a mistake, but I know now what's important."

Eric and Ethan stared at his crotch, as if their father had programmed them as to how this ritual ended. If the Lord rewarded you with life, it was an insult not to celebrate it. This was Abel's gift for his steadfast devotion, and he planned to enjoy it without guilt. The days of denying or shunning his urges were over.

"Take your pants off now," he said forcibly, feeling joy and freedom for the first time in years when they did.

❖

"Why does your hair always smell so good?"

"I saw the brand of shampoo you wear on your right sleeve and decided to try it," Sydney said. She was curled up on the bed with Parker pressed against her back.

"Keep it up and I may have to spank you."

"That's an interesting thought, but Logan's due back any minute and I want to be dressed when he arrives."

"Where's your sense of adventure, baby? Wouldn't Mother Parish love to read about her little girl's wild and sexy ways if Logan sells his story?"

"Keep it up and my mother will give you a lecture you won't soon forget. She already thinks you're a bad influence on me."

"I can't be that bad since I can't talk you out of these shorts."

Sydney turned and ran her finger along Parker's lips. "Maybe after you win the Open we can spend some time with my mom? I want her and Margo to get to know you."

"How about even if I don't win the Open we invite them to the beach for as long as they'd like?"

"You wouldn't mind?"

Parker kissed her before she got up. "You can invite anyone you like since we'll be a team," she said from the bathroom. Any teasing she had planned flew from her head when Parker's phone started to ring. "Could you answer that for me? It's probably Beau."

"Parker King's phone," she said.

"God, she has her playthings answering for her now." The female voice was slightly slurred but Sydney couldn't mistake the venom in the statement. "Run along, dear, and fetch Parker for me, would you?"

"Can I ask who's calling?"

"Are we trying to make points for being a good little girl? Trust me, sweetheart, Parker lives her life in a candy store. That's a fine way to exist if you aren't a glutton, but my Parker was born with quite the sweet tooth. So, gumdrop, don't get delusions of grandeur that she'll keep you around once she's bedded you, and put her on the goddamn phone."

"Who is it, baby?" Parker asked as she bent to get her shoes.

"I don't know, but she really wants to talk to you." Sydney held the phone out, then pressed close when Parker sat on the bed.

"Hello." Parker's back stiffened in reflex when she heard the voice on the other end. "No, Mother, and I'd prefer you didn't use that word when it comes to Sydney."

"And I won't have you use that tone with me, Parker. Besides, we both know just how capable you are with women. You and your sisters are hard to miss every time you make the headlines because of some slut or other. If this one gets upset, I'm sure a dozen are ready to take her place."

"Do you need something, or are you just in the mood to share your Jack haze?" She relaxed a bit when Sydney kissed the side of her neck. Despite the circumstances, she gave her the best smile.

"Parker?"

"What? We both know our realities as well as our shortcomings, so why pretend they don't exist?" Judging by the clink of ice against glass, Susan King took a sip of her ever-present cocktail, thereby proving her point. Her favorite was Jack Daniel's with a splash of Coke, though by now the mixer had become almost a garnish. "What do you want?"

"I called to congratulate you for your win."

Parker pinched the skin on her forehead, trying to stave off the headache she felt coming on. Conversing with her mother was like taking a huge swig of ipecac. She was suddenly nauseous. "I'm in the middle of a tournament, so your call's a little premature."

"I'm talking about England. I watched it on television and you did well. Jorge said your win even inspired my play."

"Who's Jorge?" she asked reluctantly, because she wasn't anxious to hear the answer.

"My new tennis instructor, and he's a big fan of yours. I'm sure your ears must be ringing from all the conversations we've had about you."

"What happened to the other guy you were taking lessons from?"

"Your father had a run-in with him and he moved on. Not that you'll ever ask about your father, but he's become more righteous than ever. He's completely insufferable, and you and your sisters aren't making it any easier for me, you know."

"We've been through this and nothing changes, so just tell me what you want." Sydney pulled her hand away from her head and placed it over her heart since she now sat on her lap.

"The check's late and I have bills. You're so wrapped up in yourself you forget about my responsibilities."

"I'm sure keeping Jorge in new tennis whites and your country-club dues current takes money. I'd hate to think how you would've managed if I hadn't been any good." She tried for sarcasm but her pain made her fail.

"Just call Nick and find out what the holdup is."

"It'll have to wait for a few days. I'm sure the transfer will appear in your account soon. Nick never forgets to send it."

"Well, your little faggy friend did, so check on it."

She sighed and prayed for patience. "I'm in the middle of a major tournament so your allowance isn't a priority. If you need money that bad, ask Dad."

"I haven't seen your father in weeks. Not that I care, but I think the high-and-mighty one has finally run off with someone." The sound of ice came again and Susan laughed hysterically right afterward. "That asshole. All these years of pointing out everyone else's sins, and he runs out on me. You all did, so don't think about cutting me off."

"Where is he?"

"How the hell should I know, Parker? It's not like I'm dying for him to come home. All I care about right this minute is that transfer." With that the line went dead.

"It's okay, baby," Sydney said softly as she pulled her head to her shoulder when the tears started. "Whatever it is, it'll be okay."

Parker felt drained when the tears finally stopped, but the feeling was familiar. These calls from her mother came routinely, and no amount of strength she imagined she had made a difference. To have the one woman who shouldn't want her only for materialistic things make such a call cut into places she didn't even realize could hurt so bad.

It took fifteen minutes of holding Parker and running her fingers through her hair, but Sydney finally got her to go to sleep. Even in sleep she could see the sadness on Parker's face. The story Parker had started that night in her house had many more chapters, Sydney was sure of that, but she refused to stop until she knew all of it. That was the only way to help Parker through it.

Quietly she slipped out of bed and dressed in the bathroom, not wanting to disturb Parker. She left a note on the pillow still warm from where she lay, then took Parker's cell and went to the kitchen. She didn't think Parker would mind what she was doing as she searched for Gray King's number.

"Hey, runt."

The greeting made her smile, and a bit of the horror of what Parker had gone through during the call from her mother disappeared. And that's what it had been. She'd seen it etched on Parker's face. "The runt's taking a nap, so you're stuck with me."

"Sydney, this is a good surprise."

"Do you have time to talk?" She pulled herself up on the kitchen counter so she wouldn't have to sit on the floor.

"I'm all yours. What's up?"

She described the call and how Parker had been after it was over. She was almost betraying Parker's trust, but she couldn't help her if she didn't understand her family dynamic. "Your mother's a different kind of parent, isn't she?"

"Susan is no one's parent, Sydney. I've always believed all of us are born with a special talent. Mine and Kimmie's is volleyball, and Park's is tennis, among other things, but Susan's only talent is taking care of Susan."

"Can anyone keep her from getting to Parker?"

"When the tournament is over, we need to have another family meeting. We cut this deal with her a long time ago and Nick set it up, but now might be the time to renegotiate the terms."

"Renegotiate how?" She listened for Parker but the apartment was still quiet.

"We all need to face the facts that neither of our parents will ever accept anything about us. If that's true, why subject ourselves to the abuse as well as pay for the privilege?"

"Do you think that's best for Parker?" As much pain as the strained relationship with her parents brought Parker, cutting them completely out of her life could bring its own slew of mental land mines.

"The best thing for Parker is you, and all she needs from you is love. If she has that, the rest will take care of itself. Kimmie and I tried to give her what our parents stole from her, but we always knew when she found the right person, we'd fade a little into the background of her life. That's okay with me, though, because you really are the right person for her."

"Thanks," Sydney said, not needing to be validated, but the words made her smile anyway. "Can I do anything to make this better?"

"Just be with her, and know that you aren't alone. We love Parker, and we'll all get over hurricane Susan just fine together. And, Sydney," Gray said softly.

"Yes?"

"Please call me whenever you like. Parker's the best, but sometimes it's good to consult somebody who wrote her instruction manual. If you ever need to talk, I promise to listen and give advice sparingly."

Gray's soft side made her laugh. "You got it, and thanks."

"One more thing, she's nuts about hot chocolate, but after a talk with our mother, take her somewhere that has a great red velvet cake. Works every time, no matter how deep the funk."

Sydney checked on Parker one more time forty minutes later, finding her awake. The buzzer made her look toward the front door, but she didn't move. "Are you okay?"

Parker nodded before moving her head from side to side to crack the bones. "Those calls always get to me, but they don't happen often, so I try not to dwell on them." The buzzer rang again and Parker nodded toward the front of the house. "Go ahead, I'm fine."

"How goes the manhunt, Logan?" Parker asked when she joined them.

"Interesting."

"I'd offer you a place to sit, but Sydney hasn't gone furniture shopping yet. How about the three of us go grab an early dinner? When you're finished telling me about the psycho who's chasing me, I'll give you some tennis pointers."

Logan gave them a ride to a small family-owned Italian restaurant Sydney had read about and waited for them to settle at a table before he started talking about the case. "We sent the last note you received to the FBI for analysis, and the findings surprised us."

"Surprised like finding prints everyone's missed up to now?" Parker asked.

"No prints, but there's one distinct clue."

"What's that?" Sydney took the fifth bread stick Parker was about to eat away from her.

"What? I'm hungry."

"It'll spoil your appetite for the tremendous amount of food you ordered, so be quiet and pay attention." She turned back to Logan and nodded for him to continue.

"The FBI tested the ink, thinking there might be something unique about it that we could use to narrow our search. The ink's common, but they did find rattlesnake venom mixed in. That's unique, but it doesn't point us in a certain direction."

Sydney stared at the salad the waiter delivered, but next to her Parker started to twirl the fettuccini she'd ordered as an appetizer, getting ready to take a bite. Parker acted as unaffected as if Logan had been discussing the weather.

"Where do you buy rattlesnake venom?" Parker asked. "Is there a special section of eBay I've never heard of?"

The joke made Sydney get up and run toward the back in search of the bathroom. She picked the last stall, and after she'd locked herself in she heard someone come in and, under the next stall, saw Parker's tennis shoes. For some reason they made her cry harder.

"Can I come in?" Parker asked, but she didn't answer. "Please don't shut me out." Parker's head was visible over the divider, which meant she was standing on the next toilet.

"What will it take for you to start taking this seriously? It doesn't seem fair that I just found you and someone's trying their damnedest to kill you. No matter what, though, you laugh it all off like it's some joke. These people are serious. The scar on your chest that's still red should be proof enough."

"Open the door for me a second, please?"

After she unlatched the lock and the door swung back and hit the wall, Parker's body seemed to fill the opening. Parker knelt before her.

"I can't live in fear, Syd. It's not who I am. While nothing of this magnitude has happened before, I won't let it change who I am inside. If I do that, I'll have to walk away from you, and no one, especially you, can ask me to do that. As long as they're after me, I don't have to worry about you, and I want to keep it that way. I love you, and I know you worry, but this isn't going to beat us or me."

"You can't promise that."

"I can and I will. I promise you, baby, this creep with the snake ink won't get near me. You might think I'm brushing this off, but I'm careful."

"You were careful outside that restaurant and look how close they got. This guy hurt you. The only lucky thing about that was he didn't kill you."

Parker held her hands and nodded. "He did hurt me, and Alicia tried as well. Nothing in life is a guarantee except how I feel about you. If I'm afraid all the time, it'll harm our relationship, so that's why I fight hard against giving in to it."

"Is it wrong to want you to be careful?"

"No, and I'll check my surroundings even more carefully. If this madman went to all the trouble to milk some deadly snake to pen me a letter, I think he's seriously deranged, so I'll take whatever steps I have to for us to be safe. Come on before your salad gets cold."

"It's a salad, Parker, it's supposed to be cold." She accepted the hand up, but appreciated the hug she got more when she was on her feet.

"Yeah, but I'm thinking Alfredo's turning over in his grave when he sees what a congealed mess my fettuccini has turned into."

"Sorry, Logan," she said when they made it back to the table.

"I understand what you're going through, Sydney, don't worry about it. I just don't understand why this guy's so fixated on Parker. There are plenty of gay athletes out there. Maybe because she makes the papers a little more than the others with her life off the court."

Sydney stabbed her salad and looked up at Parker with an arched brow. "Those days are over, I can promise you that. Otherwise she'll be making the papers for another set of reasons."

"It was bound to happen," Parker said.

"What's that, honey?" She took Parker's hand.

"I've gone from being the Hugh Hefner of the courts to being henpecked so fast I'm getting whiplash."

Logan laughed at the confession, and she joined him. "Getting back to your case, besides the venom-laced ink, the letters contained no fingerprints, and thousands of stores across the country sell the stationery. My friends at the bureau did agree to work up a profile on our stalker and see where exactly we should concentrate our efforts. I keep saying *he*, but in reality this could be a woman."

"Well, if part of the profile includes throwing drinks on Parker for any reason, you may have your work cut out for you," she said, and Logan looked at her like he didn't understand.

"Happens that often, does it?" Logan asked, with the same teasing tone she'd used.

"I'm guilty of doing it myself once, but you can count me out now since I'll let you know my whereabouts when the notes were sent. That and the fact I'm terrified of snakes." She kissed Parker's cheek, trying to get rid of the pout she'd helped put there.

They spent the rest of the meal talking about Logan's tennis game. Sydney decided to buy a racquet and try to learn the basics. With any luck she'd be able to talk Parker into playing a slow game with her on her great court at home.

"Red velvet?" Parker asked when she ordered dessert.

"They say it's the best in the city."

"What else did Gray tell you about me?" Parker asked as she cut off a piece with plenty of icing.

"Nothing terrible." She accepted the piece Parker offered her. "Are you mad?"

"Not likely, if you can find cake this good."

After Parker paid for dinner, Logan gave them a ride home with a promise to keep them informed about what both the NYPD and FBI discovered in the investigation.

"Hurry up, honey, I have a promise to keep," she said when she put her hands under Parker's shirt as she tried to unlock the door.

"If you don't behave you'll have to get naked out here in the hall."

The lock finally relented and Parker picked her up and she wrapped her legs around Parker's waist for the ride to the bedroom. She bit Parker's bottom lip softly to try to rile her up, but from Parker's breathing she was as ready as she was. It was good to feel the bed under her and Parker on top of her when they reached the bedroom, but the out-of-place sound stopped them both.

"Syd, don't move." Parker glanced up slowly and saw the lump right next to Sydney's head under the sheet. Caught up in each other, neither of them had noticed it when they walked in, and even if they had studied the bed, the spot that was now moving looked like a fold in the sheet.

"What is that?" Sydney asked when the rattling got louder, and Parker saw how fast her pulse was when she glanced at her neck.

"It's either a really big motion-controlled vibrator—"

"I don't own a vibrator," Sydney whispered, "and do not make me laugh and shake the bed."

"Or it's a rattlesnake."

"What're we going to do?"

"Lock your legs around my waist and slowly put your arms around my neck."

"Why?"

"Baby, I love talking to you, you know that, but having long conversations in a bed with a pit viper isn't my idea of a hot time." The snake uncoiled and slithered closer, which made the rattle sound twice as loud.

They moved off the bed together and toward the door, with Sydney hanging on to Parker like the thing had become airborne and was close to landing on her head. When she last looked the fangs had broken through the sheet inches from where Sydney's head had been. Whoever had done this had gone too far now, and she hoped the bozo was finally ready to come out of hiding.

"Wait here," Parker said when they reached the living room. She had to get rid of the snake before the damn thing crawled off somewhere in the apartment and laid eggs. It was a long shot, but she'd seen too many movies in hotel rooms around the world not to take the chance. She unzipped her bag and pulled out a practice racquet.

"You can't leave me here all by myself. I'm coming with you. Can I borrow one of those?" Parker took another one out of the bag and handed it to her. "This is the first time you've let me touch these things." Sydney grasped it with two hands.

"Make a note for the future. If any type of dangerous serpent is in the room, don't hesitate to come out swinging."

The rattle was visible when they opened the door, but thankfully the dangerous end was still caught up in the bedding. She didn't have a lot of experience with reptiles, but it was so thick whoever this one belonged to must have fed it well. The first swing she took made the rattler stand almost rigid before it soon started in again. She kept at it until there was a visible bloodstain and the damn thing wasn't moving.

"I bet PETA would have me beaten if they'd had witnessed this."

Sydney shivered as she clutched the racquet to her chest. "How do you think it got in here?"

"Are rattle snakes indigenous to New York?"

"Depends on who you ask, but they're usually referring to the two-legged kind."

"Then someone must have left it as a present, since it's too chunky to slither under the door." The snake lay motionless, but it still made her skin crawl. "Are you okay?"

"I should be more freaked out to find a snake in my bed, but having you here made it all right. You make me feel safe." Sydney dropped her racquet and ran to her for a hug. "It's creepy that someone we don't know was in here."

"Let's call Logan to come and do whatever needs to be done, then check ourselves into a nice hotel. Maybe I can have the thing skinned and made into a headband for the finals."

"Are we buying a new bed?"

"A bed and a couple of chairs so I can put my socks on in the morning." The siren outside signaled Logan's return, along with a team of officers who dusted the apartment for prints and interviewed the neighbors in case they'd seen something.

They left as soon as the police finished their questions, and Logan promised to lock up when he was done. When their cab arrived at the hotel, Gray, Kimmie, Nick, and Beau were waiting for them to make sure they were all right. Once they were finally alone, Parker held on to Sydney as the shock of what happened leaked out in a jag of hysterical crying.

The stalker had gotten so close that she made no more promises. Keeping Sydney safe had been paramount in her mind from the moment she heard that rattle, and now would be no different. She planned to accept the bodyguards Beau had hired, if only to keep Sydney in her arms and whole.

The rest of it wasn't important, the tournament included.

❖

The activity in Times Square beneath their window was constant, but their room was tomb quiet. Sydney had almost made herself sick crying, but had finally given in to her exhaustion. The situation with this stalker had always been frustrating, but now Parker's sense of helplessness left her floundering. Not that she had a death wish, but it was time for this to be over. She'd said repeatedly that she wouldn't change who she was, but she couldn't lie to herself anymore.

This situation had changed her. She was tense everywhere except her house, and this summer even that had changed when the letter was delivered there. Now, finding that snake in Sydney's apartment meant nowhere was safe. She was still alive, but whoever this was had succeeded in making her afraid of every shadow that crossed her path. Before, this person could only take her life, but now she had Sydney. Not being able to protect Sydney made the fear flourish in every recess of her mind.

She stared down at the crowds. Their room was too far up for her to see anyone's face clearly, but she still wondered if her pen pal was down there…waiting, wanting, relentless. She stared down at her billboard across the street, trying to spot anyone fixated on it. The likelihood she'd find them like that was small, but then she hadn't thought she'd find love on a flight.

"Are you looking for a way to escape the hysterical woman who's prone to crying jags?" Sydney lay on her stomach with her hands under her head. Her hair was in disarray, but Parker found her sexy and lush with the sheets pooled at the small of her naked back. "I'm pretty sure those windows don't open, so you'll have to use the door."

"Get away from you?" Sydney rolled on top of her as soon as she lay down. "I'm trying to figure out how to keep you locked in here until my match."

The skin along Sydney's back was warm as Parker gently ran her fingers down to the curve of her butt. She loved not only the feel of Sydney but the curves that defined her feminine body.

"I'm sorry," she said as Sydney placed her thigh between her legs. "After everything you've been through, I'm sure you weren't anxious to sign up for such a crazy relationship."

"You didn't ask for some wing-nut stalker either, baby." Sydney slightly lifted her head so they could make eye contact. "Are you comfortable with all this?"

"At the moment, I'm plenty comfortable."

Sydney laughed and slapped her shoulder. "Not that. My long-term relationship track record isn't wonderful, but—"

When Sydney hesitated, she said, "At least you have one."

"I would've put that differently, but I want to know if you need to talk about anything. I really want this to work."

She held on to Sydney and rolled them over until she had Sydney mostly under her. "This is new to me." She smiled and slipped her fingers into Sydney's hair. "Even though it is, being with you completes me. I know that sounds corny, but sitting on the beach with you was the first time I felt at peace with a woman. The restlessness that always came after I got what I wanted from someone didn't with you." She laughed. "That didn't exactly come out right, did it?"

"Don't worry, I know what you mean. I wouldn't describe what happened to me as restlessness, but once I'd committed I wondered why I wasn't happy. I had what a lot of people want, but I was still lonely. Does that make sense?"

"Yes, it does." She lifted Sydney's head and kissed her. "If you're worried I'll disappear after the weekend, don't be." She moved so her pelvis pressed into Sydney's. "And if you're waiting for me to freak out, I won't."

Sydney moaned when she lowered her mouth and sucked her nipples into two rosy points, then reached down and opened the lips of her sex with her index finger. She loved sex, making a woman wet and hard, and driving her to the brink of need. She'd loved it from the first time she'd touched someone, but this was so much more than sex.

She moved down and immediately sucked Sydney's clitoris into her mouth because she was the one at the brink. She needed to taste Sydney, put her fingers inside her and give her what she wanted. She needed Sydney to be hers.

That desire multiplied tenfold when Sydney drew her legs up and her knees fell open as if she was giving herself over. Parker sucked harder when Sydney thrust her hips up like she was desperate. Her mouth and chin were slick with Sydney's essence, and she stroked faster, meeting Sydney's movements.

"Parker, I'm coming," Sydney said, her back arched, her eyes shut tight.

She thrust hard and deep, never taking her mouth or eyes off her. No tournament in the world had given her this complete satisfaction when she'd won, and she'd never been so honored to put her hands on someone and watch her get lost in her touch. Sydney's hips stopped midair and she moaned as the walls of her sex squeezed her fingers, taking the last bit of pleasure from them as she orgasmed.

She loved sex, but it had taken on new meaning the first time she'd made love to Sydney. It was no longer an act of physical release, but a demonstration of how she felt.

"I love you," she whispered when she held Sydney after she was done. "And I'll be here until you don't want me."

"You're in for a long haul, then." Sydney reached for her hand.

If she thought their night was over, she smiled when Sydney took her hand and placed it between her legs again. One long and mind-numbing orgasm obviously wasn't enough, because Sydney was hard again.

"How turned on are you?" Sydney asked.

Parker spread her legs wider when Sydney tapped the side of her thigh and tried not to come when she laid her entire hand between her legs and stroked firmly. "You tell me." Not even three sets of tennis made her sound this winded.

"If you're desperate," Sydney lifted her ass and spread her legs as well, "I won't be cruel. Put your fingers back in."

"You said something about not being cruel?" Sydney appeared decadent as she took her in again. It was the only word she could find to describe the ecstasy on her face.

"I'm in the mood for slow, but I won't be a glutton if you can't wait."

"How can I refuse a request like that when you—" Sydney entered her fast, her thumb slamming into her clit with enough force to make her come if she didn't have much control. "Sneaky, Syd," she said, trying desperately to hang on.

This time Sydney's stroke was gentler, but she already had her attention. No matter how much control she possessed, she wouldn't last much longer. "So, fast or slow?" Sydney asked.

Parker bent her hand back a little so the knuckle of her index finger rolled over Sydney's clit. Her reaction would help her answer the question. Sydney's hips jerked and she brought her mouth down and kissed her. *Fast it is*, she thought as Sydney's touch became more urgent. Her mind imploded and all she could concentrate on was the spot between her legs.

If they kept this up until she played, her legs would give out after the first game. Hell, it wouldn't be the first time she'd lose this thing. Sydney was here—open, ripe, wet—and she loved her. Where it most counted, she'd already won.

CHAPTER SEVENTEEN

Good morning, do you need help finding your seats?" The usher at the Open seemed eager to escort Sydney and the others to the box courtside. Every available seat allotted to Parker would be full since she had gotten Margo and her mother tickets for the final. She'd joked that maybe great seats would soften Lucia's stance.

"Thanks, we can find them. Have any of you spotted Bobbie?" Sydney asked. The match was set to begin in an hour and Bobbie was nowhere in sight. One row up from them, Logan shook his head. He appeared out of place in a suit, but the jacket was necessary to conceal his weapon. He was there to keep an eye on both of them, but she was afraid he'd be so engrossed in the match, a rabid gorilla could join them and he wouldn't notice.

"She's parking the car. The sweetheart dropped us off at the gate, saying she didn't want us out in the open too long," Kimmie said. Behind her Gray and Natasha sat holding hands and sharing a bagel.

"This place looks so much smaller on TV," Lucia said as she adjusted her hat.

"I wish it was." Sydney scanned the crowd, even though she didn't know what or who she was searching for.

"She'll be fine," Margo said. "For what these seats cost, the mob will take out anyone who tries anything to stop this thing."

Sydney smiled and nodded. She wouldn't relax until they caught this guy. "It's not fair that she has to stress about some nut as well as this match. You have no idea how hard she works for days like this."

"Put that monster out of your head," Lucia said. "Don't give him the satisfaction of depriving you of the fun of watching Parker win today. Trust me, when she does, that's the memory you'll have of this moment."

"I hope so, Mom."

"I know so, and I'm your mother, so sit back and relax. Besides, after all this is over I have plenty more questions for Romeo, so she's not getting off that easy."

❖

Downstairs, Parker thought about all the games it had taken to get her to this point. She'd made it this far on numerous occasions, only to fall short of the goal. On the other side of the locker room, Lee Darnell sat with her eyes closed, so loose she appeared to be sleeping. Lee was the underdog who'd fought her way through the ranks to become the hero of the tournament. All the seeded players who'd underestimated the up-and-comer from Texas had gone home surprised at her level of play.

In a change of pace, Parker let her mind wander to other things besides the final as a way to try to make her stomach settle down. It never failed, and her pre-play jitters had scared Sydney that morning when she found her puking in the bathroom. It'd taken a while to convince her that she did it before every final she played in, so she should get used to this unfortunate side effect of winning. The churning usually went away when she set her feet for the first serve of the match.

Their friend the snake charmer had been quiet since their scare at the apartment, and she hoped it stayed that way until this match was over. With Logan so close to Sydney, she had one less thing to worry about, so she turned her attention to Lee Darnell.

Lee had opened her eyes, but her posture and relaxed breathing made her appear bored and uninterested in what they were about to start. Only when they were called out for practice did she stir at all.

The sound of cameras going off started as soon as they emerged from the tunnel, and Parker took time to peer up and smile at Sydney. Warm inside, she unzipped her bag and removed a racquet.

The tension had finally started to melt away and she was ready to play.

❖

"I do this to please you, Lord," Abel said softly as he unbuttoned the middle of his shirt.

"I'm sorry, did you say something?" the older woman sitting a row up from him asked.

"I said, may the Lord be with you."

"Thank you." The woman looked at him like he was crazy but continued her conversation with the man next to her.

When Abel was sure her attention was on Parker and Lee, he slowly put his hand into his shirt so he could remove the knife he'd taped to his chest. The weapon belonged to Eric, and the sharp porcelain blade hadn't set off the metal detectors on the way in. This was the moment he'd waited for and had planned for years.

Across from him much farther up in the stands, Eric sat and watched him with a smile so wide he appeared somewhat deranged. All he had to do was fulfill his part by killing Parker, and Eric would tell their father about it. Even if he died as well, Parker's death would buy his father's forgiveness. He'd have no choice.

On the court, Parker grabbed the towel off the back of her seat and tried to wipe away the dust in her eyes. It wasn't debilitating, but whatever the wind had kicked up had made her start blinking furiously.

She had the towel pressed to her eyes when she heard a woman scream, followed by the crowd's reaction. When she turned a large man was closing the distance between them, but all she zeroed in on was the knife he held out in front of him, aimed at her chest.

"Death to those who go against God." The statement was the same, but the voice was different. She was sure this wasn't the same guy, which meant stalkers—plural.

"Shit," she said as the pain shot through her side and blood instantly stained her tennis whites.

She used the towel to keep the end of the knife away from her when the guy pulled back for another swipe. When she picked up her racquet and swung to disarm him, the sharp blade cut right through the strings. "What is it with you people and my racquets?"

Ignoring the pain of the cut, she swung again and connected with his jaw, which sent him back a few paces, shaking his head as if to clear the blow away. He staggered forward again but she was ready. The racquet flew forward again and knocked the knife out of his hand.

Logan and a group of officers were on the guy before he had the chance to rearm himself. The attacker struggled and freed his hands but didn't get completely away before one of the officers Tasered him. That knocked him unconscious. Once they cuffed him and rolled him over, Parker felt like someone had stabbed her through the heart.

He'd aged since the last time she'd seen him. His faced was lined, his dark hair was completely gray, and he'd lost a massive amount of weight, but the woozy man starting to come to was her father.

Everyone sat in silence when she dropped her racquet and walked off the court. An official announced there'd be a delay in play until everything was sorted out.

Sydney and Parker's sisters watched her walk out without another look at the man Kimmie and Gray said was their father, Francis. He was cuffed, awake, and screaming at Logan and the others who were trying to drag him off.

"She's an affront to God in heaven," Francis said. "Let me go or face the fires of hell for keeping me from what needs to be done."

"Carry this asshole out, if you have to, but get him out of here," Logan said to the four uniformed officers who surrounded Francis.

"I can't believe he tried to kill her," Gray said, her eyes glued on her father.

"Or that he's been the one harassing her all this time," Kimmie said. "Who does that to his child?"

"I know he had a problem accepting your choices, but this is unbelievable," Sydney said. She wanted to run down and take Parker home, but she didn't have a choice except to wait and see what Parker would do. The blood that'd soaked her shirt proved she was hurt, but she hadn't outright forfeited—yet. Beau had gone down to see about her injuries, and waiting for him to get back was killing her.

"Parker's a survivor, though, Sydney," Kimmie said as she put her arm around her.

"The cut she'll get over," Gray said, "but we need to be there for her until she completely heals because of the mental wounds that bastard inflicted."

"You're what she's going to need, my love," Lucia said. "I might've given Parker a hard time, but I don't doubt she loves you. Love her and she'll be fine."

"Thanks," Sydney said, turning her head to Kimmie, then her mother. "I only want to know if she's okay right now. We'll deal with the rest until I know she's over it."

❖

The medic knelt next to Parker and injected a topical anesthetic around the still-bleeding wound. She'd sat, numb from what had happened, as the guy cleaned the area right under her rib cage. Beau sat next to her and held her hand, but remained quiet as if he was in as much shock as she was.

"I can't believe he sent all those letters." She nodded when the guy held up the needle to start suturing. "I would've never guessed he hated me that much."

"All you can think is that he's sick and didn't know what he was doing," Beau said.

"That's why something about them looked vaguely familiar. When I saw him running at me, I thought of all those Christmas seasons he used that old pen and inkwell. He'd meticulously address all the cards he'd send out with even rows of calligraphy he said he could do only with that pen." Her mind seemed trapped in some bizarre highlight reel—she kept seeing her father running at her with that knife.

"It was the only time he sat for hours, making sure every letter in every name was perfect. I guess he took the same care when it came to sending out death notices."

"Try not to think about it. Let's go home so you can heal and we can all relax. At least you know he can't hurt you anymore."

"Go home? I've got a match to play, and I intend to play it. That righteous bigot won't take this away too. He put that damn snake in Sydney's bed, and that's unforgivable. Sydney could've been seriously hurt. There's no going back from this. And my so-called mother, she had to have had some hint of what he was doing."

"Parker, are you okay?" Sydney stood back with Nick as if not sure she'd want to see her.

"I'm probably doing better than you. You look like you're tied up in knots."

"Is your life always this action-packed?" Sydney asked, her eyes glassy.

"Only in big cities. At home Abby and I usually just sit and howl at the moon for entertainment."

"That sounds oddly blissful. You ready to go?" Sydney held her other hand as the medic finished making a row of small, tight stitches.

"I promised you joint custody of this trophy, and I'm not about to renege on that."

"Are you sure?"

She nodded. "Probably tomorrow you'll have to run out for tissue when I break down and cry a lot, but right now I don't want to think about it. If I can, I want to play, even if I last only a few games. If I lose, then I do, but I want to try."

"I love you. You know that, right?"

She kissed Sydney. "I do, and I love you too. Now, take a peek across the room and tell me if the Texas Tarantula's looking confident of victory."

Sydney glanced over her shoulder and kissed her neck. "She looks like you don't even have to play since she has it all sewn up."

"All done, Miss King." The medic placed a pressure bandage after he'd applied more deadener to the area.

"Are you sure about this? I don't want you getting hurt any more than you already are," Sydney said as she stared at the white bandage.

"I'm sure. Everyone out there paid to see good tennis, not the King family drama, so that's what I plan to give them. I think I can make it through the entire match, but I might not play my usual finesse game."

"Finesse game?" Sydney sounded like she was trying not to laugh. "Not that you don't possess finesse in other aspects of your life, honey, but playing tennis isn't on the list."

"Then there's nothing to worry about."

"Since you're so willing, I should do my share." Sydney whispered the rest of what she had to say in her ear, and Parker's face got hot. She kissed Sydney on the lips and Beau on the forehead before she changed her shirt.

"Come on, Darnell, it's time to kick some ass."

"I'm glad you're willing to go along so graciously, sugar, cause that's exactly what I'm planning to do. I'm sorry you got hurt, but when we go out there I'm going to shove every ball down your throat."

Beau and Nick grabbed Sydney around the waist when Lee finished her taunts, and her protective nature made Parker feel like she'd gotten a shot of painkiller.

❖

"Well, sports fans, barring any other crazies running out of the stands wielding sharp implements, we're ready to play tennis," the radio announcer said.

Gray King stood up and glared in the direction of the booth to cut off any other smart comments. Then she turned to Sydney and offered her some peanuts. "Try these, they taste a lot better than nails."

"I can't help it, I'm nervous for her." She kept her eyes on Parker, who was sitting and sipping from a bottle of water.

"Believe me, she's nervous enough for the both of you. This is Park's year, Syd, I can feel it."

"She deserves it after everything she's been through."

"Service, Miss King." Parker walked to the baseline and waited for the balls to be thrown to her. She took a deep breath and let it out with a slump in her shoulders.

Beau and Nick held their breath and hands as she threw a ball into the air, preparing to send it over the net. "This will tell the tale of the next couple of hours," Beau whispered to her. "We'll see how much power she can put behind the ball."

Sydney heard Parker's usual grunt then the pop when she served. It was so loud it sounded as if Parker was standing right next to her. "I swear I saw fuzz fly off it."

"No kidding," Beau said, appearing as if someone had taken a piano off his back. "Those meditation sessions must've paid off. She didn't even wince on the downstroke."

"Fifteen-love." The chair pointed toward Parker's side of the net. The players had to wait for a couple of minutes until the crowd calmed down. It sounded as if the fans appreciated Lee for her struggle to get to the final, but now that play had started, their loyalties were firmly ensconced on Parker's side of the net.

They were battling out the third game of the first set when Logan returned to his seat. He'd removed his jacket and, without the shoulder holster, looked like every other fan there to enjoy the tennis.

"Everything okay?" Sydney asked.

"Mr. King is on his way downtown for processing, and the uniforms I placed around this place should make everyone behave until the match is over. How's she doing?"

"She won the first game and came close to breaking in the second, but Lee hung on." She stopped talking as soon as Parker put the ball back in play. Parker stood on the baseline and sent Lee for quick sprints around the court with her ball placement.

"Forty-love." Again the chair pointed toward Parker's side of the net. Her ace won the game.

The first set was over in less than fifty minutes, and Parker seemed relaxed and pain-free. Sydney said a prayer the second one would go as well and as quickly, and her mom hugged her as if she'd read her mind.

Disaster struck in the third game of the second set. Parker had won the first two games easily, and Lee had started to show signs of fatigue from the running and from the heat, since her shots lacked the accuracy of her earlier play even to Sydney's non-expert eye. In a desperate chase to get a ball Parker had sent in a direction Lee didn't seem to expect, she hit back a high lob. When Parker reached up to smash it over the net Sydney almost heard the stitches pop, and from Parker's facial expression she knew the pain was instant. The ball fell outside the baseline as a point for Lee, followed by Parker dropping her racquet.

"Miss King?" the sideline judge asked when she grimaced as she bent to pick up her racquet.

"I'm okay."

"Thirty-fifteen," the chair said. Parker was still ahead but Lee seemed to have finally found her weakness.

The lobs became more frequent and Parker had more and more difficulty getting the ball over the net, no matter what angle she hit it from, losing her the second set quicker than Lee had lost the first. During the break she ran into the tunnel and had the pressure bandage replaced, hoping it'd last the entire third set. As the medic worked she reminded herself that, despite the wound, physically she'd outlast Lee when it came to stamina.

"Are you sure?" the medic asked once the old bandage was off.

"As tight as you can make it."

When play resumed she felt good enough to make Lee pay for the number of lobs by returning them with such force, some of them bounced into the stands. The pain almost paralyzed her, but she tried to ignore it, which helped her hold her serve.

They were tied at six games apiece when she finally had to call time. The constant stretches had taken their toll, and the bandage could no longer hold back the blood.

"Miss, King, you have fifteen minutes to return to the court," the chair judge explained. "If you can't, you'll have to forfeit. Do you understand?"

"Yes, sir, and thank you." She ran out holding her side, grateful the medic was waiting just out of sight of the crowd, like she'd asked. She had her shirt off before she reached him, and the movement was excruciating.

"I need you to fix it so it'll last at least ten more serves."

"Miss King."

"Call me Parker, and I don't want to hear about how bad it looks. You have thirteen minutes before I have to forfeit the game."

He did as she asked and injected another round of anesthetic to the area before he placed a fresh pressure bandage over it. "You've popped a couple of stitches, but this might hold until you're done. Watch out for those lobs and good luck."

"Miss King, are you ready to resume play?"

"Yes, sir."

"Tie break for the match. Miss King will serve first."

She looked up into the stands and searched for Sydney before she made any move to serve. Sydney stood up, making herself easier to find, and smiled when their eyes met. Sydney put her hands over her heart and nodded, which made her smile and tap over her heart with her fingertips.

The first serve went over the net, and she was surprised how pain-free her side was all of a sudden. Lee hit a backhand and the volley began. It was hard-hitting and fairly straightforward back and forth without a lot of flare for about twelve strokes. At her first opportunity, Lee sent a high lob over the net. She gauged it and stood waiting for the right moment.

"Point, Miss King." She'd sent it over the net almost directly at Lee Darnell. If the kid won it'd be playing tennis, not by exploiting her injuries.

For fifteen minutes they traded points as each of them tried to gain the advantage. The shots became more difficult as the pain got worse, but she played through it.

"Advantage, Miss King, match point." She'd waited a lifetime to hear that one phrase. The crowd seemed pumped as they stood and chanted "Kong."

"Quiet, please."

She bounced the ball four times, closed her eyes, and took a deep breath in an effort to center herself. Even if she lost, she was sure no one would fault her play or her courage for getting this far. That was the noble way of looking at the situation, but another thought popped into her head.

Fuck that. All those hours of practice, all the running and the time in the gym had to be good for something. It was time to prove it.

She hit the ball like she wasn't hurt and Lee scrambled after it to try to connect. It should've been the winner that'd end her misery, but the line sensor went off and the serve was called out. All Lee had to do now was jump all over her second serve, which was traditionally slower, and bring the game back to deuce.

But Parker had never in her life bowed to tradition when it came to her game, so why start now? It was time to go home to her stretch of beach, her dog, and, most important, her girl.

"Quiet, please."

No one in the arena appeared more shocked than Lee Darnell when her second serve flew past her. It had hit perfectly in the corner without touching the net. She'd finally lifted the monkey off her back and delivered the Grand Slam.

"Game, set, and match, Miss King."

The center court stadium came alive with camera flashes as she held the trophy at chest level, in too much pain to lift it over her head. She walked the circuit around the court, stopping when she saw her family. No one ever accomplished something like this alone, and she was grateful for the love and support from every one of them who, like Sydney, was crying in joy.

The day had brought its losses, but she was through mourning the possibility of a relationship with her parents. They'd given away both her and that right a long time ago, and she had no guilt about what would happen to them now. If they fell into a black hole, it was of their own making.

Beau had been right all along. Family sometimes was built with the people God put in your path, not those you were born to. And with the group she'd found along her road in life, the losses would be easier to get over as long as they loved her.

CHAPTER EIGHTEEN

L ong month, huh?" Beau asked as they sat in the airport waiting for their plane.

Parker was grateful they were the only ones sitting in the VIP lounge. "Turned out okay, so it was worth the hassles." She scratched around the first cut, which was for the most part healed. The emotions of who'd done it and why would take longer, but time would resolve that as well.

Francis King had been placed in a state hospital until he was competent to stand trial, and based on his ramblings Eric and Ethan had been arrested as well for their part in the attacks. Over Beau and her sisters' objections, Parker had made a statement on Alicia's behalf for her part in the melodrama the tournament had turned into. That was all she was willing to do for Alicia, and she hoped Alicia would crawl out of the bottle long enough to get the help she needed.

They'd stayed in the city longer than she'd planned, but she'd wanted to participate in the investigation into all her father and his family had done to hurt her and her sisters.

"You doing okay?" Beau asked.

They really hadn't been alone together in days, so this was his first chance to ask how she was feeling. "You know, all this time, a small piece of me really missed him."

"That's 'cause you're a good kid." Beau put his arm around her, and she was grateful he was always so affectionate. He'd filled all those missing pieces her father couldn't and wouldn't in her life. Beau's presence was making her less numb.

"I'm sure the story will come out eventually. A lot of press attended all his court appearances and Francis was really anxious to talk to them. Logan's only going to be able to filter that for so long." She stretched her legs out and felt physically older.

"I'm from the hills of Tennessee, so I thought I'd heard it all, but your daddy's family is a little out there."

She laughed and, considering the disgust of it all, she was happy she still could. "You think?"

Her father's history had been littered with things that made her recoil and become angry, considering Francis had had the nerve to question her and her sisters' choices. He'd abandoned their mother emotionally long before because he preferred sex with men, but his true loves were his brothers, the twins Eric and Ethan. At least that's how he'd explained it. His brothers backed up his story as soon as they were brought in for questioning.

The only moment she'd felt any compassion for Francis was when Logan showed her Ethan's interrogation. All three brothers had been a product of their sadistic father, who thought himself a preacher with a congregation of three. Her grandfather's strange religious teachings had started when their mother died when the twins were four.

Being the oldest, Abel Prophet had run not only from his home but from his history and become Francis King. He'd tried to start over with a family of his own, but his father's influence was too engrained to ignore. Francis didn't like being overpowered in their barn, but he'd learned well how to prey on the weak. When he'd gone home and his father wasn't there, he'd taken his place in Eric and Ethan's life. He'd explained for the first time in that dreadful place full of musty straw and rusty equipment that he'd been the strong one.

"You're right about that," she said, not yet able to reconcile her father's past. "According to his brother Eric, Francis snapped when he sent word their father had died."

It hadn't been hard to find Eric and Ethan after Francis mentioned them, since they were in the room he'd rented. And Ethan had admitted that Eric had attacked her outside the restaurant.

She couldn't understand why all this had happened, since hearing that her abuser had died would've relieved her. She certainly wouldn't have become obsessed with making something up to him by killing someone. That's what Francis had done, though. When his father was gone, he thought he could make amends only if he sacrificed his children.

"You might be his child, but you should remember only those years you were all a family. Leave the rest to Francis and the hell he'll have to live with."

"What I'm going to remember is Sydney, you, Nick, my sisters, and Sydney's family. And I'll keep repeating that I was hatched from an egg and my parents had nothing to do with it."

Beau hugged her again and laughed.

"Miss King, if you'd like, you and your friends can board early," the lounge hostess said as another agent offered to take their bags. Only Nick was missing, but he hadn't gone far, just to buy some magazines for the flight. "Congratulations on your win."

"Thank you." She followed the brunette through the door, already missing Sydney, who'd left for work earlier that morning. It would be two days before she'd make it down so they could decide their future living arrangements.

She had a sense of déjà vu as they turned the corner and the crew stood waiting to greet them. "Welcome aboard, Miss King, I hope you enjoy your flight and congratulations on your win." It was exactly what Sydney had said the day they met.

"Yeah, yeah, but if you really loved me…"

Sydney narrowed her eyes and tried to look mad. "I'd do what?"

"This." She dropped her bag and kissed her. "Though a chicken salad sandwich and some hot chocolate might just hit the spot," she said when they parted.

"Go sit down, smart ass, I'm taking us home."

EPILOGUE

Almost a year later, they'd furnished Sydney's apartment for the occasions they were in the city, but Sydney now lived in Alabama. The move was the easiest decision she'd ever made, and she didn't regret the life she'd left in New York. The airline had made the transition easy by allowing her to change her departure hub to New Orleans, which was a short flight from the Mobile airport.

Parker liked to cook, read, and take walks on the beach with her. If she were any more perfect, she was sure she'd wake up and find she'd dreamed her up. Sydney watched from the kitchen window as Beau and Natasha put Parker through her workout in preparation for the French Open and Wimbledon. She'd taken a few months off so she could make both tournaments, and this was her first free week of vacation.

Sydney turned the oven off and took out the roast she'd made for dinner before she headed outside. "If you go anywhere near that pan, I'll drive you to the pound myself, mister, and come back with a cat," she said to Abby.

The dog put his paw over his eyes and whined, giving her his best innocent routine. "Don't give me that 'who me' act, Abby King. You're just like your mother, so I'm not buying it."

He followed Sydney out to the court, tail wagging, and when Parker shot one over the fence in their direction Abby was in doggie heaven.

"Go home, people, the boss has arrived for her tennis lesson," Parker said to Beau and Natasha.

"Can we tell her good-bye first?" Beau asked.

"Make it quick. She's cuter than you, and being out here all day with the two of you made me miss her."

Sydney laughed and waved to their two departing friends. "You aren't too tired?"

"Nah, I'm never too tired for you. How about an incentive game as our lesson for today?"

"An incentive game, huh? Run down the rules for me."

"You lose a piece of clothing for every point you lose." Parker wiggled her eyebrows as she made her suggestion.

"You want me to play strip tennis with the number one player in the world?"

"Um, yeah. Come on, it'll be fun and I'll give you first serve."

"Oh, I'm sure that'll clinch it for me." She took the racquet Parker held out and walked to the baseline. When Parker was ready she tried to remember everything she'd learned about serving. Abby barked from behind her, and the ball flew off at an odd angle when she hit it. "Enough from the peanut gallery. It's not like I'm holding any cards here."

She tried again and Parker, true to her word, slowed her game down, a lot. Even with that advantage Parker won the first point. With exaggerated slowness Sydney stripped her shirt off and threw it behind her. It had barely hit the ground when Abby took off with it clutched in his mouth. She bounced the next ball longer than normal when Parker's eyes stayed glued to the dark-green silk bra she was wearing.

On the next shot Parker seemed to forget herself and hit the ball back so hard she didn't even try to hit it, and took off her shorts. "Could you come over here, please?" Parker stood at the net, and she guessed the matching panties had proved to be too much for her concentration.

"Do you give up?"

"I surrender, baby." Parker lifted her over the net and kissed her. She wrapped her legs around Parker's waist as she walked them off the court to the water's edge. She put her down long enough to get all their clothes off before heading out into the surf. The water was still on the cold side, but having their hot bodies pressed together made it comfortable.

"I love you," Sydney said.

"I love you too. You like it here?" Parker held her high enough so she could kiss the side of her neck.

"I love it here. I get to be with you, and I get my clothes buried on a regular basis by our dog. What's not to love?"

"He buries your stuff to keep it safe, it means he likes you," Parker said before she kissed her neck.

"How about you, do you like me?"

"I more than like you, baby. How about I take you inside and show you just how much?"

Her feet never touched the sand as Parker walked them to the back door. As always, Parker had checked the closest house that morning to make sure it was still tenant-free, not wanting to upset her with peeping neighbors.

The house décor had changed a little over the months since Sydney had moved in, which made it a home for both of them. Mixed in with the tournament pictures were shots of Sydney's family that her mother had given them on one of her numerous visits. Lucia Parish and Parker shared a great relationship, much to Sydney's relief, and Margo was crazy about her. Both of them admitted that the way Parker looked at her showed how she felt.

It was the same look on Parker's face as she set her on the bed. Parker's touch showed desire and love, never a sense of obligation, and the more Parker touched her, the more she wanted.

"You're so beautiful." Parker lay next to her and ran her hand up from her hip to cup her breast. The nipple instantly puckered under her palm and Parker smiled when she moaned. Parker replaced her hand with her lips and sucked it against the roof of her mouth.

"I love when you do that." Her hands kept Parker's head in place in case she didn't know what she was talking about. The suction increased as Parker's hands went back down her body. "Let me feel you, baby."

Parker moved so she covered her but held most of her weight up by resting on her elbows. She loved this position since it allowed every inch of their skin to touch, and Sydney lay still to enjoy the sensation before she moved her hands to Parker's hair to drag her up for a kiss.

"Make love to me," she said as she moved her legs farther apart to allow Parker to get closer to her. Parker had to lift her hips up a little to reach the spot she wanted, but by doing so, she opened enough space for Sydney to touch her in return.

Both their centers were so wet and they were both so ready it didn't take much, and Parker's grunts close to Sydney's ear fueled her orgasm. The grunts were similar to the ones on the court during her play, but this was her very private version.

Amazingly, making love with Parker now was as exciting as their first time. And even on days like this when the end snuck up on her sooner than she'd like, she felt cherished as Parker went rigid over her before turning into a giant marshmallow.

"If this is how you learned to play tennis, don't tell me, okay?"

"You don't care for my teaching techniques?"

"I didn't say that, honey. I just don't want to know where you learned your technique, Romeo. Especially who you practiced with, got me?"

"Gotcha."

"Are you hungry?"

"You cooked, so I'll get it and bring it back here, how's that sound?" Parker asked as she rolled off and stood, not bothering with clothes.

"Like you'll be in there eating roast directly from the pan while I'm back here starving," she said as she held her hand out as a request to be helped up.

She was still laughing at Parker's antics when they walked into the kitchen. She noticed two things right off. Abby was sitting there looking like if he could whistle he'd be doing it, and half the roast was gone. He opened his eyes wider and shook his head when she took a step toward him.

"What happened to my roast?" she asked, and it was hard to keep a straight face when Abby lifted a paw and pointed at Parker.

"No way, buddy, she's done a detailed search of my mouth," Parker said with her arms crossed over her chest, and as if he'd learned from Parker's mistakes when it came to upsetting her, he put his paw down and backed toward the door slowly. He made a break for it when he cleared the doggie door.

"I swear you two were separated at birth. What am I going to do with you?" She turned around and put her arms around Parker's waist. She'd let Abby know later that there was another roast in the oven and the one he'd eaten was for him.

"You could keep us."

"Oh, I'm keeping you and Abby all right, don't worry about that," she said, and laid her head on Parker's shoulder. She cherished her life filled with fun moments like this with Parker and Abby, but also the sense of place they gave her. "I want to sit by a fire, eat, and listen to you read me a poem," she said, and shivered from the warm rush of emotion.

Parker's smile was hard to tame as she pulled Sydney closer. "You sure are easy to please." She carried Sydney into the library and set her on one of the comfortable couches while she prepared a tray for them.

A fire was burning by the time she made it back and found Sydney staring into it so profoundly that she hated to disturb her. "We have a fire, wine, and a nice spread."

"All I need is you," Sydney said as she held up her hand.

"That you have, sweetheart."

"Read me something."

She rolled the ladder to a section at the end, climbed it so she could reach the top shelf, and selected an old leather-bound book with faded gold lettering on the cover. When she opened it, the pages appeared almost translucent.

Her voice faded away to nothing on the last word of the sonnet, and Sydney sat staring intently at her. For some reason her choice had brought tears to Sydney's eyes, and Parker knelt to wipe them away.

"If it's going to make you cry, I won't read you any other love poems."

"I'm crying because you love me enough to do it."

"Actually I'm kneeling for another reason."

"Why's that?" Sydney sniffled and wiped her face with the back of her hand.

"Abby wanted to come and apologize about the roast, and I thought I'd butter you up for him."

Sydney ran her finger along her top lip. "It'll take a lot more reading out of this book to accomplish that, Shakespeare."

With a snap of Parker's fingers, Abby ran in and sat next to Parker. He held a basket in his mouth and put a paw up for Sydney to shake.

"Sydney, Abby and I love you, and we wanted to give you something that'd show you how much you mean to us. If I were a poet this would be much more eloquent, but I'll try my best. Will you give me the chance to make you happy for the rest of your life? If you say yes, you'll never spend another moment without feeling like the center of my universe. I love you and I'll do so until there's no breath left in my body." Abby put his basket down on Sydney's lap, put his paw next to it as if he wanted her to look inside, and let out a soft woof for his part of the proposal.

Sydney cried again when she saw the ring box lying on the straw inside. "Yes," she said, without even opening it.

"Is that yes to me, or the dog?"

"To both of you, goofy. I know you come as a pair." Sydney leaned forward for a kiss.

"Shall we have a toast?" Sydney laughed when Parker picked up two mugs from the tray she'd brought in. Hot chocolate was the one memory Parker had chosen to keep of her father.

They didn't need any other words as they tapped the mugs against each other and took sips of the hot, almost velvety drink. Sydney rested her head on her shoulder and closed her eyes. "I give thanks you live your life by always choosing the road less traveled. It brought you to me, and I promise to always love you the way you deserve. This is only our beginning," Sydney said.

"And I promise that the long stretch of miles we have to go before we're done will be memorable."

And they were.

About the Author

Originally from Cuba, Ali Vali has retained much of her family's traditions and language and uses them frequently in her stories. Having her father read her stories and poetry before bed every night as a child infused her with a love of reading that carries till today. In 2000, Ali decided to embark on a new path and started writing.

Ali now lives in the suburbs of New Orleans with her partner of twenty-eight years, and finds that living in such a history-rich area provides plenty of material to draw from in creating her novels and short stories. Mixing imagination with different life experiences makes it easier to create a slew of different characters that are engaging to the reader on many levels. Ali states that "The feedback from readers encourages me to continue to hone my skills as a writer."

Books Available From Bold Strokes Books

Ladyfish by Andrea Bramhall. Finn's escape to the Florida Keys leads her straight into the arms of scuba diving instructor Oz as she fights for her freedom, their blossoming love...and her life! (978-1-60282-747-9)

Spanish Heart by Rachel Spangler. While on a mission to find herself in Spain, Ren Molson runs the risk of losing her heart to her tour guide, Lina Montero. (978-1-60282-748-6)

Love Match by Ali Vali. When Parker "Kong" King, the number one tennis player in the world, meets commercial pilot Captain Sydney Parish, sparks fly—but not from attraction. They have the summer to see if they have a love match. (978-1-60282-749-3)

One Touch by L.T. Marie. A romance writer and a travel agent come together at their high school reunion, only to find out that the memory of that one touch never fades. (978-1-60282-750-9)

Night Shadows: Queer Horror edited by Greg Herren and J.M. Redmann. Night Shadows features delightfully wicked stories by some of the biggest names in queer publishing. (978-1-60282-751-6)

Secret Societies by William Holden. An outcast hustler, his unlikely "mother," his faithless lovers, and his religious persecutors—all in 1726. (978-1-60282-752-3)

The Raid by Lee Lynch. Before Stonewall, having a drink with friends or your girl could mean jail. Would these women and men still have family, a job, a place to live after...The Raid? (978-1-60282-753-0)

The You Know Who Girls by Annameekee Hesik. As they begin freshman year, Abbey Brooks and her best friend, Kate, pinkie swear they'll keep away from the lesbians in Gila High, but Abbey already suspects she's one of those you-know-who girls herself and slowly learns who her true friends really are. (978-1-60282-754-7)

Wyatt: Doc Holliday's Account of an Intimate Friendship by Dale Chase. Erotica writer Dale Chase takes the remarkable friendship between Wyatt Earp, upright lawman, and Doc Holliday, Southern gentlemen turned gambler and killer, to an entirely new level: hot! (978-1-60282-755-4)

Month of Sundays by Yolanda Wallace. Love doesn't always happen overnight; sometimes it takes a month of Sundays. (978-1-60282-739-4)

Jacob's War by C.P. Rowlands. ATF Special Agent Allison Jacob's task force is in the middle of an all-out war, from the streets to the boardrooms of America. Small business owner Katie Blackburn is the latest victim who accidentally breaks it wide open, but she may break AJ's heart at the same time. (978-1-60282-740-0)

The Secret of Othello by Sam Cameron. Florida teen detectives Steven and Denny risk their lives to search for a sunken NASA satellite—but under the waves, no one can hear you scream... (978-1-60282-742-4)

Andy Squared by Jennifer Lavoie. Andrew never thought anyone could come between him and his twin sister, Andrea...until Ryder rode into town. (978-1-60282-743-1)

Finding Bluefield by Elan Barnehama. Set in the backdrop of Virginia and New York and spanning the years 1960–1982, *Finding Bluefield* chronicles the lives of Nicky Stewart, Barbara Philips, and their son, Paul, as they struggle to define themselves as a family. (978-1-60282-744-8)

The Jetsetters by David-Matthew Barnes. As rock band the Jetsetters skyrocket from obscurity to superstardom, Justin Holt, a lonely barista, and Diego Delgado, the band's guitarist, fight with everything they have to stay together, despite the chaos and fame. (978-1-60282-745-5)

Strange Bedfellows by Rob Byrnes. Partners in life and crime, Grant Lambert and Chase LaMarca are hired to make a politician's compromising photo disappear, but what should be an easy job quickly spins out of control. (978-1-60282-746-2)